D1223249

STATE
LIBRARIES

3 2001

TALLAHASSEE, FLORIDA

JAMES HOGG

# *Anecdotes of Scott*

THE STIRLING / SOUTH CAROLINA RESEARCH EDITION OF
THE COLLECTED WORKS OF JAMES HOGG
GENERAL EDITOR – DOUGLAS S. MACK

THE STIRLING / SOUTH CAROLINA RESEARCH EDITION OF
# THE COLLECTED WORKS OF JAMES HOGG
## GENERAL EDITOR – DOUGLAS S. MACK

Volumes are numbered in the order of their publication in
the Stirling / South Carolina Research Edition

JAMES HOGG

# Anecdotes of Scott

Anecdotes of Sir W. Scott

and

Familiar Anecdotes of Sir Walter Scott

Edited by
Jill Rubenstein

With a Note on the Genesis of the Texts by
Douglas S. Mack

EDINBURGH UNIVERSITY PRESS

1999

PR
5338
.H55
1999

© Edinburgh University Press, 1999

Edinburgh University Press
22 George Square
Edinburgh
EH8 9LF

Typeset at the University of Stirling
Printed by The University Press, Cambridge

ISBN 0 7486 0933 4

No part of this publication may be reproduced or transmitted
in any form or by any means, electronic or mechanical, including
photocopying, recording, or any information storage or retrieval
system, without prior permission in writing from the publisher.

A CIP record for this book is available
from the British Library

The Stirling / South Carolina Research Edition of

# The Collected Works of James Hogg

**Advisory Board**

*Chairman* Prof. David Daiches

*General Editor* Dr Douglas S. Mack

*Associate General Editors* Dr Peter Garside, Dr Suzanne Gilbert, and
    Dr Gillian Hughes

*Secretary* Dr Gillian Hughes

*Co-ordinator, University of South Carolina* Prof. Patrick Scott

*Ex Officio (University of Stirling)*
    The Principal
    Head, Centre for Scottish Literature and Culture
    Head, Department of English Studies
    Head, School of Arts

*Members*
    Prof. I Campbell (University of Edinburgh)
    Thomas Crawford (University of Aberdeen)
    Ms Jackie Jones (Edinburgh University Press)
    Ms G. E. McFadzean (University of Stirling)
    Dr Christopher MacLachlan (University of St Andrews)
    Prof. G. Ross Roy (University of South Carolina)
    Prof. Jill Rubenstein (University of Cincinnati)
    Prof. Roderick Watson (University of Stirling)

## The Aims of the Edition

James Hogg lived from 1770 till 1835. He was regarded by his contemporaries as one of the leading writers of the day, but the nature
of his fame was influenced by the fact that, as a young man, he had
been a self-educated shepherd. The third edition (1814) of his poem
*The Queen's Wake* contains an 'Advertisement' which begins as follows.

> The Publisher having been favoured with letters from gentle-
> men in various parts of the United Kingdom respecting the
> Author of the *Queen's Wake*, and most of them expressing doubts

of his being a Scotch Shepherd, he takes this opportunity of assuring the public, that *The Queen's Wake* is really and truly the production of *James Hogg*, a common Shepherd, bred among the mountains of Ettrick Forest, who went to service when only seven years of age; and since that period has never received any education whatever.

The view of Hogg taken by his contemporaries is also reflected in the various early reviews of *The Private Memoirs and Confessions of a Justified Sinner*, which appeared anonymously in 1824. As Gillian Hughes has shown in the *Newsletter of the James Hogg Society* no. 1, many of these reviews identify Hogg as the author, and see the novel as presenting 'an incongruous mixture of the strongest powers with the strongest absurdities'. The Scotch Shepherd was regarded as a man of powerful and original talent, but it was felt that his lack of education caused his work to be marred by frequent failures in discretion, in expression, and in knowledge of the world. Worst of all was Hogg's lack of what was called 'delicacy', a failing which caused him to deal in his writings with subjects (such as prostitution) which were felt to be unsuitable for mention in polite literature. Hogg was regarded as a man of undoubted genius, but his genius was felt to be seriously flawed.

A posthumous collected edition of Hogg was published in the late 1830s. As was perhaps natural in the circumstances, the publishers (Blackie & Son of Glasgow) took pains to smooth away what they took to be the rough edges of Hogg's writing, and to remove his numerous 'indelicacies'. This process was taken even further in the 1860s, when the Rev. Thomas Thomson prepared a revised edition of Hogg's *Works* for publication by Blackie. These Blackie editions present a bland and lifeless version of Hogg's writings. It was in this version that Hogg was read by the Victorians. Unsurprisingly, he came to be regarded as a minor figure, of no great importance or interest.

The second half of the twentieth century has seen a substantial revival of Hogg's reputation; and he is now generally considered to be one of Scotland's major writers. This new reputation is based on a few works which have been republished in editions based on his original texts. Nevertheless, a number of Hogg's major works remain out of print. Indeed, some have been out of print for more than a century and a half, while others, still less fortunate, have never been published at all in their original, unbowdlerised condition.

Hogg is thus a major writer whose true stature was not recognised in his own lifetime because his social origins led to his being smothered in genteel condescension; and whose true stature has not been recognised since, because of a lack of adequate editions. The poet Douglas Dunn wrote of Hogg in the *Glasgow Herald* in September 1988: 'I can't help but think that in almost any other country of Europe a complete, modern edition of a comparable author would have been available long ago'. The Stirling / South Carolina Edition of James Hogg seeks to fill the gap identified by Douglas Dunn. When completed the edition will run to thirty-one volumes; and it will cover Hogg's prose, his poetry, and his plays.

## Acknowledgements

The research for the early volumes of the Stirling / South Carolina Edition of James Hogg has been sustained by funding and other support generously made available by the University of Stirling and by the University of South Carolina. Valuable grants or donations have also been received from the Carnegie Trust for the Universities of Scotland, from the Modern Humanities Research Association, from the Association for Scottish Literary Studies, and from the James Hogg Society. The work of the Edition could not have been carried on without the support of these bodies.

I am particularly grateful to Dr Gillian Hughes, the Associate General Editor responsible for the present volume. For access to letters quoted in the Note on the Genesis of the Texts, thanks are also due to the Beinecke Library (Yale University), to the Bodleian Library (Oxford University), to the Huntington Library (California), and to Stirling University Library.

Douglas S. Mack<br>General Editor

## Volume Editor's Acknowledgements

Peter Garside, Gill Hughes and Douglas Mack have patiently and unstintingly shared their wide knowledge of both Hogg and Scott. In addition, I have received valuable help from Nancy Armstrong on the Hogg family, John Cairns and David Daiches on Scott's legal career, Kenneth Johnston on Wordsworth, Emily Lyle on songs and ballads, and Jane Millgate on Scott's nonfiction prose. Janet Horncy and David Retter of the Alexander Turnbull Library in Wellington viii

generously extended warm hospitality and expert professional assistance during my visit to New Zealand. I thank that institution and the Pierpont Morgan Library in New York for access to manuscript material and permission to publish it. I am indebted as well to the National Library of Scotland, to the Special Collections Department of the University of Cincinnati Libraries, and to Stirling University Library. The Charles Phelps Taft Memorial Fund and the Research Council of the University of Cincinnati provided travel support, without which this edition could not have been completed. Above all, Gill Hughes worked on this volume as Associate General Editor with extraordinary attention and generosity. To all these individuals and organizations I express my sincere gratitude.

Jill Rubenstein

# Contents

# Introduction

## 1. Hogg and Scott.

James Hogg and Walter Scott met in 1802. They were young men of almost the same age, and they shared many of the same passions: for outdoor pursuits; for poetry; for the richness of the Scots language; and for the intricately intertwined traditions, history, landscape and lore of the Borders. However, they emerged from radically different worlds. Hogg knew poverty early and grew up in the country, loved, cheerful, and almost wholly self-educated, unabashedly devoted to whisky, the lasses, and his fiddle. Scott was a child of middle-class Edinburgh, the son of a stern and pious lawyer and a somewhat ineffectual mother, carefully educated but always cautious to separate imaginative life from family and, later, professional life.

Both men possessed and cultivated a natural genius for friendship. Despite the cultural and social distance between them, they established a warm regard for each other that would endure for thirty years. The *Anecdotes of Scott* is Hogg's testament to this friendship and to his deep respect for Scott as artist, a respect the more profound because it is granted to an equal in a realm where social distinctions can have no real meaning.

However, those differences do mean a great deal in more mundane realms. In the class-ridden, intensely political world of early nineteenth-century intellectual Edinburgh, they were exacerbated by a highly competitive, commercialised, literary market-place and a set of self-conscious gentlemen-literati, sometimes brilliant, usually arrogant, increasingly worried by the time's strident assaults on privilege. This context necessarily impinged upon the relationship between Hogg and Scott, and it is powerfully present in every paragraph of the *Anecdotes*.

Hogg writes about Scott from the perspective of one man of letters recollecting another, an authorial self-image inextricably intertwined with the cultural conditions of his time. Hogg attained his first real literary success at the age of forty-two with the publication in 1813 of *The Queen's Wake*, the poem which established his reputation. Scott, by contrast, had been widely lauded since the 1803 edition of *Minstrelsy of the Scottish Border*; and when his first novel appeared in 1814, he had already written and profited from an unprecedentedly successful series of narrative poems. Hogg's early literary failures (at least in terms of sales and reception, which were almost nil) inevitably irritated his considerable natural vanity and rendered him extremely sensitive to what he perceived as slights or rejection. This sensitivity informed his friendship with Scott, whom Hogg regarded at various times as mentor, literary father-figure, patron, colleague, influence peddler, impercipient critic, and somewhat inferior fellow artist.

The image of himself which Hogg cultivated, tolerated, enjoyed or lamented (depending upon mood and circumstances) additionally complicated their relationship. Understanding well that literary Edinburgh would not accept him on its own terms, Hogg fashioned a persona sufficiently novel and engaging to enlist the amused tolerance, if not always the affection, of the social and intellectual world he sought to enter. He played simultaneously the rustic buffoon—dirty, crude, drunk, stretched out on the chintz sofa in Lady Scott's drawing room, the good-humoured butt of sophisticated jokes in the *Noctes Ambrosianae*–and the inspired bard of nature, successor to Burns and foremost amongst the fashionable 'uneducated poets' (the title of Southey's 1831 volume) of his day. At times, Hogg apparently thrived on this strategy, as in this account by N. P. Willis of a conversation with John Wilson (alias 'Christopher North'), chief architect of the *Noctes* :

> I spoke of the *Noctes.*
> He smiled, as you would suppose Christopher North would do, with the twinkle proper of genuine hilarity in his eye, and said, "Yes, they have been very popular. Many people in Scotland believe them to be transcripts of real scenes, and wonder how a professor of moral philosophy can descend to such carousings, and poor Hogg comes in for his share of abuse, for they never doubt he was there and said everything that was put down for him."
> "How does the Shepherd take it?"
> "Very good humouredly, with the exception of one or two occasions, when cockney scribblers have visited him in their tours, and tried to flatter him by convincing him he was treated disrespectfully. But five minutes' conversation and two words of banter restore his good humour, and he is convinced, as he ought to be, that he owes half his reputation to the Noctes."[1]

A more contemplative although perhaps equally patronising assessment comes from the pen of Carlyle, describing a meeting in London early in 1832:

> Hogg is a little red-skinned stiff sack of a body, with quite the common air of an Ettrick shepherd, except that he has a highish though sloping brow (among his yellow grizzled hair), and two clear little beads of blue or grey eyes that sparkle, if not with thought, yet with animation. Behaves himself quite easily and well; speaks Scotch, and mostly narrative absurdity (or even obscenity) therewith. Appears in the mingled character of zany and raree show. All bent on bantering him, especially Lockhart; Hogg walking through it as if unconscious, or almost flattered. His vanity seems to be immense, but also his good-nature. I felt interest for the poor 'herd body,' wondered to see him blown hither from his sheepfolds, and how, quite friendless as he was, he went along cheerful, mirthful, and musical. I do not well understand the man; his significance is perhaps considerable. His poetic talent is authentic, yet his intellect seems of the weakest; his morality also limits itself to the precept 'be not angry.' Is the charm of this poor man chiefly to be found herein, that he *is* a real product of nature, and able to speak naturally, which not one in a thousand is? An 'unconscious talent,' though of the smallest, emphatically *naïve*. Once or twice in singing (for he sung of his own) there was an emphasis in poor Hogg's look—expression of feeling, almost of enthusiasm. The man is a very curious *specimen*. Alas! he is a *man*; yet how few will so much as treat him like a *specimen*, and not like a mere wooden *Punch* or *Judy*![2]

To what extent did this multi-faceted role-playing limit Hogg's literary development? One can merely speculate. Most assuredly it affected his relationship with Scott, who, while genuinely fond of Hogg, tended to regard him *de haut en bas* in the company of those whom he perceived as his own literary or social equals. He wrote to Byron on 6 November 1813:

> The author of the Queen's Wake will be delighted with your approbation. He is a wonderful creature for his opportunities, which were far inferior to those of the generality of Scottish peasants. Burns, for instance—(not that their extent of talents is to be compared for an instant)—had an education not much worse than the sons of many gentlemen in Scotland. But poor Hogg literally could neither read nor write till a very late period of his life; and when he first distinguished himself

by his poetical talent, could neither spell nor write grammar. When I first knew him, he used to send me his poetry, and was both indignant and horrified when I pointed out to him parallel passages in authors whom he had never read, but whom all the world would have sworn he had copied. An evil fate has hitherto attended him, and baffled every attempt that has been made to place him in a road to independence. But I trust he may be more fortunate in future.[3]

'Poor Hogg', 'the poor herd body', 'poor man': well-meaning condescension permeated the contemporary perception of Hogg and, to a large extent, defined his friendship with Scott. He sincerely wanted to help the somewhat feckless Hogg, and his correspondence abounds with schemes to extricate Hogg from recurring financial disasters. He tried to secure him a position as appraiser of sheep farms for the Duke of Buccleuch; he hoped to have him appointed to the Excise, citing the precedents of Burns, Henry Mackenzie, and Adam Smith; he invited Hogg to accompany him to the Coronation so that he might write 'some sort of Shepherd's Letters' about the great event (an invitation which was regretfully declined); and he pulled every available lever attempting to obtain for Hogg a pension from the Royal Society for Literature. He was even willing to be 'Chappit back' (i.e., rebuffed) by Lord Montagu, 'a risk of all others which I detest incurring rather than leave his cause unpleaded'.[4]

Nonetheless, Scott regarded Hogg as something of a loose cannon, disapproving of his love affairs, intemperance, and financial improvidence. Writing to the Duchess of Buccleuch (20 March 1812), he wonders if Hogg is beyond help: 'The poor bard [...] is I fear a person whom it will indeed be difficult to serve to any essential purpose yet nature has been liberal to him in many respects and it is perhaps hard for those born under better auspices to censure his deficiencies very severely'.[5] Scott's ambivalence was compounded by his own temperamental aversion to risking his literary reputation, so that he never reviewed Hogg's work in print, refused to lend his name or support to *The Spy*, Hogg's venture into the periodical press, and declined to contribute to his projected collection of contemporary poetry, *The Poetic Mirror*.

At the same time, Scott was undeniably fascinated by the authenticity of Hogg's genius and, most likely, flattered by his adulation. The rustic poet's deeply-rooted sense of place and of the past appealed to Scott's own predilections, and he recognised in Hogg a true poet's ear for both verbal and musical melody. Hogg's relaxed, almost intuitive use of folklore and the supernatural attracted Scott's admiration and, perhaps, envy, as Scott never quite managed to integrate these elements into his own work without awkwardness.

## 2. Genre and Performative Biography.

The reader of the *Anecdotes of Scott* approaches the text and probably finishes it as well with two questions in mind: what is it, and is it true? However, the *Anecdotes* is inherently unclassifiable: part biography, part autobiography, part memoir, and part apologia. To attempt to categorise it under a single generic label is ultimately reductive. Always the nonconformist and the self-designated outsider, Hogg sought in the *Anecdotes* to deconstruct genre, thus demystifying literary authority and subverting those established forms of discourse which he resented. Similarly, to expend significant amounts of time and scholarly energy trying to determine the correspondence between Hogg's account of events and their actuality brings to bear an inappropriate judgemental criterion that diminishes the imaginative vitality of this text. Was Hogg a liar? Did he fabricate stories? Possibly, even probably, but why revoke the artistic license here that we so readily grant him elsewhere? If language even partially constructs rather than mirrors reality, assessment of a work of life-writing in terms of its assumed referentiality to truth becomes a critical fallacy.

The *Anecdotes* constructs Scott in terms of Hogg's perception of Scott's conception of their relationship; all other elements of character are either subsidiary or absent. Whatever fidelity to truth is present, therefore, is at best only a fragment of the whole. Certainly the title implies Hogg's consciousness of this fragmentary quality and is designed to counter the paradoxical assumption that auto/biography should be simultaneously a work of imagination and a repetition or even a representation of actual lived experience.

Hogg's writing is habitually multi-voiced, and the *Anecdotes* is no exception. Given this habit of composition, as well as the relational nature of human character and the ever-changing social and temporal construction of identity, both Scott and Hogg in the *Anecdotes* may be regarded to a large extent as protean fictive creations, interacting within a very specific socially, culturally and economically determined milieu that is as much aesthetic conceit as it is historical time and geographical place. The questions raised by this text, then, concern representation rather than referentiality, subjectivity rather than personality, and the social and artistic *construction* of identity rather than any objectively demonstrable traits of character.

There would seem to be three possibilities for the 'I' of this auto-biographical narrative: the self that speaks in the narrative present; the self that acts in the narrated past; or the self as other, that is, Scott. Even the simplest alternative, the speaking voice, elicits ambiguity: is this one more of Hogg's created personae; is it, near the end of his life, the totality of all his created personae; or is it something apart from them, the real James Hogg, whoever that might be? Or is there no stable identity at all signified by that 'I'?

Of course the 'I' that narrates and reflects cannot be identical to the 'I' that participates in the narrated event; no one can write of his own existence disinterestedly. Hogg exhibits no overt awareness of this distinction. He also seems unconcerned that the self comes into existence only in its differentiation from some other as expressed in language, so that neither the narrative 'I' nor the created 'Scott' can refer to any individual located beyond the immediate frame of the text. Nevertheless, Hogg's instincts serve him brilliantly; and the created tension amongst these three versions of the self–the narrating self, the acting self, and the surrogate self in the person of Scott–gives the *Anecdotes* its special flavour.

There is another ontological ambivalence implicit in both titles. These are **Familiar** *Anecdotes*, **Domestic** *Manners*, thrust through public occasions of writing and publishing into the scrutiny of strangers. Hogg repeatedly emphasises his intimacy with Scott, who reads him unpublished material from proof, receives him warmly at Parliament House, and feels quite at liberty to stop by for breakfast unannounced. From this vantage point of apparent intimacy and equality, Hogg represents Scott's private life as immediately accessible, commenting freely on his verbal abuse of his sons, his apparently duplicitous attempt to conceal Lady Scott's parentage, even his ability to hold whisky. Scott's choice not to confess to Hogg the authorship of the Waverley novels provoked considerable pain and indignation, and Hogg may very well have regarded the *Anecdotes* as balancing Scott's 'lees' to him. In any case, the apparent shabbiness of the act, the transformation of private to public, inevitably calls into question both veracity and motive.

Frequently and quite justifiably on the defensive, Hogg rightly sees the assumed reader as a suspicious sceptic, probing the narrative for revelations of the author, even as he reveals the 'familiar' and 'domestic' components of someone else's life. No matter how tenaciously the life-writer evades self-revelation in favour of self-dramatisation or fictionality, he cannot evade the implicit tension between the representational (the portrayed self) and the reflexive (the writing self). They are co-present but never identical, and the reader is constantly aware of the performative nature of the act of narration. This is what John Sturrock calls the inescapable stipulation of autobiography; 'whatever an autobiographer writes, however wild or deceitful, cannot but count as testimony. It is impossible [...] for an autobiographer not to be autobiographical'.[6]

To structure this testimony, Hogg enlists the conventions of 'associative autobiography', loosely organised not by chronology but by recollection and association. The writer is present, even prominent, in the text, seemingly dependent upon linguistic accident and random memory to elicit and structure his meditations. Because the reader is intensely aware of the writer writing, this strategy privileges the present (i.e., Hogg's voice) rather than the past (i.e., Scott's life). The account of their final meeting provides a perfect example:

> When I handed him into the coach that day he said something to me which in the confusion of parting I forgot and though I tried to reccollect the words the next minute I could not and never could again. It was something to the purport that it was likely it would be long ere [he] leaned as far on my shoulder again but there was an expression in it conveying his affection for me or his interest in me which has escaped my memory for ever. (pp. 74–75)

We are left with Hogg's regret that he cannot *now* remember some word of praise bestowed upon him *then*, focusing our attention on *Hogg's present emotion* rather than on *Scott's past behaviour*.

The *Anecdotes* might best be read as what H. Porter Abbott terms a series of 'identity-related performative acts'.[7] There are acts of praise, acts of self-promotion, acts of self-concealment, acts of piety, of revenge and of other emotions, linked only by their origin and end in the consciousness of Hogg. Thus the focus is always on the discursive act, the self portraying itself through language, writing about itself or about its surrogate. This is what Hogg calls his 'ruling passion of egotism', and it is most apparent in those passages that are designed either as boasts or disclaimers. Here, for example, having claimed that Scott's dread of democracy killed him, Hogg reverts to his own centrality, or rather to the centrality of his discourse:

> He not only lost hope of the realm but of every individual pertaining to it as my last anecdote of him will show for though I could multiply these anecdotes and remarks to volumes yet

> I must draw them to a conclusion. They are trivial in the last
> degree did they not relate to so great and so good a man. I
> have depicted him exactly as he was as he always appeared to
> me and was reported by others and I revere his memory as
> that of an elder brother.  (p. 73)

This sort of thing, oft-repeated, spotlights authorial manipulation
and writing as performance. Because these performances are discursive, not actual, representational rather than mimetic, they cannot rightly be judged as sincere or insincere, accurate or inaccurate.
This reiterated emphasis on writing as a form of speech act posits
an implicit bargain between Hogg and his reader. The constant focus on himself as *writer* not only asserts equality with Scott; it also
places the reader in collusion with Hogg as a party to a performative compact, in which Hogg writes while the reader respectfully
suspends disbelief, just as in reading, say, a Waverley novel. Relating the quarrel between Scott and himself over a passage in *The Spy*,
for example, Hogg reprints the disputed excerpt, justifies his attack
on Scott (even though he changed his mind the following morning
and changed it back again later), and shamelessly solicits sympathy:

> At that period the whole of the aristocracy and literature of
> our country were set against me and determined to keep me
> down nay to crush me to a nonentity; thanks be to God I have
> lived to see the sentiments of my countrymen completely
> changed. (p. 50)

Hogg presents Scott's indignation but not his arguments and provides no evidence to substantiate the purported conspiracy. Nevertheless, the discourse itself—in this case the quoted passage framed
by narrative—functions performatively, i.e., as action, to assure the
reader's collusion.

To render somewhat less obtrusive his omnipresence in a text at
least ostensibly about someone else, Hogg employs several com-
pensatory strategies. To counter the reader's suspicion, he offers
the narrative voice as a disinterested observer with unique access to
special information. Although Lockhart may be 'the only man who
is thoroughly qualified' to write Scott's biography, Hogg will relate
his own 'simple and personal anecdotes which no man can give but
myself' (p. 37). Unsurprisingly, therefore, the paragraph of most
heartfelt praise of Scott ends with the focus squarely on Hogg:

> He was truly an extraordinary man; the greatest man in the
> world. What are kings or Emperors compared with him? Dust

and sand! [...] here is a name who next to that of William Shakespeare will descend with rapt admiration to all the ages of futurity. And is it not a proud boast for an old shepherd that for thirty years he could call this man friend and associate with him every day and hour that he chose? (p. 66)

By labeling the *Anecdotes* a 'miscellaneous narrative' and ceding to Lockhart the sole privilege of writing an authoritative biography, Hogg gains certain distinct advantages. He grants himself license to include and exclude as only he sees fit, answerable to no one. Thus in delineating his literary quarrels with Scott, he provides self-gratifying excerpts from *The Spy* and *The Queen's Wake*, ostensibly to spare the reader hours of fruitless research. Although the text published in 1834 (the *Familiar Anecdotes* in America or *Domestic Manners* in Britain) is more structured and less fragmentary than the unpublished one (the *Anecdotes of Sir W. Scott*), both versions of this 'miscellaneous narrative' are choppy and abrupt. The result is that only the continuing presence of the narrative voice gives the text whatever coherence it possesses. That is, the Scott-Hogg relationship becomes the sole unifying principle in this otherwise haphazard, or seemingly haphazard, collection of anecdotes. The apparently random arrangement cries out for some imposed unity, allowing Hogg to transform it into a generic hybrid held together only by his own consciousness. Although these are *Anecdotes of Scott*, Hogg is always there, his subjectivity filtering the presence and conversation of the Ballantynes, Laidlaw, and any others, all of whom are clearly peripheral to the central Scott-Hogg relationship. Hogg unabashedly places himself in the foreground, enlisting the reader as co-conspirator and thus cleverly subverting the charge of special pleading for Scott, and this strategy works admirably because Hogg has already exempted himself from the understood conventions of biography.

## 3. The *Anecdotes* and Ideology.

Why does Hogg's *Anecdotes of Sir W. Scott* elicit so much discomfort? It certainly made Lockhart uncomfortable; his furious response to the manuscript led Hogg to withdraw it from publication in Britain, but Lockhart's reaction was surely more irrational, biased, and offensive than anything in Hogg's text. Perhaps it is its uncertain ideological status—the implicit conflict between Romantic individualism and bourgeois economics in both figures and their radically divergent visions of communal conservatism—that provokes a sense of

disequilibrium in even the most well-disposed of readers. This ideological *disjunction* is reinforced by class envy, an inherently invidious
emotion, and by Hogg's unresolved anger. The result is a split subjectivity, a phenomenon certainly familiar to readers of Hogg's
fiction, but one which is more complicated to assimilate in an ostensibly biographical text.

Class envy and resentment pervade the *Anecdotes*. If Hogg could
be candid about these emotions, they might not poison the atmos-
phere, but his ambivalence interferes. Even as he expresses his disdain for and alienation from the hegemonic culture, he longs to be
part of it, all the while envisioning himself as the victim of a class
conspiracy. Sturrock argues that the writer of a 'work of self-presen-
tation' is, by definition, 'a conspiracy theorist' determined to correct
an inaccurate image of himself. While he need not be paranoid, 'it
surely helps [...] to be able to believe that one has been the victim
either of ill-informed attention in the past or else of an unmerited
neglect'.[8] Hogg believes both and stations himself on that semiper-
meable border through which influence can flow in only one direc-
tion; that is, the hegemonic culture cannot contaminate the traditional culture of common life, but the writer may retain his roots
therein while crossing beyond it into the more sophisticated realm.[9]

Thus Hogg begins with the feast at Bowhill, representing Scott as
actuated by his 'devotion for titled rank' and himself by a preference
for 'talents or moral worth' (p. 3). Even while he plays the outsider,
however, excluded from the high table, rescued by Scott from his
social faux pas, and mistaking Scott of Harden for an English clergyman, Hogg is very much present at the feast and, by his account,
very much admired. He employs this anecdote and others as what
Eagleton calls 'a crucial ideological instrument [...] to [...] seal the
contradictory unity of those social classes which compose the
hegemonic block'.[10] As a result, the text manifests that series of 'dis-
locations and contradictions' reflective of 'a conflict of antagonistic
ideologies appropriate to a particular stage of the class struggle'.[11] In
this case, however, the conflict is strictly an inner one, as Hogg tries
and fails to resolve his own confused class identification.

Both Hogg and Scott were acutely aware of the radically changing
social spectrum of their culture, and they both responded with pre-
dominantly conservative instincts. However, theirs were two very
different kinds of conservatism. Scott's Burkean vision of a proto-
feudal, harmoniously hierarchical society provokes Hogg's condescending amusement, so that Scott's desire to 'have one dinner in
the feudal stile' is a rather silly but harmless 'whim' gratified by the

Duke of Bucccleuch (p. 5). By contrast, Hogg's conservative ideology manifests itself in a profound sense of the rights granted by
rootedness in place and in tradition. At the same dinner, Hogg re-
grets not realising that he is seated next to Scott of Harden 'for I
would have liked so well to have talked with him about old matters
my forefathers having been vassals under that house on the lands of
Fauldshope for more than two centuries [...].' (p. 44)

The difference is farther exemplified in the argument over the
respective historical accuracy of *The Brownie of Bodsbeck* and *Old Mortality*. Scott upbraids Hogg for his 'exaggerated and unfair picture!'.
Hogg defends himself on the grounds of tradition and origins:

> "I dinna ken Mr Scott. It is the picture I hae been bred up in
> the belief o' sin' ever I was born and I had it frae them whom
> I was most bound to honour and believe. [...]" (pp. 50–51)

Hogg's use of dialect here, of course, is hardly accidental. In a familiar strategy, he represents himself as the Scots-speaking voice of
indigenous wisdom, authenticating his own view, distancing Scott,
and employing language as the vehicle whereby the subordinated
group preserves its identity within the prevailing culture.

Another unresolved ideological dimorphism in the *Anecdotes* concerns the desired role of the artist. The dominant convictions of the
hegemonic class valorised capitalism and those bourgeois social and
property arrangements which enabled it; at the same time, however, the Romantic ideology sanctified individualism, subjectivity
and the alienation of the artist (on grounds of class, gender, region,
nationality, or sensibility) from those dominant values. Hogg seems
to see both Scott and himself at times, usually different times, playing both roles, with resultant confusion for the reader. Hogg emphasises his outsider status; he has been 'living in the wilderness [...] for
the last twenty years' and thus 'know[s] very little of what is going
on in the literary world' (p. 56). For Hogg as self-designated exile,
Scott becomes a series of mirrors whereby the outsider's identity
may be reflected, examined, and constructed: the self as family man,
the self as artist, the self as financially successful and socially accepted writer.

The *Anecdotes* invariably depicts Scott in a social context and Hogg
almost always either alone or alone with Scott; the last scene of the
second version, in which the author is turned away from Abbotsford
while Scott is dying, exemplifies this discrepancy. Martin Danahay
suggests that in nineteenth-century masculine autobiographies, the
other, often the feminised other, stands for the excluded social context,

leaving the male writer to represent himself as an autonomous individual.[12] This is a persuasive argument which might help to explain why Hogg so sedulously places Scott in a social or domestic context, stressing by contrast his own detachment as an artist from the social and material realities in which all texts are embedded.

Hogg constructs Scott as a surrogate for his partial self, and the composite of the two represents the inevitably split subjectivity of the man of letters in a capitalist society. Because the Scott half of this composite brings to it that complex of economic, social and domestic relations we call ideology, his greatest monument is, of course, Abbotsford, 'a thing altogether of his own creation' (p. 30). The Romantic quest for a complementary self is a familiar theme, and here, as in so much Romantic writing in general and Hogg's fiction in particular, the confrontation with the other becomes also a confrontation with the self.

Danahay writes of 'the dark side of Romantic autobiography' in terms suitable for *The Confessions of a Justified Sinner*: 'The self is double, not single. The individual is split and conceals a secret, illicit double that represents the antisocial and violent impulses [...] that in fact are an aspect of the self'.[13] Hogg regarded himself (and was regarded by others) as an anomaly, a resident of that ideological border between the hegemonic and subordinate cultures. Barred from radicalism by both temperament and ambition, he projects himself through Scott, the ultimate insider and belonger. At the same time, however, in their literary quarrels, Hogg invariably speaks for the integrity of artistic impulse, spontaneous feeling untrammelled by those lesser considerations of prudence and expediency which Scott voices. As in the best of Hogg's fiction, the unstable nature of this simultaneous repression and indulgence of selfhood renders it a volatile mixture of divided ideological allegiances and aspirations.

# 4. Hogg and his Double.

Hogg's Scott has no inner life; he exists only as object of Hogg's consciousness, an adjunct of his perception. Like Tennyson's Hallam, Scott becomes a screen onto which the author projects various fragments of his subjectivity. Occasionally Scott plays Mr Hyde to Hogg's respectable Dr Jekyll, as Hogg blames Scott for unworthy acts and illicit desires of his own. Thus it is Scott, not Hogg, who fawns on the aristocracy, lies to his friends, and advocates vandalism and vigilante justice. Or Scott is cast as Victor Frankenstein, glorying in

domesticity and professional triumph, while Hogg plays the creature, alienated through manners, appearance, and poverty but des-
perately desiring what Scott possesses.

This use of the biographical subject as a partially mirroring, partially contrasting subjectivity has a disconcerting impact on form.
While the title of the *Anecdotes* and its fragmentary nature would
seem to suggest a kind of humility, the narrative actually has the
opposite effect. As the ostensible biographer writes his autobiography, he ignores the flux of identity that, of course, comprises the
actual Scott, those multiple existences that have nothing to do with
James Hogg. That is, he defines his main character wholly in terms
of James Hogg's perception of Walter Scott's perception of their relationship, and everything else is absent or relegated to a subsidiary
function.

Throughout his fiction, Hogg is preoccupied with the ambiguous
subject—on the one hand an agency possessed of will, on the other, a
character deprived of self-possession, created by and submissive to
narrative authority. Scott becomes another version of those paradoxical characters who abound in Hogg's fiction, simultaneously
powerful and passive, regarded from outside by the normative writer
or reader with both desire and contempt. Scott, in short, becomes
feminised. These are **Familiar** *Anecdotes* and **Domestic** *Manners*, focusing our attention on 'what he was in the parlour in his family and
among his acquaintances' (p. 37), that is, placing Scott always in a
social context. This emphasis clearly departs from the more familiar tradition of the nineteenth-century masculine author as 'autonomous individual' detached from the social matrix of labour and production.[14] Regenia Gagnier has demonstrated that 'in the canonical
literary autobiographies, having a woman at home is necessary to
the self-conception of authorial men'.[15] The woman behind the scenes
creates that refuge from worldly and material distractions necessary
for the great writer and thus enables the implicit bourgeois aesthetic
of individualism, self-realisation and the autonomy of the creative
imagination. However, by placing him always in a domestic or social context and never alone, Hogg implicitly feminises Scott in a
text in which women are reduced to objects of male consciousness;
the actual female voices are either irksome (Margaret Hogg mo-
nopolising Scott's attention on a visit), or simple (Sophia Scott as a
cute but not-terribly-bright three year old), or mysteriously silent
(Lady Scott's dubious origins and opium addiction).

Hogg farther marginalises Scott by highlighting his status as an
outsider in Ettrick Forest, the locus of authenticity and value. First

Hogg's mother chastises the editor of the *Minstrelsy* for spoiling the traditional ballads: 'They were made for singing an' no for reading; but ye hae broken the charm now, an' they'll never be sung mair' (p. 38). Then Scott, 'who had come into that remote district to [...] preserve what little fragments remained of the country's legendary lore', finds himself bored by 'the everlasting question of the long and short sheep', a rebuke of the antiquarian Shirra, too worldly for the mundane reality of the Borders (p. 38). By thus feminising and marginalising Scott, Hogg asserts his otherness, trivialises the communal conception of his social role, and suggests that it is himself, the other half of this split subjectivity, who exemplifies the true nature of the man of letters.

Although Hogg's praise of Scott is eloquent and sincere, to some extent the *Anecdotes* comprises a sort of declaration of independence, an assertion of creative and political autonomy. It includes all those elements of 'idealization, revision and rejection' which Freud argues are characteristic of literary biography.[16] Harold Bloom's conception of the 'anxiety of influence' as a version of the Freudian family romance also illuminates the *Anecdotes*. Bloom distinguishes between 'strong poets', or 'figures of capable imagination', who 'wrestle their strong precursors, even to the death', and 'weaker talents' content to idealise. The appropriation of 'imaginative space', however, brings with it 'the immense anxieties of indebtedness', the poet's shameful sense that he is not creating from within but simply being 'found' by great poems already outside himself.[17] Hogg's occasional hostility to Scott might be understood as a sense of bondage, the resentment attendant upon involuntary servitude. In Bloom's terms, the *Anecdotes* functions as a 'ritual of separation', Hogg's salvational misreading not so much of specific texts as of the relationship between the two writers:

> Poetic influence—when it involves two strong authentic poets —always proceeds by a misreading of the prior poet, an act of creative correction that is actually and necessarily a misinterpretation. The history of fruitful poetic influence [...] is a history of anxiety and self-saving caricature, of distortion, of perverse willful revisionism without which modern poetry as such could not exist.[18]

This 'act of creative correction' is nowhere more obvious than in Hogg's famous rebuke to Scott distinguishing their two 'schools' (p. 61), and it is equally apparent in his defence of his 'traditionary' tales (p. 47). Neither passage in any way denigrates Scott, but both stake a claim for Hogg in what he regarded as his own province. While his memoir of Scott frequently strains the reader's patience and requires an unusual degree of forbearance, it nevertheless succeeds as a poignant memorial, all the more affecting, perhaps, because the reader must actively confront the unease it elicits. Beneath the author's egoism and tender vanity lie commendable qualities of honest regard, deep affection and sincere gratitude. It is the tribute of one remarkable man to another, both flawed and both admirable, living in a remarkable time.

## 5. Reception of the *Anecdotes*.

Hogg's memoir of Scott, published in the United States in April 1834 as *Familiar Anecdotes of Sir Walter Scott* and in the United Kingdom two months later as *The Domestic Manners and Private Life of Sir Walter Scott*, elicited surprisingly little reaction in print. The dearth of formal reviews may be attributable in part to Lockhart's indignation; the powerful editor of the *Quarterly Review* may have wielded his influence to minimise notice of the book. *Fraser's Magazine*, to which Hogg had been and remained a contributor, did publish a lengthy review in its number for August 1834 (vol. X, no. lvi). It ran unsigned but was written by the magazine's founder William Maginn, the 'Morgan Odoherty' of the *Noctes* and the clever, sarcastic, and alcoholic friend of Lockhart.

Maginn's 32-page review exudes mean-spiritedness while including generous extracts from the *Domestic Manners*. He regards both Hogg and Hogg's American memoirist (Simeon De Witt Bloodgood) as opportunistic, unprincipled liars, and he writes with vicious class disdain:

> If by domestic manners he had intended the manners of Sir Walter's domestics, there is no doubt that he is fully qualified, from taste, relationship, congeniality of sentiment, and considerable social intercourse with them, to do the subject justice; but as to the manners of Sir Walter himself, as well might we expect from a costermonger an adequate sketch of the clubs in St. James's Street. (p. 125)

Maginn reiterates the all-too-familiar puns on Hogg's name, refers to him repeatedly as 'the Herd', and flatly denies the possibility that there might have existed any degree of intimacy between him and Scott. He confuses Hogg's egoism with presumptuousness and can forgive neither: 'In all the pages of his sketch, not five names of the gentlemen acquainted with Sir Walter occur' (p. 156). The review is notable primarily for the degree of its small-minded nastiness, a vivid reminder of what Hogg endured as the accompaniment of any literary success he enjoyed in his lifetime.

The *American Monthly Magazine* offers a much more charitable assessment. The first part (vol. III, no. 2, April 1834) does not mention the *Anecdotes* but chronicles 'A Visit to the Ettrick Shepherd' by the unnamed author. To his surprise, he finds the establishment at Altrive remarkably genteel and its inmates thoroughly charming. The Shepherd is

> a man, born in humble life, without education, without patronage, without adventitious aid of any sort, rising from obscurity by the force of genius alone, to enviable fame–the associate alike of the peasant and the peer.–A man whose unaffected simplicity of manner, whose boundless but unoffending egotism, whose goodness of heart, and sincerity of feeling, make him loved by all men, whether he be seen with his family at Altrive, or in the fashionable vortex of England's or of Scotland's metropolis. (p. 91)

The following number (vol. III, no. 3, May 1834) reviews the *Familiar Anecdotes*; it, too, is unsigned but most likely attributable to the same author as the previous month's 'Visit'. Like Maginn, the reviewer inescapably notes Hogg's egoism, but unlike Maginn he accepts it as an intrinsic part of his persona:

> These anecdotes are strongly characteristic of the Shepherd's mind. He has often said, "I like to write about myself,"–and, in the work before us, he has very decidedly evinced his liking, for the greater part of it records scenes in which, with Scott, he was present, and opinions which Scott expressed of him. The Shepherd writes as he speaks, and we like him the better for it. Those who have familiarly conversed with him, while reading his prose, see the old man before their eyes, with all his náivete [*sic*], his good humor, self-complacency, and unoffending egotism. The sincerity with which he writes, atones for his rambling narrative, and–we might say–for the graceful carelessness of his style. (p. 23)

This reviewer mildly chastises Hogg for making Scott appear 'in some respects, unamiable and jealous' (p. 181) but concludes by urging his readers to purchase the book so that 'a few hundred dollars could be sent to its industrious and deserving author' (p. 184).

Later assessments tempered and deplored the ferocity of the initial response in Britain. Christian Johnstone's 1837 review of the *Life of Scott* in *Tait's Edinburgh Magazine* chides Lockhart for his treatment of Hogg, 'a man whom he ought to have understood too thoroughly to indulge in anger against him'.[19] The reviewer approvingly quotes Hogg's 'graphic and diverting' description of Lady Scott and mocks Lockhart for barring it from his 'filial and decorous pages' (p. 220). Similarly, in Willis's account of his interview with 'Christopher North', Wilson calls the *Fraser's* review (which he assumed to have been written by Lockhart) 'a barbarous and unjustifiable attack' and defends Hogg's particular brand of veracity:

> he is perfectly honest, no doubt, and quite revered Sir Walter. He has an unlucky inaccuracy of mind, however; and his own vanity, which is something quite ridiculous, has given a coloring to his conversations with Scott, which puts them in a very false light; and Sir Walter, who was the best natured of men, may have said the things ascribed to him in a variety of moods, such as no one can understand who does not know what a bore Hogg must sometimes have been at Abbotsford.[20]

Comparing the manuscript of the *Familiar Anecdotes of Sir Walter Scott* to the version published in 1834 farther illuminates the work's reception. The American editor regularised Hogg's idiosyncratic spelling, although Scottish place names (Lawrieston, Drumlanrig) correctly spelled by the author are occasionally misspelled in the printed version. The editor added a wealth of punctuation, sometimes clarifying meaning, occasionally cluttering it. Minor details of punctuational convention, such as periods after abbreviations, differ between the American and British editions.

The editor eliminated Hogg's colloquial offences against religious decorum; so that 'a devil of a run' becomes 'a prodigious run', 'for God's sake' is rendered respectable as 'for goodness' sake', and Scott's reaction to Mr Paterson, the Galashiels preacher, is diluted from 'G— d— him!' to simply 'D— him!'. Other alterations seem designed to shield the reader's delicate sensibilities, as when Hogg's poignant description of the dying Scott as 'reduced to the very lowest state of degradation to which poor prostrate humanity could be subjected' is changed to the considerably more bland 'state of weakness'. The *Familiar Anecdotes* occasionally deprives Hogg's Scots of some of its zest, so that his ingenuous but pointed observation on the Buccleuch property holdings—'how could they hae gotten haud o' a' the South o' Scotland'—is rendered as the less emphatic 'gotten hand'.

The British edition includes a series of intrusive editorial footnotes, generally either patronising or denigrating. These express snide observations on Scott's character as well as the usual invidious aspersions against Hogg. Scott is admonished for his love of role-playing:

> Sir Walter, practical, and with a strong grasp of real life in his poetry, was always endeavouring to live in a world of fiction. His Abbotsford, the dinner [at Bowhill] here narrated, and the reception of the king at Edinburgh were continuous efforts to transplant himself into another age—not unlike children playing Crusaders, Reavers, Robinson Crusoes, &c. (p. 74)

Similarly mean-spirited footnotes draw the reader's attention to Scott's 'uncourteous treatment of Lord Holland' (p. 77), his 'anxiety to be connected with nobility by a wife's illegitimacy' (p. 94), and his fawning on the young Duke of Buccleuch, 'this boy idiot [...] who valued a moorfowl more than a poet' (p. 133). The editor mocks Hogg for believing himself the victim of a conspiracy and for concluding with a passage from Horace: 'Saul among the prophets! Hogg quoting Latin!' (p. 136). The footnotes are clearly not Hogg's. They are not present in the manuscript, and he had no opportunity to read or correct proofs for either published version. In the case of the American *Familiar Anecdotes*, distance rendered it impossible; in the case of the British *Domestic Manners*, the edition was unauthorised. These non-authorial footnotes are transcribed and identified here in the Notes as additions to the *Domestic Manners*.

## Notes

1. N. P. Willis, *Pencillings by the Way: Written during Some Years of Residence and Travel in France, Italy, Greece, Asia Minor, and England* (New York: Morris & Willis, 1844), p. 198.

2. James Anthony Froude, *Thomas Carlyle: A History of the First Forty Years of his Life*, 2 vols (New York: Scribner's, 1882), I, 189.

3. *The Letters of Sir Walter Scott*, ed. by H. J. C. Grierson, 12 vols (London: Constable, 1932–37), III, 373.

4. Scott to William Laidlaw, 26 March [1828], in Grierson, X, 405.

5. In Grierson, III, 91.

6. John Sturrock, 'The New Model Autobiographer', *New Literary History*, 19.1 (1977), 51–63.

7. H. Porter Abbott, 'Autobiography, Autography, Fiction: Groundwork for a Taxonomy of Textual Categories', *New Literary History*, 19.3 (1988), 597–615.

8. Sturrock, p. 27.

9. Terry Eagleton, *Criticism and Ideology: A Study in Marxist Literary Theory* (London: NLB, 1976).

10. Eagleton, p. 11.

11. Eagleton, p. 96.

12. Martin A. Danahay, *A Community of One: Masculine Autobiography and Autonomy in Nineteenth-Century Britain* (Albany: State University of New York Press, 1993), p. 3.

13. Danahay, p. 91.

14. Danahay, p. 3.

15. Regenia Gagnier, 'The Literary Standard, Working-Class Autobiography, and Gender', in *Revealing Lives: Autobiography, Biography, and Gender*, ed. by Susan Groag Bell and Marilyn Yalom (Albany: State University of New York Press, 1990), p. 96.

16. Sigmund Freud, *Leonardo DaVinci*, trans. by A. A. Brill (New York: Dodd, Mead, 1932), p. 116.

17. Harold Bloom, *The Anxiety of Influence* (New York: Oxford University Press, 1973), pp. 5, 26.

18. Bloom, p. 30.

19. *Tait's Edinburgh Magazine*, n.s. 4 (April 1837), 205–20 (p. 219).

20. Willis, pp. 198–99.

# Note on the Genesis of the Texts

> Is there, for honest Poverty
> > That hings his head, and a' that;
> The coward-slave, we pass him by,
> > We dare be poor for a' that!
> For a' that, and a' that,
> > Our toils obscure, and a' that,
> The rank is but the guinea's stamp,
> > The Man's the gowd for a' that.— [...]
> > > (Burns, 'For a' that and a' that')

By the summer of 1829, Hogg was a writer of established reputation in his late fifties. Perhaps not quite yet a Grand Old Man of Scottish letters, he was nevertheless approaching that condition; and two articles he published during that summer suggest that he had already reached the stage of life in which reminiscences about the old days come naturally and flow freely. The two articles in question look back to events that had taken place about a quarter of a century earlier, and are entitled 'Reminiscences of Former Days. My First Interview with Allan Cunningham'; and 'Reminiscences of Former Days. My First Interview with Sir Walter Scott'.[1]

These articles are spirited accounts of the origins of two of Hogg's most important and long-lasting friendships; and towards the end of the Scott article, having warmed to his theme, Hogg writes as follows.

> There are not above five people in the world who, I think, know Sir Walter better, or understand his character better, than I do; and if I outlive him, which is likely, as I am five months and ten days younger,[2] I will draw a mental portrait of him, the likeness of which to the original shall not be disputed. In the meantime, this is only a reminiscence, in my own line, of an illustrious friend among the mountains. (p. 52)

Hogg, it would appear from this, feels that his long and close friendship with Scott has given him insights into the character of the great man. Further, Hogg wishes to record these insights: their subject makes them important, and they ought not to be lost. Another motive can perhaps also be detected. Hogg (like Burns before him) had been a manual labourer in early life; and he was therefore a member of what would have been thought of as 'the lower orders' by members of the intensely class-conscious literary world of early-nineteenth-century Edinburgh. Earning much of his living in later life in that society as a professional writer, Hogg, as a working-class boy made good, experienced a great deal of patronising condescension (and worse) from people who assumed themselves to be his superiors. For example, his novel *The Three Perils of Woman* (1823) was reviewed by his friend John Wilson in the following terms in *Blackwood's Edinburgh Magazine*. As will be seen from this extract, Hogg's name provided his gentlemanly friends with hours of harmless fun, as they thought up new and ever-funnier pig puns which would help to remind the talented but presumptuous former shepherd that he ought not to get ideas above his station. Wilson writes:

> It is indeed this rare union of high imagination with homely truth that constitutes the peculiar character of his writings. In one page, we listen to the song of the nightingale, and in another, to the grunt of the boar. Now the wood is vocal with the feathered choir; and then the sty bubbles and squeaks with a farm-sow, and a litter of nineteen pigwiggins. [...] It is impossible to foresee whether we are about to help ourselves to a pine-apple or a fozey-turnip—to a golden pippin or a green crab—to noyau or castor-oil—to white soup, syllabub, and venison, or to sheep-head broth, haggis, and hog's flesh. The table-cloth, too, is damask, and richly figured; but villainously darned and washed in its own grease—a china tureen, filled to the brim with hodge-podge, undergoes unceasing domiciliary visits from a huge wooden spoon, fitter to stir tar for sheep-smearing.[3]

As he coped with this kind of thing, Hogg must have found Scott's friendship a source of great comfort and support; and no doubt he hoped that his projected 'mental portrait' of Scott would provide an opportunity to set the record straight for the benefit of people like Wilson. In writing an extended account of his friendship with Scott, Hogg would be able to assert: *Scott* took me seriously, and no-one can dispute the value of *his* good opinion.

Scott in general did full justice to Hogg's worth and talent; but he was not above an occasional lapse into patronising condescension in the Wilson manner. For example, Scott writes as follows to Lord Montagu in a letter of 8 June 1817.

There is an old saying of the seamens every man is not born

to be a boatswain and I think I have heard of men born under
a six penny planet and doomd never to be worth a groat. I
fear something of this vile sixpenny influence has gleamd in
at the cottage window when poor Hogg first came squeaking
into this world.

The 'squeaking' is of course yet another pig joke; and Scott elsewhere refers to Hogg as 'the honest grunter'.[4] Patronising condescension from Scott must have been particularly painful and humili-
ating for Hogg, precisely because of the value he placed on Scott's
opinion. Real pain is an uncomfortable presence in both versions of
Hogg's anecdotes of Scott; and much of this pain seems to derive
from Hogg's uneasy and unwilling perception that, sometimes, Scott
did not entirely believe, with Burns, that 'The rank is but the guin-
ea's stamp, / The Man's the gowd for a' that'. This, perhaps, generated an anger that Hogg, given his deep affection and admiration for
Scott, was unwilling fully to acknowledge even to himself.

In the event, Hogg did indeed survive his friend; and when on 21
September 1832 death at last released Scott from the pain and distress of his long final illness, Hogg's thoughts turned to the promised 'mental portrait'. This project was clearly in his mind when he
wrote as follows to Scott's son-in-law John Gibson Lockhart on 4
October 1832, some two weeks after Scott's death. The 'Kaeside'
mentioned in this letter was the home of William Laidlaw on Scott's
Abbotsford estate. Laidlaw had been one of Hogg's closest friends
since the 1790s, when Hogg had worked as a shepherd on Laidlaw's
father's farm, Blackhouse in Yarrow; and Laidlaw had later became
Scott's steward at Abbotsford.

My dear Lockhart
Having been dissapointed in seeing you at Kaeside which I
hardly expected to do considering the confusion and distress
you were in yet I cannot help writing to you thus early as I
find that now having lost the best and most steady friend that
I ever had in the world I have none now to depend on for
advice or assistance but yourself. I never applied to any body
for these but to him and they never were wanting
I am then going to begin by giving you a piece of advice  It
is "That you will write Sir Walter's life in my name and in my
manner" I think it will give you ten times more freedom of
expression both as a critic and a friend and you know you can
never speak too kindly of him for me. As I have promised
such a thing to the world I really wish you would do it and I

am sure it would take for there is no biographer alive equal to you[5] but for a son brother or husband to write an original and interesting biography is impossible Therefore be sure to take my name and forthright egotistical stile which you can well do and I think you will not repent it. It will likewise do me some credit as a biographer and in fact there is no man can do it but you not having command of the documents As for Laidlaw he cannot write at all. Think of this my dear Lockhart and depend on it it shall be an Adam Blair[6] no living shall ever know of it and if you think it necessary I shall copy it all with my own hand or get the sheets copied here as you write them and let them all be transmitted from this to the publisher[7]

What could have prompted Hogg to make this extraordinary proposal? It is worth remembering that, when he suggests that Lockhart write 'in my name and in my manner', Hogg is in fact proposing an extension of an already well-established arrangement. Since 1822, Hogg had regularly appeared as 'the Ettrick Shepherd' in the immensely popular *Noctes Ambrosianae* of *Blackwood's Edinburgh Magazine*, a series of articles written (for the most part) by Wilson and by Lockhart. The *Noctes* purport to record the table-talk of the *Blackwood's* group of writers; and in these articles 'the Ettrick Shepherd' speaks in a very distinctive 'forthright egotistical style'. Hogg himself used 'the Ettrick Shepherd' as a pen-name; and he cultivated his own version of the Ettrick Shepherd's 'forthright egotistical style'. The *Blackwood's* caricature, however, represents Hogg as an absurd, vain, and opinionated clown who, nevertheless, can sometimes get to the heart of the matter with the inspired, intuitive simplicity of a child. Hogg's attitude towards the Shepherd of the *Noctes* varied between good-natured amusement and angry resentment; but by 1832 he had undoubtedly become accustomed to being used as a mouthpiece by Wilson and Lockhart. The suggestion that Lockhart should make use of the Ettrick Shepherd's 'forthright egotistical style' in writing a biography of Scott *is* an extraordinary one; but in a sense it grows naturally enough out of the extraordinary use of Hogg's 'name' and 'manner' by Wilson and Lockhart in the *Noctes*.

Hogg's suggestion is a ploy for proposing that he and Lockhart should co-operate on a biography of Scott, on terms that would be advantageous to Hogg: 'It will likewise do me some credit as a biographer'. Such an arrangement would have had many attractions for Hogg: as we have seen, he had strong reasons for wishing to create a permanent record of his friendship with Scott. Furthermore, as Hogg points out in his letter to Lockhart of 4 October 1832, only

Lockhart (as Scott's son-in-law and literary executor) had 'command of the documents'. Lockhart's biography was clearly destined to become the standard one; and co-operation with Lockhart would be likely to secure the best possible home for the material Hogg wished to make public about his friendship with Scott. Hogg, then, had strong motives for proposing a collaboration with Lockhart; but what would be in it for Lockhart? Hogg's suggestion is that the old tried and tested *Noctes* device of using the Shepherd as a mouthpiece might offer Lockhart a welcome freedom to move beyond the kind of hagiography demanded by filial piety; and Hogg does have a certain point when he says 'for a son brother or husband to write an original and interesting biography is impossible'.

It would appear, then, that Hogg's suggestion is not, on closer examination, quite as wildly absurd as it seems to be at first sight. Nevertheless, it remains a hare-brained notion; and it comes as no surprise that Lockhart did not rise to Hogg's bait, preferring to write the biography in his own name and manner. This left Hogg no further forward in his efforts to place on record his own account of his friendship with Scott. Fortunately, a little later in the autumn of 1832 an opportunity began to take shape, as a result of Hogg's links with the London publisher James Cochrane.

Hogg had spent the early months of 1832 in London as a guest of Cochrane at Waterloo Place, the object of the visit being to make arrangements for the publication by Cochrane of a multi-volume collected edition of Hogg's works. The projected series was given the title *Altrive Tales*, the name deriving from Altrive Lake, Hogg's remote moorland farm in the Scottish Borders. The first volume of the series was duly published by Cochrane shortly after Hogg's return to Scotland in March 1832; but Cochrane became bankrupt very soon after the publication of this volume. The financial consequences of this turn of events were extremely serious for Hogg, who wrote to Cochrane on 3 May 1832 as part of his attempts to save as much as possible of the *Altrive Tales* project from the wreck. As the tone of this letter suggests, Hogg was to remain on friendly terms with Cochrane in spite of the bankruptcy.

> I wondered day after day that I did not hear from you with my promised remittance but a very painful letter which I recieved yesterday[8] has explained the cause I assure you I am truly grieved that you should have been forced to give in by inveterate creditors at a time in which no man could stand if pushed to the uttermost. But it is for you & for your lovely family that I grieve far more than for myself. Because I know well you

will join with my friends in securing the remaining 2000 copies for me. I have appointed Mr M‚Donald and Mr Pringle to
wait on you to get the matter arranged for you know no credi-
tor can touch any edition unless my share of one fifth of it is
first paid up and then indeed I can go no farther. [...] Now I
beseech you my dear Cochrane as you hope to be respected
to go hand in hand with my friend in securing the remaining
copies for me and I shall stick by you in literature as long as I
live.    (Beinecke Library, Yale University)

While he was Cochrane's guest in London in the spring of 1832,
Hogg got to know his host's business associate John M'Crone (also
known as McCrone, MacCrone, or Macrone). Indeed, on leaving
London in March 1832, Hogg had presented M'Crone with a shepherd's plaid as a souvenir.[9] Following Scott's death in September
1832, M'Crone (having a keen eye for what would be likely to sell)
began to make plans for a book that would mark the passing of the
great novelist; and, naturally enough in all the circumstances,
M'Crone turned to Hogg as a potential source of material for his
book. As a result, M'Crone paid Hogg an extended visit at Altrive
in the autumn of 1832, in the aftermath of Scott's death. During this
visit, Hogg used his good offices to arrange for M'Crone to be shown
round Abbostford. In a letter of 2 November 1832 to William
Laidlaw at Kaeside, Hogg writes:

The bearer hereof is a Mr John M‚Crone from London to
whom I when there was much indebted for the kindest attentions. He has been here for some time on a visit and being a
great enthusiast in all things relating to literature he cannot
leave Scotland without seeing all that can be seen about
Abbotsford. I therefore commit him to your care for a day
and request your attentions to him.    (Beinecke Library, Yale
University)

M'Crone's visit to Hogg in the autumn of 1832 duly yielded the
hoped-for material for the projected book on Scott. At the beginning
of March 1833, M'Crone (by now established in a new publishing
business in partnership with Cochrane) received a package by post
from Hogg; and this package consisted of a manuscript containing
Hogg's anecdotes of Scott. Hogg writes about this in a letter of 1
March 1833 to the publisher William Blackwood in Edinburgh. Hogg
and Blackwood had quarrelled very seriously some time before,
and this letter forms part of tentative exploratory moves towards a
reconciliation. In these circumstances, Hogg has an opportunity to

enjoy himself by teasing Blackwood about the anecdotes of Scott, a highly desirable literary property which might well have gone to *Blackwood's Edinburgh Magazine* ('Maga'), but for the quarrel.

> Before I got Dr Gray's letter yesterday which has quite turned me to you I had just sent off to London familiar anecdotes of Sir Walter which would at least have filled forty pages of Maga. What a pity as you will see when they are published (NLS, MS 4036, fols 98–99)

The manuscript 'sent off to London' at the beginning of March 1833 survives in the Alexander Turnbull Library, Wellington, New Zealand (MS Papers 42 item 1), where it forms part of a collection of papers donated to that library over the years by Hogg's descendants.[10] This identification of the manuscript can be made with confidence. Turnbull Library MS Papers 42 item 1 consists of anecdotes of Scott in Hogg's hand, and the final leaf (which contains part of the text) has been folded and sealed to form the outer wrapper of a postal package. This outer wrapper is addressed in Hogg's hand to M'Crone in London; and it carries the postmark date 7 March 1833. This postmark date suggests that Hogg had not in fact 'just sent off' his package to London when he wrote to Blackwood on 1 March 1833; rather, he was about to send it off in a few days. No doubt Hogg felt an irresistible temptation to tease Blackwood about the anecdotes, while seeing the need to send a signal that the Edinburgh publisher was already too late to lay claim to this highly desirable literary property.

The leaf that has been used as a postal wrapper for this manuscript carries the title 'Anecdotes of Sir W. Scott'; and in the opening paragraph of the text of Hogg's manuscript, M'Crone, as narrator, is made to mention his visit to Hogg at Altrive in the autumn of 1832. This is in effect a linking device designed to pave the way for the integration of Hogg's anecdotes of Scott into M'Crone's text. The manuscript begins:

> When I was in Scotland last year I got an invitation to the house of The Shepherd which I accepted and remained with him for several weeks. On every occassion I tried to bring out his sentiments regarding his great patron and prototype and as these sentiments were never meant to meet the public eye or ear I deemed them of the greater importance to keep in record as they arose spontaneously from the heart while every trait in the character of so great a man is of the highest importance.

To take the Shepherd's own words as nearly as I could
reccollect them every night he said to me one day on the hill
"The only blemish or perhaps I should say foible [...]

And so we plunge into a rendering of the Shepherd's anecdotes
about Scott. This device is designed not only to link Hogg's anecdotes into M'Crone's book; it is also designed to stress the status of
Hogg's anecdotes as oral rather than written narrative.[11] For Hogg,
the distinction is an important one. Again and again in Hogg's fiction, the oral carries with it associations of unaffected honesty; it
provides a guarantee of 'nature, simplicity, and truth', to use a favourite Hogg expression of approval. The opening of *Anecdotes of Sir
W. Scott*, then, seeks to stress that this text will offer the real, un-
guarded, and unaffected opinions and insights of the Shepherd about
'his great patron', the anecdotes being recorded 'as they arose spontaneously from the heart'. The opening of Hogg's text also stresses
that the insights offered by Hogg's anecdotes are valuable because
their subject is Scott: 'every trait in the character of so great a man is
of the highest importance'.

As we shall see, however, the *Anecdotes of Sir W. Scott* did not pro-
ceed smoothly to publication as planned. Hogg's manuscript duly
arrived in London in March 1833; and what happened next can be
gathered from letters exchanged by Hogg and Lockhart towards the
end of that month. This exchange refers to letters to Hogg, from
Cochrane and from M'Crone, which do not seem to have survived.
Hogg writes as follows to Lockhart on 20 March:

My dear Lockhart
    I have recieved such a letter from M,Crone this moment as
would put me in a rage at any man alive but you. I must explain matters to you on this head and I am sure you will ex-
culpate me for what I have attempted to do. Now you must
know that from a jocular hint given in one of my *reminiscences* I
was applied to from all quarters even from a place called
Albion in America for something original or anecdotes about
Sir Walter. I refused them all saying to every one of them "If
I can furnish any thing original about him it must be to my
friend Lockhart his legitimate Biographer" Mr M,Crone came
here on Summer (or Autumn I believe) soliciting the same
thing I positively refused on the same grounds Now read the
following extracts

    Waterloo Place Febr 20th "Mr Lockhart called a few days
    back on the subject of Mr M,Crones life of Sir Walter

+ + + so satisfied is he that you will assist our friend that
he wishes him to give out the work as your own. Lockharts
materials he says are so abundant he hardly knows how
to bring in one half of them. Now I would not give a sheet
or two of your anecdotes &c &c"

This suggests that, towards the end of February 1833, Hogg received assurances from Cochrane that Lockhart had no objection to
his providing anecdotes of Scott for use by M'Crone. It would seem
that Hogg then wrote his anecdotes quickly and spontaneously, before sending the completed package to M'Crone early in March
1833. At all events, Hogg's letter to Lockhart of 20 March 1833
continues as follows:

It was this approbation of your's that fairly misled me and Mr
M,Crone says "I should like very much if you could give me
some little information regarding the more prominent features
of Sir Walter's character. Such as your opinion on his POLITICS
RELIGION and literary matters. I want some insight also into
his family circle such as none but you can give. Sir Walter in
his study is pretty well known How was he in the parlour"
These I have attempted to do. But not for the world would I
have published one of them without your cognizance. My
positive instructions were that the M.S. was to be referred to
you. That you were at liberty to take out or add whatever
you pleased or to cancel the whole! Could any man in the
world pay more deference to a friend than this? I'll defy him.
Then your best plan would have been as the whole was submitted to you just to have popped the M.S. into your desk and
have said "I think Mr Hogg is wrong I must suppress this till
he and I correspond about it" and not have fallen on and
abused me in such a manner. I am sorry you did but I am not
angry I thought when Cunningham and Chambers[12] had both
given sketches of his life and character one who was a thousand times oftener in his company than they both should have
as good a right. I assure you if Sir Walter despised me and
held me in the lowest contempt his behaviour and his letters
to me testified the reverse. Of that I shall make you sensible
when you like. But though I was to be highly paid and am
paid in part which is the worst of it not for any worldly consideration would I hurt the feelings of any one of Sir Walter's
family less your own than any other however deeply you
have wounded mine. Therefore the whole are cancelled and I

write to M,Crone this very day to return the M.S.S.–They
will no doubt see the light some time but they shall not as long
as I live. What can I do more? The worst thing of all is that
Mr M,Crone has taken a copy for he says "As I was copying
them for the press it struck me" &c Now I am perfectly certain
that all or most of my anecdotes will be retained and detailed
in quite a different stile. If there is any preventative for this it
must be used else I lose the work altogether I do assure you
on the word of an honest man ("although a vulgar clown")
that there is not one of the anecdotes which [is] not literally
and positively true and the first thing I shall do when the work
is returned to me I shall read it over to Laidlaw and the
Fergusons[13] and appeal to them if I have given an unfair or
untrue estimate of his private character and deportment. If I
have *in one single instance* in their opinion I shall alter it as I am
certain those anecdotes and remarks will be held in more estimation yet when I am laid in the dust than many volumes
that shall be written on the same subject. I am sorry you despised even to look at it else you would *perhaps* have formed
another estimate of it before the end. But no more of it. The
work as far as I am concerned is cancelled and if I have erred
in merely putting down my reminiscences on paper I beg
your pardon and hope you will remain my friend the same as
ever. I can do no more in extenuation and am your's most
respectfully

James Hogg
(NLS, MS 1554, fols 75-76)

Lockhart's reply is dated 22 March 1833:

Dear Hogg
   You have been grossly misinformed as to every part of my
conduct and feeling on the occasion to which your letter of
this morning refers. The facts are these Seeing an advertisement that Mr. McCrone was about to publish a life of Sir W.
Scott including many "private letters" of the deceased, & "materials furnished by his friend Hogg" I called at Cochrane's to
warn *him* that no private letters of Sir W. Scott could be legally
published without the sanction of his executors and that if he
persisted in doing so I should call for an Injunction–but that
wishing to save *him* needless expense I gave him this notice.
Mr. McCrone of whom I know nothing was in the shop and
immediately asked how we had suffered Mr Polewhele[14] to

publish private letters of Sir W. S. without interference? I answered that if he would look into Polewhele's book he would
find Sir W's own note, allowing him to print these letters—
and that *we* now stood in the room of the dead, and must be
consulted on all such occasions, as *he* had been when alive.
He then said—"Have we no right to print anecdotes such as
Mr. Hogg's?" I replied "—thats another affair—I have no right
to prevent Hogg or any man from publishing what he pleases
on the subject—Always excepting *letters.*" This was all, as far as
I recollect. I may very probably have added that if we interfered in such a case, it was not for any jealousy as to materials
that might have been of service to *me* being given to another
person—that our materials were more than abundant: but as
to my conferring confidentially on this subject with either
McCrone or Cochrane that was out of the question—I know
and desire to know nothing of either of them. Observe that all
this was after repeated announcements in the newspapers of
*your* having supplied Mr McCrone with your reminiscences
of Sir W. Scott.

The next time I saw him, he produced in this room a bundle of your *M.S.* and told me here were your anecdotes. I
confess I was exceedingly hurt and angry not that you should
have sent him such a M.S.—no—but that you should have sent
it them *unseen by me*: For I well knew that altho' you had always
loved and respected Sir W. you could not write so many pages
about him without saying things that would give pain to his
children, and I strongly suspected that, tho' on my representation you would willingly shake out any offending passages,
he would have made a copy for himself, and that some day or
other all would be out! Did I not judge aright? You confess
that he has made such a copy, and that you have no doubt all
you wrote will be published, after *you are gone*—aye, after you
are gone—after you can suffer nothing from my answer—Perhaps after I and all that could have answered you are gone
also!—I cast my eye hastily over the *M.S.* and the first thing I
lighted on was your statement about Lady Scott & *opium*! and
then indeed I was wroth, and abused you heartily, & said the
next thing would be to get Sir Walters valet and explain the
secret history of his toilette. I felt that you had permitted yourself to put before the public a statement which would cause
misery to my wife and her sister, and I perceived that there
was no remedy—that it would be worse ten years hence than

now–& that some day it must come–I hope the scoundrel who has dared to repeat to you the words of my momentary passion uttered in my private apartment, into which he had no right to intrude, has reported them truly He may or he may not. He who has for his own purposes copied without leave your *M.S.*, must be a person of very loose feelings. I know not. I *probably* said said [*sic*] that it would be easy for me, if I chose, to give to the world scraps of letters and diaries which would induce the belief that Sir W. Scott dispised James Hogg– & so I could: but did he dispise him–No–he condemned some parts of his conduct and smiled at his vanity, but he admired his genious and knew his heart was in the right place and if I published *all* that I could of what he has left written *anent* Hogg *that* would be visible

But surely this fool has misunderstood *me*–I doubt if he is capable of understanding any thing–His book called *Waverley Anecdotes*[15] shows him ignorant of all things human and divine, except the art of making a title page lie, and the outside of a volume swindle–On reading afterwards your M.S. I declined giving this man any opinion of its contents. They seem to me very unworthy of the subject and of the writer–And they contain among other things, several gross mistatements as to matter of fact–one of them what must be a mere dream of yours, and which directly impeaches the personal veracity of Sir W. Scott–You may jocularly talk of *leeing* but the man who says that which is not *from malice* is a villain *from vanity* is a slave. Is it thus that James Hogg talks *now* of Sir W. Scott– what would he have said had he been so charged in his life time by any man? I shall say no more but that if I said any thing seriously derogatory to your character or implying that I attributed to you any worse fault than that of rashness and indiscretion I recall the words of hasty and outraged feeling and assure you that I remain now as ever

Your sincere friend

J G Lockhart

(NLS, MS 1554, fols 77-78: copy of the original)

Another account of Lockhart's confrontation with M'Crone is to be found in a letter of 19 April 1833, written home to Edinburgh by William Blackwood, then on a visit to London.

We sat nearly a couple of hours with Mr Lockhart, and had a great deal of talk with him. He is just the old man, as friendly

and satirical as ever. He gave us a most ludicrous account of
some interviews he has had with this fellow McCrone,
Cochrane's partner. This worthy you know has announced a
Life of Sir Walter Scott, and told Mr L. he had got a number
of Sir W's letters to Constable which he intended to incorpo-
rate in his work. Mr L. made him aware that the law would
entitle Sir W's executors to get an injunction to prevent these
being published without their consent; this however McCrone
did not at first credit, but he soon found Mr L. was right. His
next interview, and this is the best joke of all, was to consult
Mr L. with regard to a large MS. which he had received from
his friend Hogg, containing most interesting anecdotes of Sir
W.–Mr L. knowing well what a bundle of lies the whole would
be, at first declined to look at it, but McC. pressed him so
much that he opened the scroll. The very page he glanced at
contained such beastly & abominable things that he could not
restrain his indignation, and poured out his indignation against
Hogg in such unmeasured terms that his poor auditor was
quite dumfoundered. He however left the M.S. for Mr L's
consideration. He went over it, and was filled with utter disgust & loathing     (NLS, MS 4035, fols 51–54)

Blackwood does not exactly make Hogg's manuscript sound tame
and boring: it contains 'beastly & abominable things', and it fills
Lockhart with 'utter disgust & loathing'. Lockhart's own comments
likewise fall some way short of warm approval; witheringly, he points
out that one of Hogg's anecdotes 'directly impeaches the personal
veracity of Sir W. Scott', while another contains a 'statement about
Lady Scott & opium'. The present volume prints Hogg's anecdotes
from the manuscript in question, and readers will be able to form a
judgment for themselves. It may be, however, that some readers
will feel that Blackwood and Lockhart are perhaps getting a little
over-excited about Hogg's suggestion that Scott told lees with regard
to the authorship of the anonymously-published Waverley novels
(p. 11); and about Hogg's mention of the fact that Lady Scott took
opium (then widely used as a pain-killer) 'for a complaint which
(poor woman!) was never revealed until the time was past for curing it' (p. 11).

In short, Lockhart's anger seems disproportionate, even absurdly
so. But it is worth remembering that Hogg's mention of the lees about
the authorship of the Waverley novels appears in the context of a
claim by Hogg that Scott had once told him that Lady Scott was the
illegitimate child of the Earl of Tyrconnel. If this story were true, the

person in question would be George Carpenter (1750–1805), who was the second Earl of Tyrconnel. Scott's future wife, Charlotte Charpentier, had been born in Lyons in 1770. It is tempting to speculate that the real cause of Lockhart's anger may have been that Hogg had let the cat out of the bag with regard to a family secret concerning Lockhart's mother-in-law. This, however, is not a matter that can be settled with confidence one way or the other, because confusion and uncertainty still surround Lady Scott's parentage.

However that may be, Hogg decided to abandon his original plan for publishing his anecdotes of Scott, because of Lockhart's anger. As we have seen, Hogg writes as follows in his letter to Lockhart of 20 March 1833:

> not for any worldly consideration would I hurt the feelings of any one of Sir Walter's family less your own than any other however deeply you have wounded mine. Therefore the whole are cancelled and I write to M,Crone this very day to return the M.S.S.–They will no doubt see the light some time but they shall not as long as I live.

Hogg's letter asking M'Crone to return the manuscript containing *Anecdotes of Sir W. Scott* does not seem to have survived; but the manuscript must indeed have been returned to Hogg, because, as we have seen, it forms part of the collection of Hogg's papers donated in due course to the Alexander Turnbull Library in Wellington by Hogg's descendants. In the letter to Lockhart quoted above, Hogg writes that the anecdotes of Scott written for M'Crone 'will no doubt see the light some time but they shall not as long as I live'. In the event, the anecdotes written for M'Crone in 1833 were not published until 1983;[16] and the present edition represents only their second appearance in print.

In spite of their dispute in March 1833, it would appear that Lockhart and Hogg were once again on friendly terms by September 1833. This is confirmed by the tone of a letter to Hogg of 23 September 1833, in which Lockhart discusses Hogg's continuing dispute with William Blackwood ('Ebony'):

> My dear Hogg
> I was pleased to see your hand writing once more this morning but regretted to find that your affairs are not as they ought to be. [...] Tis a pity you & Ebony cd not patch up your senseless dispute–I did what I could when he was in town in the spring but saw he was very angrily obstinate & thought himself seriously injured [...]. I am glad to know that Wilson &

you at least are on friendly terms again. To hear of a quarrell
between you two was indeed painful—but I knew that cd not
last long. God knows friends are dropping so fast into the
grave that we had need to think well before we suffer estrange-
ment to arise among those that survive. (NLS, MS 2245, fols
232–33)

It will be remembered that Lockhart, in his letter to Hogg of 22
March 1833, gives an account of his acrimonious interview with
M'Crone. In that letter, Lockhart states that he told M'Crone 'I have
no right to prevent Hogg or any man from publishing what he pleases
on the subject—Always excepting *letters*'; and it appears that Hogg in
due course began to consider the possibility of publishing a new
version of his anecdotes of Scott. A letter to M'Crone of 12 May
1833 seems to suggest that a plan for a new version of this kind was
already forming in Hogg's mind. This letter is worth quoting in full,
as it offers a glimpse of some of Hogg's various concerns and activi-
ties during the period in which he wrote his anecdotes of Scott.

My dear Mac.
I am sure I have no reason to be angry with you though you
may have some to be angry with me for withdrawing the M.S.
which I wrote purposely for you and at your request. But
though I think Lockhart was very wrong and behaved very ill
I do not see that I could behave otherwise than as I did. And
moreover as he and Chambers are both quite mad at you and
considering the power that they possess over the whole British press I saw that they would damn the work in the very
outset.[17] I got a kind letter from Lockhart in answer to mine
acknowledging that he got into ill temper at our taking the
start of him and saying there were some things in it that I *durst*
not have published if Scott had been living There he was
wrong; for saving for good friendship's sake I cared as little
either for Sir Walter's good or ill-will as I do for his though I
have always considered myself honoured in both and wish
never to make an enemy whom I can retain as a friend. He
asked pardon for any rash expressions he might have used
but still he gave me no liberty to publish I therefore think that
it would be better to suppress the work for a while till we see
if the bowls will rowe right for I have the warmest wish to
further it for your sake and if I set my old shoulder to it freely
depend on it I'll give it a heeze in spite of the devil the world
and the flesh. I can add a great deal more but I would not like

to have these original anecdotes garbled every one of which are strickly and literally true. They should either be published just fully and fearlessly as I have written them or not at all. I got a tempting offer from a place called ALBANY somewhere in America for some original anecdotes of Scott but I wrote an answer declining it. I have likewise put off the Messers Blackie for two or three months until I see how you come on.[18] I would like at all events if practicable that your names were in as publishers and as the Blackies are good men and sell to all the TRADE at half price you cannot be wrong in taking a few hundreds of each vol. What are become of all the vols of my tales which Cochrane and Mason contrived to preserve for me?[19] Am I never to realize any thing from them? Why do you not tell me any thing about the Cochranes? You should remember that there is no family in England whom I love so much as the Cochranes. Kiss dear sweet Mary Anne[20] for me and give her the old shepherd's blessing. I would like to kiss Mrs Cochrane myself but I wont depute you so all that you have to do is to give my kindest love to her. There is a lady I think Mrs Norman Lamont[21] who wrote to me for *holographs*! I told her that you had some hundreds of mine and all the literary men in Britain so that you may depend on it she will apply to you therefore have plenty ready and as I shall ad-dress this under cover to her husband who is I think member for Leeds it is likely she will deliver it with her own hand as she lives very near your door in St James's. I have five gen-tlemen living with me just now but I have some hopes there is one going away to morrow. I will however be happy to see you though we should make you a *shakedown*. Tell honest kind-hearted Christie[22] that his brother James is still with me and has been I know not how long as I cannot turn him away. He does little odd jobs for us about the garden and hedges and I pay him 11/ a week discounting four for bed and board He is a clever obliging fellow. I have been trying my whole interest to get him established as the Duke of Buccleuch's slater and I believe there is not a better tradesman in Britain but the devil is I cannot answer for his steadiness for though perfectly so-ber the greater part of the year

> One single glass will set him on
> And simple is the spell
> But he never will give over again
> Not for the devil himsel'[23]

I have hopes however that I will succeed in getting him established as secondary headsman at any rate. It is very seldom that I read a letter now and far seldomer that I write but Margaret[24] reads them and then she says there are such and such letters that I *must* answer and then what can one do? I got a severe cold last winter and disregarding it went to Edin[r] and joined my old favourite Duddingston club wrought wonders at the curling fell through the ice over the head and got exceedingly ill was long confined in Edin[r] and Mrs Hogg had to come in and wait on me.[25] I have never been well since and find that I never will be well again. If Mrs Lamont calls with this letter say that your holographs are all at home but that you will look them out for her and wait on her with them at 3 Rider Street St James's

Yours very truly
James Hogg
(Bodleian Library, Oxford, MS AUTOGR. d. 11, fols 321–22)

It is possible to see a hint of troubles to come when Hogg asks M'Crone 'Why do you not tell me any thing about the Cochranes?' The above letter was written in May 1833, and just over a year later Cochrane discovered that his wife had been carrying on an adulterous love affair with M'Crone. This became generally known to the friends and associates of the people involved; and on 8 November 1834 Hogg wrote to his friend Allan Cunningham in London for further news of the affair:

I write this at Mrs Hogg's earnest request who sends her kindest respects to Mrs C. and you and requests to know all that you know about Mr M,Crone and Mrs Cochrane for there are so many things one cannot ask a husband. How were they discovered? Was the thing found out and proved to a certainty? If so it has been an amour of some standing for during the time he was here the summer before last there was a constant correspondence carried on between him and a Miss Salem which I am almost certain was in her hand. [...] My wife is so shocked at it that she is like to faint whenever it is spoken about. Poor woman she kens very little about London morality. I am going to venture a few vols with Mr Cochrane[26] I am not greedy of remuneration but I would like to do him some good if I could without doing ill to myself. (Beinecke Library, Yale University)

Hogg's reference to 'the time he was here the summer before last' suggests that M'Crone had been at Altrive in the summer of 1833, in addition to his visit in the autumn of 1832; and this is confirmed by other references in Hogg's correspondence. Indeed, M'Crone seems to have packed a great deal of activity of various kinds into the 1830s, before his early death in 1837 (he had been born in 1809). In September 1834, when his partnership with Cochrane came to its dramatic end, M'Crone set himself up in business on his own account at 3 St James's Square, London. He was a close friend of the very promising young writer Charles Dickens; and M'Crone was the publisher of Dickens's *Sketches by Boz*, which appeared early in 1836. A dispute with Dickens followed towards the end of 1836; and by the time of his death in 1837 M'Crone was in severe financial difficulties.[27]

With regard to the anecdotes of Scott, the crucial sentence in Hogg's letter to M'Crone of 12 May 1833 is the following one: 'I got a tempting offer from a place called ALBANY somewhere in America for some original anecdotes of Scott but I wrote an answer declining it'. This sentence can be read as a hint that Hogg would like to accept the tempting American offer, Lockhart's disapproval having made British publication impractical. M'Crone's reply to Hogg's letter of 12 May 1833 does not survive; but as we have seen, M'Crone visited Altrive later that summer. Surviving letters to Hogg suggest that M'Crone set out for Scotland after 29 May 1833, and returned to London before 24 July 1833 (see NLS, MS 2245, fols 222–23 and MS 2245, fols 228–29). Hogg accepted the 'tempting offer' from Albany in a letter of 22 June 1833; and it may well be that he wrote this letter with M'Crone's encouragement, while M'Crone was at Altrive. Hogg writes as follows to S. De Witt Bloodgood, his Albany correspondent:

> Altrive by Selkirk the 22ᵈ the longest day of 1833
> Dear Sir
>     There is such a genuine spirit of kindness in both your letters that I cannot resist complying with your request. I therefore send you the best article that I have in my own estimation. It was written for a young friend in London with a reference to Lockhart for correction but he got into such a violent rage at my intrusion on his sphere that I thought proper to withdraw it. It is therefore wholly unappropriated and your own. I make you my trustee for it  Publish it in what shape or form or as many shapes and forms as you like. But attend to this. I would like if you could confine it to America and not let the right of publishing reach Britain at all. But if you cannot

effect this and if it is contrary to the law of nations then be sure to send every sheet as it comes from the press to Messrs Cochrane & Co 11 Waterloo Place London which secures the copyright to me here provided the articles or work is published in Albany and London at the same time

There is likewise a poem of mine which I would have liked much to have added to this work. It was written about 1820 and addressed to Sir Walter on first hearing that he was made a baronet but I cannot lay my hands on it and where to direct you to find it I cannot tell. I know it was published at the time but whether in a Magazine or in the fourth vol of my Poetical works published by Constable I am quite uncertain[28] If you can find it add it to this here inclosed and then you will have all embodied that I have ever written about Scott

(Beinecke Library, Yale University)

Thus it was that Harper and Brothers of New York, in 1834, published Hogg's *Familiar Anecdotes of Sir Walter Scott*, with a memoir of Hogg by Bloodgood. This book does not contain Hogg's poem 'written about 1820 and addressed to Sir Walter on first hearing that he was made a baronet'. However, the poem in question introduces the *Familiar Anecdotes* in the present edition, thus giving effect to Hogg's wishes.

In his letter to Bloodgood of 22 June 1833, Hogg seems to imply that he is enclosing the manuscript he had prepared for M'Crone; but this is not the case. In fact, Hogg wrote a new manuscript for Bloodgood, and this new manuscript survives in the Pierpont Morgan Library, New York. At the end of the first paragraph of the new manuscript, Hogg writes '(*then copy the whole of the Reminiscences of him in The Altrive Tales*)'. The volume of *Altrive Tales* published by Cochrane in 1832 contains Hogg's autobiographical *Memoir of the Author's Life*; and the *Memoir* includes a section on Scott which is a reprint (with some minor alterations in wording and one long insertion) of Hogg's 1829 article for the *Edinburgh Literary Journal*, 'Reminiscences of Former Days. My First Interview with Sir Walter Scott'. This material from *Altrive Tales* duly appears in the New York *Familiar Anecdotes*; but the version printed in the *Familiar Anecdotes* differs somewhat from the *Altrive Tales* version. No doubt some of the changes can be attributed to Bloodgood, but many of them appear to be authorial. It would appear that 'this here enclosed' (as Hogg puts it in his letter to Bloodgood of 22 June 1833) comprised not only the new manuscript of the anecdotes of Scott, but also a copy of *Altrive Tales* in which Hogg had marked some revisions.

In the original version prepared for M'Crone, Hogg's anecdotes of Scott are presented as the Shepherd's spontaneous oral reminiscences of 'his great patron', these reminiscences being carefully elicited and recorded by the alert M'Crone (who, as it were, acts as Boswell to Hogg's Johnson). The circumstances in which the second version was published were entirely different from the circumstances of publication that had been envisaged for the first version; and as a result the second version is organised along very different lines. For the second version, Hogg's plan seems to have been to bring together everything he had previously written about his friendship with Scott: that is to say, the celebratory poem (first published in the *Poetical Works* of 1822) which he had written on learning about Scott's elevation to a baronetcy; the article containing reminiscences of his first meeting with Scott, published in the *Edinburgh Literary Journal* in 1829; and the anecdotes prepared for M'Crone in 1833. As these anecdotes were no longer to be presented as an informal record of spontaneous conversations, they are reshaped into a more coherent sequence. Likewise, the material to which Lockhart had specifically objected is omitted; and some new anecdotes are added. This new material includes, for example, the anecdote about the poem by Mr Gillies (pp. 61–62 below), as well as the final passage about Hogg's calls at Abbotsford during Scott's last illness (p. 75 below).

*Familiar Anecdotes of Sir Walter Scott* was published in New York in April 1834; and in June 1834 a new edition appeared, published by John Reid & Co. of Glasgow, in association with Oliver & Boyd of Edinburgh, and various London publishers. (In some copies the London publishers named are Whittaker, Treacher & Co.; and in other copies the London publishers named are Black, Young, and Young.) This new edition was given the title *The Domestic Manners and Private Life of Sir Walter Scott*, and it includes a slightly shortened version of Bloodgood's Memoir, as well as some new footnotes.

The new footnotes do not appear to be by Hogg: for example, one of them reads 'Saul among the prophets! Hogg quoting Latin!' (p. 136; p. 125 in the present edition). Indeed, the *Domestic Manners* appears to be a pirated edition. We have seen that Hogg did not wish the new version of his anecdotes of Scott to be published in Britain; and Cochrane had warned him in a letter of 9 August 1833 about the probability that a British piracy would quickly appear:

> I am afraid we shall never see the proofsheets—but the work is sure to be imported—or reprinted here within two months of its appearance in America. (NLS, MS 2245, fols 230–31)

A pirated British edition was likely to follow publication in America because of the state of copyright law in the early nineteenth century; and because, in the aftermath of Scott's death, reminiscences of the great novelist by his friend the Ettrick Shepherd were highly saleable.

Lockhart, unsurprisingly, was far from enthusiastic about the *Domestic Manners*, writing as follows to William Blackwood on 18 August 1834, a couple of months after the appearance of the pirated volume in Britain.

> In Wilson's hands the Shepherd will always be delightful;[29] but of the fellow himself I can scarcely express my contemptuous pity, now that his 'Life of Sir W. Scott' is before the world. I believe it will, however, do Hogg more serious and lasting mischief than any of those whose feelings he has done his brutal best to lacerate would wish to be the result. He has drawn his own character, not that of his benevolent *creator*, and handed himself down to posterity—for the subject will keep *this* from being forgotten—as a mean blasphemer against all magnanimity. Poor Laidlaw will be mortified to the heart by this sad display. The bitterness against me which peeps out in many parts of Hogg's narrative is, of course, the fruit of certain rather hasty words spoken by me to Cochrane and MacCrone when they showed me the original MS, but nevertheless Hogg has *omitted* the only two passages which I had read when I so expressed myself,—one of them being a most flagrant assault on Scott's veracity, and the other a statement about poor Lady Scott, such as must have afflicted for ever her children, and especially her surviving daughter [Sophia, Lockhart's wife]. Dr Maginn has handled Hogg in his own way in 'Fraser's Mag.'[30]

William Maginn was the editor of *Fraser's Magazine*, and he 'handled Hogg' with some vigour in two reviews in *Fraser's* in the immediate aftermath of the publication of the *Domestic Manners* in June 1834. The number for July 1834 contains a review by Maginn of Hogg's *A Series of Lay Sermons on Good Principles and Good Breeding*; and the number for August 1834 contains a review by Maginn of the *Domestic Manners*. Maginn and Lockhart were close associates; and, in her thesis on 'James Hogg's Fiction and the Periodicals', Gillian Hughes has suggested that the vigour and venom of these two reviews may derive directly from the animosities generated by Hogg's quarrel with Lockhart. Hughes writes:

It is not possible to say that the review [of the *Domestic Manners*] was written at Lockhart's instigation, but it pleased him and may well have been written with that intention. Perhaps the feelings roused towards Hogg by this literary quarrel also found expression in the review of another Hogg work in the preceding number of the magazine; Hogg's *A Series of Lay Sermons on Good Principles and Good Breeding* was not only attacked but deliberately misquoted and misrepresented, although it was brought out by the publisher of the magazine. The review is so cleverly managed that on a superficial reading and without comparing the reviewer's extracts with the original text it seems to be a kindly review of a grossly personal and vulgar book. It has been attributed to Allan Cunningham indeed, whose simple honesty and warm friendship for Hogg would not have permitted him to write it.[31] The review ends, for example, with ten maxims supposedly taken from Hogg's sermon on the text "It is better to marry than burn"; they all illustrate his supposed lapses from delicacy of language and idea in discussing sexual concerns, and are given references to pages subsequent to page 352. Hogg's book, however, ends at page 330, and his earlier sermon on the text decorously treats the marriage state as a companionable one, and discusses a proper conduct to be observed in it by the husband. Besides this unfair invention, the reviewer also alters Hogg's existing text to make personal and scandalous allusions to Lord Grey, to emphasise the naive and limited experience of the Shepherd, and to present a picture of a jolly convivial man trying to express himself in moral terms essentially foreign to his nature.[32]

The reaction of Lockhart amply demonstrates that Hogg's anecdotes of Scott had a capacity to touch raw nerves. This seems to be connected with a collision of different attitudes to class, a collision that is produced when these anecdotes seek to define the basis of the relationship between Hogg and Scott. I am indebted to Ian Duncan for the suggestion that Scott provides a sketch of Hogg in the character of Gurth, the swineherd (inevitably!) in *Ivanhoe*. Gurth becomes the loyal feudal follower of the knight Ivanhoe; and in this can be seen Scott's idealised conception of the relationship between the Shepherd and Sir Walter. Hogg sometimes plays up to this feudal notion of his relationship with Scott, as for example when he describes Scott in the anecdotes as his 'great patron'. Also unmistakably present in the anecdotes, however, is Hogg's desire to achieve a different kind of friendship with Scott; a friendship that will rest

entirely (rather than partly) on the kind of attitude to class given
expression in Burns's 'For a' that and a' that'.

> Is there, for honest Poverty
>         That hings his head, and a' that;
> The coward-slave, we pass him by,
>         We dare be poor for a' that!
>     For a' that, and a' that,
>         Our toils obscure, and a' that,
>     The rank is but the guinea's stamp,
>         The Man's the gowd for a' that.— [...]
>
> Ye see yon birkie ca'd, a lord,
>         Wha struts, and stares, and a' that,
> Though hundreds worship at his word,
>         He' but a coof for a' that.
>     For a' that, and a' that,
>         His ribband, star and a' that,
>     The man of independant mind,
>         He looks and laughs at a' that.— [...]
>
> Then let us pray that come it may,
>         As come it will for a' that,
> That Sense and Worth, o'er a' the earth
>         Shall bear the gree, and a' that.
>     For a' that, and a' that,
>         Its comin yet for a' that,
>     That Man to Man the warld o'er,
>         Shall brothers be for a' that.—[33]

The pain that was plentifully present in both versions of Hogg's
anecdotes (not only for the writer of these texts, but also for some of
their first readers) was a product of the gap between the aspirations
of Burns's song, and the realities of life in early-nineteenth-century
Edinburgh. That pain is still all too evident to readers of these texts
today; but in and through the pain, Hogg's anecdotes of Scott still
have much of significance to say about a long friendship between
two major writers.

## Notes

1. The article about Cunningham appears in the *Edinburgh Literary Journal*, 16 May 1829, pp. 374–75; and the article about Scott appears in the *Edinburgh Literary Journal*, 27 June 1829, pp. 51–52.

2. It appears that Hogg was baptised on 9 December 1770, but until almost the end of his life he believed that he had been born on 25 January 1772 (which is indeed 'five months and ten days' after Scott's date of birth, 15 August 1771). 'Dr Russell of Yarrow says that he was at last undeceived by the parish register and mourned over having two years less to live' (Edith C. Batho, *The Ettrick Shepherd* (Cambridge: Cambridge University Press, 1927), p. 11.

3. 'Hogg's Three Perils of Woman', *Blackwood's Edinburgh Magazine*, 14 (October 1823), 427–37 (p. 427).

4. For Scott's letter to Lord Montagu, see *The Letters of Sir Walter Scott*, ed. by H. J. C. Grierson, 12 vols (London: Constable, 1932–37), IV, 461; and for his reference to Hogg as 'the honest grunter', see *The Journal of Sir Walter Scott*, ed. by W. E. K. Anderson (Oxford: Clarendon Press, 1972), p. 35.

5. Lockhart's much-praised biography of Burns had been published in 1828.

6. Lockhart's novel *Adam Blair* (1822) had been a popular success; and presumably Hogg means that the projected book on Scott will be equally successful.

7. National Library of Scotland (hereafter NLS), MS 924, no 83. Hogg is proposing a system of copying manuscripts similar to that which Scott had adopted to preserve his anonymity as the author of the Waverley Novels.

8. Hogg learned of Cochrane's bankruptcy from a letter of 27 April 1832 sent to him by Sir Richard Phillips (Stirling University Library, MS 25 box 2(2)).

9. See Hogg's letter to M'Crone of 23 March 1832 (Huntington Library, California, Rare Book 320006, vol. 1).

10. Hogg's daughter Harriet moved with her husband and family to New Zealand in 1879; and a large collection of Hogg's papers was later donated to the Alexander Turnbull Library by her descendants.

11. For a valuable discussion of the oral in nineteenth-century Scottish writing, see Penny Fielding, *Writing and Orality: Nationality, Culture, and Nineteenth-Century Scottish Fiction* (Oxford: Clarendon Press, 1996).

12. Allan Cunningham, 'Some Account of the Life and Works of Sir Walter Scott, Bart', *The Athenaeum*, 6 October 1832, pp. 641–53; and Robert Chambers, 'Life of Sir Walter Scott', *Chambers's Edinburgh Journal* [6 October 1832], Supplement.

13. Sir Adam Ferguson (1771–1855) was one of Scott's closest friends. His sisters lived at Huntley Burn on the Abbotsford estate, while Sir Adam himself divided his time between Edinburgh, Huntley Burn, and his estate in Dumfriesshire (see *The Journal of Sir Walter Scott*, ed. Anderson, pp. xxxvi–xxxvii, and the note to 4(b) on p. 92, below).

14. The reference is to *Letters of Sir Walter Scott; Addressed to the Rev. R. Polwhele [and others]* (London, 1832).

15. In 1833 Cochrane and M'Crone published an anonymous two-volume work, *The Waverley Anecdotes, Illustrative of the Incidents, Characters, and Scenery, Described in the Novels and Romances, of Sir Walter Scott, Bart.*

16. James Hogg, *Anecdotes of Sir W. Scott*, ed. by Douglas S. Mack (Edinburgh: Scottish Academic Press, 1983).

17. Robert Chambers (1802–71) founded with his brother the successful and influential Edinburgh publishing firm of W. & R. Chambers. The brothers produced the popular weekly paper *Chambers's Edinburgh Journal*. Lockhart likewise wielded great influence in his capacity as editor of the *Quarterly Review*, a post he held from 1825 till 1853. (This note, and the notes below, draw on the work of Dr Gillian Hughes for a forthcoming edition of Hogg's *Collected Letters*.)

18. Following the failure in 1832 of the *Altrive Tales* project as a result of Cochrane's bankruptcy, Hogg attempted to make alternative arrangements for the publication of a collected edition of his writings; and early in 1833 he was in negotiation about this with the publishers Blackie and Son of Glasgow (see his letter to Blackie of 11 February 1833, NLS, MS 807, fols18–19). In this letter Hogg expresses interest in Blackie's proposals, but makes it clear that he is not yet ready to conclude a bargain. The Blackie project eventually bore fruit after Hogg's death (November 1835). Blackie published *Tales & Sketches, by the Ettrick Shepherd* (6 vols, 1837); and *The Poetical Works of the Ettrick Shepherd* (5 vols, 1838–40).

19. The reference here is to the copies of the first volume of *Altrive Tales*, printed just before Cochrane's bankruptcy in 1832. It appears that these copies remained on Cochrane's hands until 1835, when he reissued them with alterations to disguise the fact that they had been intended as the start of a whole series: see Douglas S. Mack, 'James Hogg's "Altrive Tales": An 1835 Reissue', *The Bibliothek*, 5 (1969–1970), 210–11. The identity of Mason is not known.

20. Cochrane's young daughter.

21. On 5 May 1833 (a week before the date of this letter to M'Crone) Hogg had written in response to a request from Hannah Lamont for an example of his autograph (Beinecke Library, Yale University). Hogg correctly assumed that Hannah Lamont was the wife of Major Norman Lamont. The Major had served at Waterloo, and in 1832 he was returned to parliament for Wells (not Leeds as Hogg mistakenly says). In the early 1830s, postal charges were paid by the recipient rather than the sender of a letter. Hogg proposes to send this letter to M'Crone via Major Lamont, because members of parliament could use the post gratis. The Lamonts lived in London at 3 Ryder Street, St James's.

22. John Christie seems to have been connected with Hogg through the London journal *The Metropolitan*: see a letter of 19 March 1832 to Christie from the African traveller John Lander (Beinecke Library, Yale University).

23. An adaptation of the closing lines of the 'Moralitas' from Hogg's ballad 'The Powris of Mosecke', first published in the *Edinburgh Magazine* (a new series of the *Scots Magazine*): *Edinburgh Magazine*, 9 [*Scots Magazine*, 88] (October 1821), 356–61 (p. 361).

24. Hogg's wife.

25. Hogg was always athletic, and continued to compete successfully in sports like archery and curling until late in life. Hogg's curling exploits at the Duddingston Club in Edinburgh are discussed in Norah Parr, *James Hogg at Home* (Dollar: D.S. Mack, 1980), pp. 82–85, 113–14, 116.

26. Cochrane published Hogg's *Tales of the Wars of Montrose* (3 vols) in 1835.

27. M'Crone's dealings with Dickens can be traced in the Pilgrim Edition of *The Letters of Charles Dickens: volume one, 1829–1839*, ed. by Madeline House & Graham

Storey (Oxford: Clarendon Press, 1965). There is a detailed note on M'Crone on p. 81; and numerous references to him can be traced through the Index (see the entry under 'Macrone, John').

28. The poem to which Hogg refers is 'Lines to Sir Walter Scott, Bart.', *Poetical Works of James Hogg*, 4 vols (Edinburgh: Constable, 1822), IV, 133–40.

29. That is, in the *Noctes Ambrosianae*.

30. Quoted in Margaret Oliphant, *Annals of a Publishing House: William Blackwood and his Sons*, 2 vols (Edinburgh: Blackwood, 1897), II, 123.

31. See *Wellesley Index*, II (1972), 343. [Footnote by Dr Hughes.]

32. In a footnote, Dr Hughes adds: 'For specific instances of such distortions compare the differing versions of the relevant passages in the review in *Fraser's Magazine*, 10 (1834), 1–10 (pp. 5, 6, 6) and in James Hogg, *A Series of Lay Sermons on Good Principles and Good Breeding* (London, 1834), pp. 32, 34, 205.' See Gillian Hughes, 'James Hogg's Fiction and the Periodicals' (unpublished doctoral thesis, University of Edinburgh, 1981), pp. 254–55.

33. *The Poems and Songs of Robert Burns*, ed. by James Kinsley, 3 vols (Oxford: Clarendon Press, 1968), II, 762–63.

*Anecdotes of*

*Sir W. Scott*

# Anecdotes of Sir W. Scott

When I was in Scotland last year I got an invitation to the house of The Shepherd which I accepted and remained with him for several weeks. On every occassion I tried to bring out his sentiments regarding his great patron and prototype and as these sentiments were never meant to meet the public eye or ear I deemed them of the greater importance to keep in record as they arose spontaneously from the heart while every trait in the character of so great a man is of the highest importance.

To take the Shepherd's own words as nearly as I could reccollect them every night he said to me one day on the hill "The only blemish or perhaps I should say foible that I ever discerned in my illustrious friend's character was a too high devotion for titled rank. This in him was mixed with an enthusiasm which I cannot describe amounting in some cases almost to adoration if not servility. This was to me the strangest disposition imaginable! For me who never could learn to discern any distinction in ranks save what was constituted by talents or moral worth. I might indeed except the ministers of the gospel for whom I had always a superior veneration? But this was the class that Sir Walter cared least about of any and as far as I remember at this moment with the exception of Dr Hughes and Domonie Samson I never met with a clergyman in his house. It was perhaps on this account that the Rev<sup>d</sup> and venerable Dr Rutherford of Yarrow has always been left out of the list of his genealogy. I remember however of Sir Walter one day in 1806 reading the latin epitaph to me which is engraven on the tomb-stone of that great and good divine of explaining it in English and acknowledging their propinquity but whether he was his great grandfather or grand uncle I *can not* reccollect.

However to return to our amiable Baronet's aristocratic feelings I shall give a few instances of these. Although of course he acknowledged Buccleuch as the head and chief of the whole Clan of Scott yet he always acknowledged Harden as his immediate chief or chieftain of that particular and most powerful sept of Scotts. And Sir Walter was wont often to relate how he and his father before him and his grandfather before that always kept their Christmass with Harden in acknowlegement of their vassallage. This he used to tell with a degree of exultation which I thought must has been astounding to

every one who heard it as if his illustrious name did not throw a
blaze of glory on the house of Harden even a hundred times more
than the descent from that hardy and valiant house could through
upon him. It was no matter what people thought no body could
eradicate those feelings from his mind.

There is another instance at which I was both pleased and dis-
gusted. We happened to meet at a great festival at Bowhill when
Duke Charles was living and in good health. The company being
very numerous there were two tables fitted up in the dining-room
one along and one across. They were nearly of the same length but
at the one along all the ladies were seated mixed alternately with
gentlemen and at this table all were noble save if I remember aright
Sir Adam Ferguson whose everlasting good humour is a passport
for him into all companies. But I having had some chat the young
ladies before dinner and always rather a flattered pet with them
imagined the could not possibly dine without me and placed myself
among them. But there was a friend behind me who saw better. Sir
Walter who presided at the cross table arose and addressing the
Duke of Buccleuch requested him as a particular favour and obligation that he would allow Mr Hogg to come to his table for that he
could not do without him and after some other flattering compliments he added

"And moreover

> "If ye reave the Hoggs o' Fauldshope
> Ye herry Harden's gear."

I of course got permission and retired to Sir Walter's table when
he placed me on the right hand of the gentleman next to his right
hand. That was as a matter of course Scott of Harden and yet not-
withstanding the broad insinuation about the Hoggs of Fauldshope
and Harden so completely opakue was my comprehension that I sat
beside that intelligent and venerable gentleman for a whole night
and all the while took him for an English clergyman. I was quite
dumfoundered when the Duke told me next day that it was Harden.
I knew there were two clergmen of rank connected with the family
there and all the time I took Harden for one of them. And in fact
since he chances not to be a minister of the gospel he ought to have
been one. He has the same sort of dignity jocularity and caution of
expression which you always meet with in them and thus misled me
to my great grief for my forefathers had been farmers or perhaps
rather vassals under the house of Harden on the lands of Fauldshope
for more than two centuries and were only obliged to change mas-

ters with the change of proprietors It was certainly from this connection that my father had instilled into my youthful mind every tradition relating to the house of Harden of which I have made considerable use. But as Burns says

"Whene'er divinity comes cross me
My readers then are sure to lose me"

So I may say that whenever I come to speak of myself I lose the thread of my discourse. It is a failing but certainly a pardonable one with a man in my circumstances.

The thing that I wanted to relate was this that when the dinner came to be served Sir Walter refused to let a dish be set on our table until it once had been presented on the table of the Duke and his nobility "No no" said he "This is literally a meeting of the clan and its adherents and we shall have one dinner in the feudal stile. It may be but for once in our lives."

Assoon as the Duke percieved this whim he admitted it though I believe many of the dishes were merely set down and lifted again. There was another party in the anti-room I don't know whether they persisted in the same principles but I rather think not as they got drunk long before us. At the end of our libations when we parted some time in the course of the morning the Duke set his one foot on his chair and the other on the table and sung "Johny Cope are ye wauking yet" requesting that we would all do the same and join him in the chorus. This was a most puzzling experiment and created infinite fun The Duke kept his station and finished his song with great glee but many of the Scotts and the Elliots came down with a dead weight on the floor as if a shepherd had thrown a dead sheep from his back. The bursts of laughter were far louder than the choruses but the Duke finished steadily and retired. Then a great stirrup cup was proposed to his health with triple honours which was acquiesced in without a division. But the hardest thing of all occurred afterwards. Sir Alexander Don having been so much delighted with the experiment of Johny Cope insisted on performing it again after so good an example in the same stile. He sung the song in capital stile but it was a terrible experiment The men were all so elevated with their great stirrup cup that every one would attempt the ticklish station and down went men chairs and glasses as fast as in a field of battle. In the course of one chorus I lost my balance and made a devil of a run to one corner of the room against which I fell but ran back and resumed my station which feat was hailed with applause. Sir Walter enjoyed the whole scene as indeed he did every scene of hilarity with unmitigated delight always joining in the chorusses with his straight forward bass voice without either a rise or or fall in it.

Again he was descended from the chiefs of Haliburton and Rutherford in a direct line by the maternal side and to this circumstance I have heard him allude so often and of even quartering their arms along with those of the Scotts in his escutcheon that I could not help feeling it to be quite ludicrous. He always expressed himself as if his connections with these houses shed a halo of glory round his head whereas he himself constituted the greatest halo of glory that was ever shed over any of the three families from whom he claimed his immediate descent. I once at his house in Castle Street ventured in a large evening party to attempt a quizz upon him for this propensity but he cut me short with a most laughable anecdote. I am not sure that I always got justice from him in this respect. There was no man ever testified more admiration or astonishment at some parts of my productions than he did. But this was always mixed with direct blame of other parts of my prose works but never of my poetry no not in one instance that I remember of. With regard to my speeches when before people of high rank he seemed always dubious as if afraid of what was next to come out; and he very often cut me short with a droll anecdote for of these his mind was stored with a fund which was perfectly inexhaustible and which I am convinced to this day were generally made extempore as I never in my life heard him repeat an anecdote save one which I heard him repeat year after year until really it grew very stale. After all it was not an anecdote but a saying an aphorism if you will but it was this.

When Sir Walter bought the first portion of the Abbotsford estate the name of the farm house was "Clarty Hole!" which stood on the east portion of the site on which the mansion of Abbotsford now stands and I think on the ground now occupied by the splendid library. Let nae body smile at this I am telling the plain truth for although the Rev^d Dr. Douglas in his advertisements of the sale spelled the farm *Cartley Hole* it had always been in the memory of the oldest person then living termed "Clarty Hole" which in English means a puddle in a hollow! Such was the origin of the now celebrated ABOTSFORD. There was indeed a ford of the river Tweed so named and there was also a steading on the outer part of the estate named Abbotslee which would have been a fine name for the mansion-house and estate But that portion not falling to Sir Walter at the first purchase the former was adopted which I hope will remain as long as the name of Scotland itself. In this cottage of Clarty-Hole I have spent many happy days with Sir Walter and his then young rising family and I never saw him merrier. He felt that he had a place of his own for the first time and seemed perfectly happy remarking with apparently the greatest satisfaction and determination that there was nothing like a small house for a literary man for then that though his friends favoured him with a call during the day they could not saddle themselves upon him as they were always obliged to go away at night. How this sentiment was reversed before the end!

Well this cottage of Clarty-Hole consisted merely of a *butt* and a *ben* a kitchen and parlour namely and I suppose some little garret apartments for where the family all slept God knows for never getting a chance of a bed I had no means of judging. There were two beds in the kitchen that I knew of a surety and I knew no further how matters stood in that respect The parlour or dining room was so small that the servant was always obliged to keep one side and serve across But to return to my everlasting apothegm. This being Sir Walter's original habitation he in a few years planned and begun the Gothic or western portion of the mansion with its tower and its bartizans but left the original cottage joined to it as a relic. The family being exceedingly hampered of room the architects finished always one part before another and the family took possession piecemeal and the peninsular war being raging then the everlasting aphorism began. Sir Walter showed his plan to every friend who came and always with this information in his broad Northumberland burr "We agh just like the Fghench in Saghagossa gaining foot by foot and ghoom by ghoom" I cannot spell it better to his pronounciation but whoever has heard his daughter Anne's pronounciation has heard her father's.

Well it was not long after till the large eastern portion of the mansion was begun and the cottage annihilated. Still the same system was carried on and the same eternal dogma repeated "We are just like the French in Sarragossa gaining foot by foot and room by room but we hope to get possession of the whole by and by" This going on for the space of seven years was rather too much of a good thing. I once ventured to expostulate with him on the impropriety of the latter great extension of his house bringing to his mind his own saying to me of the value of a small house to a literary man. I shall never forget the mildness and suavity of his answer. "Well I was then right Hogg and you are now right in reminding me of it. But the truth is that my faithful my beloved but eccentric friend Johny Ballantyne has left me a legacy of £2000 with a request that it shall

be laid out for the benefit of my family and I have calculated that
there is no way in which I can enhance the value of my estate more
than by making a complete mansion-house" I have great doubts that
he ever inherited a sixpense from Mr John Ballantyne's funds but
knowing Sir Walter's truth and integrity I have no doubt that he
then believed the funds forthcoming.

In all my life I never knew a more sterling and kind-hearted friend
than Sir Walter and then there was no equivocation with him he
always told his sentiments forthright whether they were favourable
or otherwise. He had my success sincerely at heart and yet I think
he once at least mistook himself. I got a letter from him in Nithsdale
informing me that he was going to purchase Broadmeadows on
Yarrow that he was the highest offerer and was he believed sure of
getting it and that he had offered for it half and more on my account
that I might be his chief shepherd and manager of all his pastoral
concerns. The plan misgave. Mr Boyd overbid him and became the
purchaser on which Sir Walter was so vexed on my account I having kept myself out of a place depending upon his that he actually
engaged me to Lord Porchester as his chief shepherd to have a riding horse, house and small farm free of rent, and £20 over and
above, but with this strick proviso that "I was to put my poetical
talent under lock and key for ever" I copy the very words. Of course
I spurned at the idea and refused to implement the bargain. I think
my friend the present Lord Porchester would have been sorry to
have put me under the same restrictions. This is the circumstance alluded to in The Queen's Wake as a reflection on Walter the
Abbot.

On the whole I have never been any thing advantaged by Sir
Walter's friendship save by the honour and undeviating steadiness
of it which I certainly set a high value on. He never would review a
work of mine Never bring me forward by the least remark in any
periodical whatsoever. He was too much of an aristocrate for that.
He once promised to review a work of mine I think Queen Hynde
but he never did it although he had expressed his warmest approbation of it before several friends. I asked him a good while afterwards why he had not kept his word "Why the truth is Hogg" said
he "that I began the thing and took a number of notes marking quo-
tations but I found that in reviewing it I would have been thought to
have been reviewing myself. I found that I must have begun with
THE WAKE or perhaps THE MOUNTAIN BARD and summed up; and upon
the whole I felt that we were so much of the same school that if I had
given as favourable a review as I intended to have done that it would

have been viewed in the light of having applauded my own works."

I cannot say that these were Sir Walter's very words but they were precisely to that purport. But I, like other dissapointed men not being quite satisfied replied in these very words which I can vouch for "Dear Mr Scott ye could never think that I was in the chivalry school like you. I'm the king o' the mountain and fairy school a far higher ane nor your's.

"Well but the higher the ascent the greater may be the fall Hogg so say never a word more about that."

A thing of the very nature happened on my putting to press *The three perils of Man*. Sir Walter requested to see a few of the proof slips which were sent to him on reading of which he sent me an express that he wanted to see me on the score of my new publication. We being both in Edin[r] I attended directly. He took up the slips which were lying on his table and I think I remember every word he said concerning them.

"Well Mr Hogg I have read over the proofs with a great deal of pleasure and I confess with some portion of dread. In the first place the meeting of the two princesses at Castle-Weiry is excellent. I never saw any thing more truly dramatic The characters are all good old Peter Chisholm's in particular. Ah man! what you might have made of that with a little care and patience but it is always the same with you just hurry hurrying on from one vagary to another. In the next place and it was on this account I sent for you. Do you not think there is some little danger in making Sir Walter Scott of Buccleuch the hero of this wild tale?

"The devil a bit" said I.

"I think differently" said he "The present chief is your patron your sincere friend and your enthusiastic admirer. Would it not then be a subject of regret not only to yourself and me but to all Scotland should you by any rash adventure lose the countenance of so great and so good a man?

"There's nae fears o' that ata' Mr Scott" said I. "The Sir Walter Scott of my tale is a complete hero and is never made to say or do a thing of which his discendant the duke winna be prood."

"I am not so sure of that said he. "Do you not think you have made him rather a too selfish character?

"Oo aye. But then that's true. Ye ken they were a' a little that gate" says I.

On which Sir Walter took to himself a hearty laugh and then pronounced these very words "Well Hogg you appear to me just now like a man dancing on a rope or wire at a great height. If he is successful and finishes his dance he has accomplished no great matter but if he makes a slip he gets a devil of a fall."

I laughed in my turn took Sir Walter's hand squeezed it and shook it and said with the tears of gratitude streaming from my eyes "Never say another word about it Scott. I'm satisfied." And with that I went home and altered the designation of the hero from Sir Walter Scott of Buccleuch to Sir Ringan Redhough of Mount-Comyn one of the Buccleuch farms. After all I might as well have let it stand as made this confession which I think due to his sincerity and prudence.

I first met Sir Walter in Ettrick Forest where I spent two days and two nights with him as narrated somewhere else. At that time on parting he invited me to his cottage on the North Esk a little above Laswade and saying as he shook my hand on parting. "I will there introduce you to my wife. She is a foreigner. As dark as a black-berry and does not speak the broad Scots so well as you and I do. Of course I don't expect you to admire her much but I shall insure you of a hearty welcome."

I went and visited them the first time I had occassion to be in Edin<sup>r</sup> expecting to see Mrs Scott a kind of half blackamore whom the Sherrif as we called him had married for a great deal of money. I knew nothing about her save from his own description but the words "as dark as a blackberry" had fixed her colour indelibly on my mind. Judge of my astonishment when I was introduced to one of the most beautiful and handsome creatures as Mrs Scott whom I had ever seen in my life. A brunette certainly with raven hair and large black eyes but in my eyes a perfect beauty. She was dressed in white satin with flowers in her hair her form rather on a small scale but the most perfect symmetry. She was quite affable and spoke English very well save that she always put the *d* for the *th* and gener-ally left out the aspiration of the *h* altogether She called me always Mr Og And I must say this of Lady Scott though I never knew a lady more jealous of the company which her lord kept many many of whom she met with no very pleasant countenance or affable ad-dress Jeffery and his sept she could not endure yet I who was the lowest of all his constant visitors never went there that I did not recieve as cordial a welcome from her as if I had been one of the family. There never was a kinder heart beat in a human breast than her's. When any of the cottagers or retainers about Abbotsford grew ill they durst not tell her because it generally made her worse than they and I have known her moan the whole day and a good part of the night for the distress of an old tailor who was dying and had a small family. She was subjected in her latter years to a habit which I

know gave Sir Walter a great deal of pain but which I do not understand and should therefore have passed over in silence if it had not
been for fear of some false aspersions getting abroad. It was the
taking of opium for a complaint which (poor woman!) was never
revealed until the time was past for curing it. She is cradled in my
remembrance and ever shall be as a sweet kind and affectionate
creature. Sophia was a baby when I saw her first yet though Anne
is much her likeness Charles always appeared to be her chief
favourite.

I am now going to make a serious charge against Sir Walter which
I confess I do not in the least comprehend and hope it has arisen
from some mistake in my comprehension which is never one of the
most acute. It will be easily seen that it is impossible I could have
made the story not knowing even the surname of one nobleman
either in England or Ireland with the exception of Piercy of Northumberland Now this was what he told me or at least as I understood
the story that "his wife and her two brothers were children of the
Earl's of Tyrconnel. But that the marriage having been made abroad
and with a foreigner he found on his return home to his estates in
Ireland that the children of that marriage were illegitimate so he
made a settlement on them and left them with his brother a rich
merch$^t$ in Lyons who brought them up and educated them. And
moreover that very night he showed me a gold watch of rather a
curious construction and some trinkets (antiques if I remember aright)
which he had once lost and recovered with difficulty and these words
I distinctly remember "I would not have lost them for ten times
there value as they were keepsakes given me by my wife's uncle
and guardian Mr Carpenter."

What to make of this story I know not. I have extolled Sir Walter
for his integrity and in all the common affairs of life he was unim-
peachable. But after the thousands of *lees* that he told regarding the
anonymous novels and even swore to them it is needless to brag
very much of his truth This is the story he told me as I concieved it.
I believed it and spread it among all my acquaintances for the space
of five and twenty years when to my astonishment speaking to Sir
Adam Ferguson about it one day he told me it was all a dream of my
own imagination for that no such thing ever was heard of. That
Lady Scott was in fact as far as he knew the daughter of a Mr John
Carpenter a merchant in Lyons. As I am an honest man I have told
this story as I understood it but am willing to admit that I may have
misapprehended him. I have tried to discover if this Mr John Carpenter was not a son of the Earl's of Tyrconnel but have hitherto

been unable to trace the connection. Some one I am sure will sift it to its foundation.

Sir Walter was always affable in his family but highly imperative. No one durst object to an order or even a hint from him. Whenever his shaggy eye-brows began to hang down it was a warning for them all to be upon their p's and their q's and to take particular care what they said. Sophia now Mrs Lockhart was always his darling while her attachment to him was boundless. Whenever he came into a room where she was her countenance changed and she was often moved to involuntary laughter. I shall never forget with what affection she used to look up in his face as he hung over her while singing the old Scottish ballads at the harp or piano. She was indeed formed by Providence to be the child of his heart completely the child of nature simple and unaffected without one grain of affectation in her whole composition. He got a way of calling his second daughter "little Anne" which term he continued every time he named her long after she was bigger than her mother. He was much prouder of Lockhart than any of his other sons and has often spoken of him to me with a degree of enthusiasm which I (knowing him a great deal better than he did) thought he hardly deserved. Whenever he spoke of Walter or Charles which he frequently did it was always in a quizzical way to raise a laugh at their expense. His description of Walter when he led in Mrs Lockhart a bride with his false mostachios and whiskers was a theme of infinite amusement to him. He was wont often also to recite some of Charles' wise sayings which in the ludicrous tone that he gave them never failed to set the company in a roar of laughter. When Sophia was a mere child the mutual affection between the father and daughter was notable. I came behind them one morning in the arbour at Ashiesteel when I do not think Sophia was much more than three years old Walter was just beginning to walk. Sir Walter was asking a great number of simple questions at her to every one of which Sophia answered YES. "You are certainly in a very complaisant mood to day my dear Sophia" said he. "Pray is there no question to which you can answer No?

"No" said Sophia on which he set her down and said smiling as he patted her head "You are a dear child Sophia and have a good heart though God knows not the clearest head in the world."

When I resided in Edin$^r$ I used to go two or three times in the week to breakfast with Scott as I was then always sure to enjoy an hour's conversation with him before he went to the court of Session. Then every morning Sophia met him with smiles and embraces "Now see Papa how nicely I have toasted your roll for you.

And see how I have steeped it with butter that you might like it Papa. And here's a slice I have toasted in a different way and I'll boil your egg to you so nicely!" On which he used to say with a careless air and the very face that Chantry has given him "Ay ay. You agh a veghy good gighle Sophia" and so ended the colloquay.

The only disagreeable thing attending these delightful dejunes was the meeting sometimes with a number of minor poets a sort of sattelites that alwas hovered around Sir Walter and no man ever knew or ever will know what he laid out for the support of those poor fellows. Lady Scott hated them. But then whenever a tale of want or misery assailed her ears her heart was malleable. Malleable! Alas it was butter it melted and then the poor fellows were made welcome to every thing in the house.

This brings to my mind another anecdote which I must relate. One morning when I went in to my breakfast Sir Walter said to me with his eyes perfectly staring "Good lord Hogg have you heard what has happened?"

"Na, no that I ken o' Scott" said I. "What is it that you allude to?

"That our poor friend Irving has put himself down last night or this morning" said he

"Oo aye I heard o' that" said I with shameful coldness "But I never heeded it; for Irving was joost like the Englishman's fiddle. "The warst fault that he had he was useless." Irving could never have done any good for his family for himself or for any other body."

"I don't know Hogg what that poor fellow might have done with encouragement" said he "This you must at least confess that if he did not write genuine poetry he came the nearest to it of any man that ever failed." These were Sir Walter's very words and I record them in memory of the hapless victim of despair and dissapointed vanity. Sir Walter moreover added "For me his melancholly fate has deranged me so much that it will be many days before I can attend to any thing again."

The truth is that Sir Walter had his caprices like other men, and when in bad health was very cross but I always found his heart in the right place and that he had all the native feelings and generosity of a man of true genius. But he hated all sorts of low vices and blackguardism with a perfect detestation. There was one Sunday when he was riding down Yarrow in his carriage with several attendants on horseback; he being our Sherrif I rode up to him and with a face of the deepest concern stated to him that there was at that instant a cry of *murder* from Broadmeadows wood and that Will Watherston was murdering Davie Brunton. "Never you mind Hogg" said he with rather a stern air in his face and without a smile on it. "If Will Watherstone murder Davie Brunton and be hanged for the crime it is the most fortunate thing that can happen to the parish. Peter drive on."

He was no great favourer of religion and never went to church that ever I heard of excepting once or twice on King's fast days as we call them. He was a complete and finished aristocrate and the prosperity of the state was his whole concern which prosperity he deemed lost unless both example and precept flowed by regular grades from the highest to the lowest. True he wrote two very indifferent moral sermons but he was no religionist. He dreaded it as a machine by which the good government of the country might be deranged if not uprooted. With regard to this feeling I may mention one or two laughable anecdotes. One day Laidlaw and he were walking together in the garden at Abbotsford. The western portion of the mansion was then a building and the architect I think was a Mr Paterson.

"Well do you know Laidlaw" said Sir Walter "that Paterson is one of the best natured intelligent fellows that ever I met with? I am quite delighted with him and he is a fund of continual amusement to me. If you heard but how I torment him! I attack him every day on the fundamental principles of his own occupation. I take a position which I know to be false and stand by it and it is quite amazing with what good sense and good nature the fellow maintains his points I like Paterson exceedingly."

"O he's a fine fallow" said Laidlaw "an extrodnar fine fallow; an' has a great deal o' comings an' gangings in him. But dinna ye think Mr Scott that it's a great pity he should hae been a preacher?"

"A preacher?" said Scott "Good lord! what do you mean?"

"Aha lad!" said Laidlaw "He's a preacher I assure ye. A capital preacher! He's reckoned the best methodist (or Baptist I have forgot which) preacher in Galashiels an' preaches every Sunday."

Sir Walter wheeled about and halted off with a swiftness which Laidlaw had never seen him before exercise, exclaiming to himself "A preacher! G–d d–n him!" From that time forth his delightful colloquays with Paterson ceased.

There was another time when he and Mr Morrit and I were sitting together at Abbotsford conversing over our bottle that he said "There is nothing in this world to which I have a greater aversion than a very religious woman. She is not only a dangerous person but a perfect shower-bath on all social conversation. The enthusiasm of our Scottish ladies about religion has now grown to such a

height that I am almost certain it will lead to some dangerous revolution in the state. And then to try to check it would only make the
evil worse. Hogg if you ever chuse a wife for God's sake as you
value your own happiness don't chuse a *very* religious one" Nevertheless he generally read the forenoon service from the liturgy in
his family on Sundays.

Sir Walter I am certain entertained an oppressive dread on his
mind of an approaching anarchy and revolution even more dreadful than that which hath as yet befallen to us for many years previous to his death; and it was that dread alone which made him quit
the country when his mind was rather growing imbecile. I have
heard him hint at that dread in a hundred ways besides the above
one about the women As an instance I heard him say one night at
Abbotsford (We had been speaking of lord Buchans statue of Wallace
which I rather admired but which he abhorred) "If I live to see the
day when the men of Scotland like the children of Israel shall every
one do that which is right in his own eyes *which I am certain either I or
my immediate successors shall see* I have long ago settled in my own mind
what I shall do first. I'll go down and blow up the statue of Wallace
with gun powder. Ay I'll blow it up in such stile that there shall not
be one member left attached to another. the horrible monster!"

I think Sir Walter had a great veneration for the character of Sir
William Wallace for I remember long ago when Miss Porter's work
THE SCOTTISH CHIEFS appeared he said to me one morning. "I am
grieved grieved about this work of Miss Porter's! It is a work of
which I wished to think highly and do think highly but as to her
character of Wallace! She has made him a brave fellow it is true and
a fine gentleman. But lord help her! He is not our Wallace at all."

When I was accustomed to breakfast with Sir Walter long ago
as mentioned we just got our roll our tea and our egg; and I have
heard him declare often that he never knew what a good breakfast
was until he came to my cottage but that he had improved upon the
hint. I however had got a previous hint that he and Sir A. Ferguson
would be with me on such a morning *very yaup* and accordingly as
we have a view of the road for more than two miles from Altrive the
moment that they sat down they were presented with abundance of
broiled salmon broiled ham and egg and mutton ham all as if it had
been my ordinary breakfast. They made a capital hand at the vi-
ands which always pleases an entertainer at least one so happy to
see his guests as I was. From that day forth no man would have
missed at Sir Walter's breakfast table a plate of rein-deer tongue
ham corned beef and eggs. Fish I never remember of seeing at

it but which is never a wanting at mine.

One day when he was dining with me at Mount-Benger he took a great deal of notice of my only son James and asked me anent his capabilities I told Sir Walter that he was a very amiable and affectionate boy but that I was afraid he would never be the Cooper of Fogo for he seemed to be blessed with a very thick head. "Why but Mr Hogg" said he "It is not fair to lay the saddle on a foal. I for my part never liked precocity of genius all my life and believe that James will turn out a very fine fellow and an honour to you and to all your friends."

The boy had at that time taken a particular passion for knives especially large ones and to amuse him Sir Walter showed him a very large gardener's knife which he had in his pocket. It contained a saw but I never regarded it and would not have known it next day. James however never forgot it and never has forgot it to this day and I should like very well if that knife was still to be found that James should get it as a keepsake. Col Ferguson percieving the boy's ruling passion made him a present of his own knife a handsome two-bladed one. But that made no impression on James he forgot Col. Ferguson the next day but Sir Walter he never forgot till he came back again always denominating him "the man wi' the gude knife."

The last time he dined with me was likewise at Mount-Benger in the Autumn of 1829 and I never saw him more merry and jocular. Were I to recite all the little droll stories he told that day they would fill half a volume by themselves but I could not do them justice for though I account myself a very good teller of a story yet that man never was born who could tell a good story in as few words as Sir Walter He seemed always particularly well pleased with Mrs Hogg and paid her a great deal of deference. As it behoved me I took her down and introduced her at Abbotsford assoon as we were married and from that day forth she became a favourite. There was a good deal of company there yet he did Margaret the honour of leading her into dinner and placing her beside him. As for her poor woman she perfectly adored him. That day when he last left Mount-Benger he snatched my little daughter Maggy up in his arms and kissed her saying "God bless you my dear child" on which my wife burst into a flood of tears. When I came back in again from setting him away I said "What ailed you Margaret."

"Oh!" said she "I thought if he had but just done the same to them all I know not what in the world I would not have given" The last time she saw him was in his own house in Maitland Street a short time before he finally left it She and I were passing by chance from Charlotte Square to The Lothian Road when I happened to say "see yonder is Sir Walter's house at yon lamp" Whenever she heard that she refused to go by without seeing him once more as she said so in we went and were recieved with all the cordiality of old friends. But he addressed his whole discourse to her never heeding me but leaving me to shift for myself. He talked to her of our family and of their education and of our prospects in life enabling us to give them a good one which he earnestly recommended He talked also to her about Mr Lockhart's family and gave her rather a melancholly account of the health of little Hugh John Lockhart (the now celebrated Hugh Littlejohn) for whom he had a great affection but of whose life he then despaired. At least he despaired of ever seeing him reach manhood. The only exchange of words I got with him during that short visit was truly of a very important nature. In order to attract his attention from my wife to one who I thought better deserved it I went up to him with a curious scrutinizing look and giving my hand a sleek down over his ribs I said "Guide us Sir Walter but ye hae gotten a braw gown!" On which he fell a laughing and said "I got it made for me in Paris (such a year) when certain great persons sometimes chose to call on me of a morning, and I never thought of putting it on since until the day before yesterday but I shall always think the higher of my braw gown Mr Hogg for your notice of it" I think it was made of black twilled satin.

The last time I saw his loved and honoured face was at the little inn on my own farm in the Autumn of 1830 He sent me word that he was to pass on such a day but that he was sorry he could not call and see Mrs Hogg and the bairns Altrive being so far off the road. I accordingly waited at the inn and handed him out of the carriage. His daughter was with him but we left her at the inn and walked down the road together till the horses rested. He then walked very ill indeed for his weak leg had become completely useless but he leaned on my shoulder all the way and did me the honour of saying that he never leaned on a firmer or a surer. We talked of many things past present and to come but both his memory and onward calculation appeared to me then to be much decayed. He expressed the deepest concern for my welfare and success in life and his sorrow for my worldly misfortunes and told me that which I never knew till that day that a certain gamekeeper on whom he bestowed his maledictions without reserve had prejudiced my best friend the young Duke of Buccleuch against me by a story which although he knew to be an invidious and malicious lie yet he durst not open his mouth upon the subject farther than by saying "But my lord Duke you must always remember that Hogg is no ordinary man although he may have shot a stray moor-cock" And then turning to me he said "Before you had ventured to give any saucy language to a low scoundrel of a gamekeeper you should have thought of Fielding's tale of — I have forgot what.*

"Dinna trouble your head about that Sir Walter" said I "It's out o' nature awthegither that the young Duke should entertain ony animosity against me. I hae sometimes shot *at* a paetrick and huntit a hare on his land without ony leave because in his father's life-time I had always free liberty for these. When auld Tam Whitson aince gae leave it was never taken away again without warning an' I still stand on the gude auld system As for the rest of the story it is a made and manifest lie for I never suffered a friend to fire a shot on his Grace's land when I could prevent it and if I found that they did so I told the gamekeepers of it directly even of my nearest friends."

"I know that" said he "at least I know instances of it and it is therefore the more painful that the Duke should be made to believe the contrary. If I were you I would take the most strenuous measures of exculpating myself."

"Na na I'll do nae sickan thing said I "I hate to rake up cauld embers to kindle a new fire with. Depend on it the thing will never be mair heard of an' the chap that tauld the Duke thae lees will gang to hell that's ay some comfort."

"You are aye the auld man" said Scott.

Before we parted I mentioned my plan to him of trusting an edition of my tales to Lockhart. He disapproved of it altogether and said he would not for any thing that Lockhart should enter on any such responsibility for that considering my ram-stam way of writing the responsibility was a heavy and a dangerous one. I use his very words. And then turning half round leaning on his crutch and fixing his eyes on the ground after hanging down his large eye-brows for a good long space he said "you have written a great deal that might be made available Hogg with proper attention. And I am certain that day or other it will become available to you or your family But in my opinion this is not the proper season. I wish you could drive off the experiment until a time when the affairs of the nation are in better keeping For at present all things and in particular literature are going straight down hill to ruin."

The real truth I believe is that the Whig ascendancy in the British

---

* If you know what he alluded to mention the place or copy it.

cabinet killed Sir Walter. Yes. It affected his brain and killed him. From that period forth he lost all hope of the prosperity and ascendancy of the British empire. Nay he not only lost hope of the success of the empire but that of every individual pertaining to it and I am sorry to see and to feel his prediction but too well verified He withstood revolution to the last—he fled from it and fell a victim to it. Honest good man! for I am speaking of him always as a man not as an author Little did I think that day when I handed him into the coach that I was never to see him again. Yet I never did for though I called twice at Abbotsford during his last illness they would not let me see him and I did not much regret it. But he said something that day when we parted which in the confusion of parting I afterwards forgot. But it was something to the purport that it was likely he should never lean on my shoulder again. I am sorry I have forgot his particular words for there was an adjective that conveyed his affection for me or his trust in me or something of that nature. This is my last anecdote of my best my most honoured and beloved friend. But I have hundreds of more a few of which I shall register ram-stam as he called it just as they occur.

When I first projected the weekly paper THE SPY I went and consulted him as I generally did in every thing regarding literature. He shook his head and asked if I did not deem it dangerous ground to take the field after Addison Johnson and Henry M‚Kenzie?"

"No" said I "I'm no the least fear'd for't. Naething venture naething won. Though my papers may not be sae elegant as their's I expect they'll be mair original."

"Yes" said he rubbing his beard with his left hand "They will certainly be original enough with a vengeance." I asked him if threepence would be a remunerating price but he answered with a sort of sneer which I never could forget. "I suspect that taking the extent of the sale into calculation she must be a fourpenny cut." He was however right in discouraging it.

I asked him if he would support me in my undertaking and he said he would first see how I came on and if he saw the least prospect of my success he *would* support me and with this answer I was obliged to be content. There never was any man in the world so jealous of lending his name to any publication. The only thing he ever contributed was one letter enclosing two poems of Leyden's for my paper which no body in Europe then had in possession but himself. While speaking of that work I may mention another singular affair between him and me. There was one morning when I went in to breakfast I found him sitting with an air as stern as a judge going to pronounce sentence on a malefactor and at the same time he neither rose nor saluted me as was always his wont. "Mr Hogg I am very angry with you" said he "and I think with good reason. I demand sir an explanation of a sentence in your Spy of yesterday.

Knowing perfectly well what he alluded to seeing him look so stern and aware that he had been as much obliged to me as ever I had been to him at least I having furnished him with the greater part of the third vol. of The Border Minstrelsy my peasant blood began to boil and I found it rushing to my face and head most violently "Then I must first demand an explanation from you Mr Scott" said I. "Were you the author of the paper alluded to that places you at the head and me at the tail of all the poets in Britain?"

What reasons had you for supposing that I was the author of it Sir?" said he.

"Nay what reasons had *you* for supposing it?" said I "by taking it to yourself The truth is that I believed Mr Southey to have been the writer of that paper for Johny Ballantyne told me so. But if the feather suits your cap you are perfectly welcome to it."

"Very well Hogg" said he "That is spoken like a man and like yourself. I am satisfied. I thought it was meant as personal to me. But never mind. We are friends again as usual. Sit down and take your breakfast and it shall never more be mentioned between us."

Mr Southey subsequently told me that he believed Scott to have been the author of that paper. If he was it was rather too bad. It was a review of modern literature in the Edin$^r$ Annual Register. As some readers of these anecdotes may be curious to read the offensive passage in THE SPY I shall here extract it that work being long ago extinct and only occassionally mentioned by myself as a parent will sometimes mention the name of a dear unfortunate child forgotten by all the rest of the world.

"The papers which have given the greatest personal offence are those of Mr Shuffleton which popular clamour obliged the editor reluctantly to discontinue. Of all the poets and poetesses whose works are there emblematically introduced one gentleman alone stood the test and his firmness was even by himself attributed to forgiveness. All the rest male and female tossed up their noses and pronounced the writer an ignorant and incorrigible barbarian. The Spy hereby acknowledges himself the author of those papers and adheres to the figurative characters which he has there given of the poetical works of those authors. He knows it is expected that in a future edition they are all to be altered–They never shall! Though the entreaties of respected friends prevailed on him to relinquish a topic which was his favourite one what he has published he has published and no private considerations shall induce him to an act of such manifest servility as that of making a renounciation. Those who are so grossly ignorant as to suppose the figurative characteristics of the poetry as having the smallest reference to the personal characters of the authors are below reasoning with. Since it has of late become fashionable for some great poets to give an estimate of their own wonderful powers and abilities in periodical works of distinction surely others have an equal right to give likewise their estimates of the works of such bards. It is truly amusing to see how artfully a gentleman can place himself at the head of a school and one who is his superior perhaps at the tail of it. How he can make himself appear as the greatest genius ever existed. With what address he can paint his failings as beauties and depict his greatest excellencies as slight defects finding fault only with those parts which every one must admire. The design is certainly an original though not a very creditable one. Great authors cannot remain always concealed let them be as cautious as they will the smallest incident often assists curiosity in making the discovery" *Spy for August 24th 1811.*

This last sentence supposing Mr Scott to have been the author of the article which I now suspect he was, certainly contained rather too broad and insolent a charge to be passed over with impunity. But luckily before writing it I went to my kind friend Johny Ballantyne whose word was sometimes as little to be relied on as any man's I ever knew excepting one and asked him who was the author of that insolent paper in the Register which placed me as the dregs of all the poets of Britain?

"O the paper was sent to our office by Southey" said he "You know he is editor and part proprietor of the work and we never think of objecting to any thing that he sends. Neither my brother James nor I ever read the article till the volume was published" There is no doubt that this was a downright lee for I learned from others that James Ballantyne greatly admired the article and had read a part of it to them in M. S. I however believed it as I did every body. At that period the whole of the aristocracy and literature of Scotland both high and low were set against me and determined to keep me down so that this was but an item in an endless sum. Thanks be to God I have lived to see the sentiments of the nation completely changed.

I once more and only once found Sir Walter in the same capricious and querulous humour. It was the day after the publication of The Brownie of Bodsbeck. I called on him after his return from the

Parliament house to speak to him about something very particular as I pretended but in fact to hear his sentiments of my new work. His eye-brows were hanging very low. a bad presentiment!

Well Mr Hogg I have read through your new work" said he "And I must tell you plainly and downright as I always do that I like it very ill—very ill indeed."

"What for Mr Scott?"

"Because it is a false and unfair picture of the times altogether.

I dinna ken. It is the picture that I hae been bred up in the belief o' sin ever I was born an' mair than that there is not *one* incident not one in the whole tale which I cannot prove to be literally true from history. I was obliged sometimes to change the situations to make one part coalesce with the other but in no one instance have I recorded in The Brownie that which is not true an' that's mair than you can say of your tale o' Auld Mortality.

You are overshooting the mark now Mr Hogg I wish it were my tale.

Na I shoudna hae said that but I forgot mysel. ye may hinder a man to speak but ye canna hinder him to think an I can sometimes yerk at the thinking. I wadna wonder at ye being angry at it if ye thought it written as a counterpoise to Auld Mortality but ye ken weel it was written lang afore the other was heard of.

Yes I know that a part of it was written the year before but I suspect it has been greatly exaggerated since.

The devil a line sir has been either added or diminished that I remember of Mr Blackwood was the only man that read it beside yoursel' an' I appeal to him.

Well well I have nothing to say to that. I have only to tell you that with the exception of old Nanny the crop-eared Covenanter who is by far the best character you ever drew I dislike the tale exceedinly and assure you it is a prejudiced and untrue picture.

It's a devilish deal truer than yours though. An' that I'll prove to the hale warld" and with that I rose and was going away in a huff.

No no stop" said he "You are not to leave me in bad humour. You did not use to be offended at my telling you my mind freely.

"It's the height o' nonsense to be sure" said I quite pacified by so great a man's condescension "But ane's beuks are like his bairns he disna like to hear them spoken ill o' especially without ony good reason."

Then Sir Walter after his customary short hearty laugh repeated a proverb which I have forgot. It was something about the Clans or rather about *one* highland Clan and then added "I wish you to take your dinner with me to day there will be no body with us but James Ballantyne who will read you something new. And by the by I wished to ask something else at you. Ay it was this. Pray had you any tradition on which you founded that ridiculous story about Eildon?"

"Yes I had" said I as far as the white hounds are concerned and the one pulling the poison twice out of the king's hand when it was at his very lips."

"That is very extraordinary said he "For whenever I read it it struck me that I had heard something of the same nature but how or where I could not reccollect. I think it must have been when I was in the cradle. It is a very ridiculous story Mr Hogg the most ridiculous I ever read with perhaps the exception of Sindbad the Sailor. It is a pity that you are not master of your own capabilities for that tale *might* have been made a good one."

I always set so high a value on Sir Walter's opinion that I could recite every sentence, every word almost, that he ever said to me about my own writings. It is somewhat curious that he never once found fault with my poetry. I never once published a poem or song which he did not approve of and some of them he openly commended very highly but I never published a prose work which he did not find fault with and always with the disagreeable adjunction that it might have been made so much better Never considering that if it was beyond my capacity what way could I help it. With my poetry it was quite different and in his correspondence with Miss Seward and Lord Byron as will be seen ere long he said it was wonderful and as the work of a common hired shepherd altogether beyond his comprehension. He once told me an anecdote derogatory to himself and complimentary to me which a poet is not very apt to do. He was quarter-master he said to the Edin$^r$ or Mid Lothian gentlemen volunteers I have forgot which. But he wrote a song for the corps and got a friend to learn it and sing it at the mess. I never either heard or saw that song but I had his own word for it and am sure there was such a thing.* It did not take And a Mr Robertson got up and said "Come come! That's but a drool of a sang. Let us hae Donald M,Donald" on which Donald M,Donald was struck up and joined in with such glee that all the mess got up joined hands and danced round the table "and I danced the best way I could among the rest" said he "And there were four chaps all of the clan of M,Donald got up and danced a highland reel to the song on the top of the table."

* If you can find this song give a copy.

There must be many of the corps living who can bear him out in this anecdote: for me I only heard it once and that from his own lips and strange as it may appear considering that I submitted all things to him he did not that night know who was the author of the song but found it out by applying to the publisher next day.

Sir Walter's conversation was always amusing always interesting I never heard any man's more so. (Perhaps I might except Tom Gillespie and John Wilson) But then there was a candour and judiciousness in his which never were equalled. His anecdotes were without end and I am almost certain they were all made off-hand for I never heard any of them before or after. The only time that ever his conversation was to me perfectly uninteresting was with Mr Murray of Albemarle Street London. Their whole conversation was about Noblemen Parliamenters and literary men of all grades every one of which Murray seemed to know with all their characters and propensities which information Sir Walter seemed to drink in with the same zest as I did his highland whisky toddy. And this discourse they carried on for two days and two nights with the intermission only of a few sleeping hours and there I sat beside them the whole time like a stump and never got in a word. I wish I had the same chance again.

Like other young authors he was vain of his early works and fond of making them the subject of conversation. He recited Glenfinlas one day to me on horseback before publishing it He read me the Lay of the Last Minstrel from beginning to end. At least James Ballantyne William Erskine (Lord Kineder) and he read book about He always preferred their readings to his own. Not so with me. I liked his reading far better than any other body's; even with its deep tone and Berwick burr I could always take the poetry and the story better along with me from him than any of them. He was a capital reader—a far better reader than he was sensible of. Every thing that he read was something like his discourse it always went to the heart.

He likewise read me Marmion before its publication but I think it was in the press for it was from the proofs that he read it He read it all himself at three sittings Mr Morison went with me one day and heard him read the two middle cantos which I am sure he will never forget When we came to the door he said "Don't ring the bell Hogg for upon my soul I dare not go in."

"What for?" said I.

Because I know there will be something so terribly gruff about him" said he.

"You never war sae fer mistaken in your life" said I and rung the bell.

The reading of Marmion began I remember perfectly well on his own part. He sought out a proof and read his description of my favourite St. Mary's Loch in one of his introductions to ask my opinion of it as he himself had never been there but once. I said there never was any thing more graphic written in this world and I still adhere to the assertion therefore it was no flattery and I liked it so well that I requested to hear the canto that followed it on which he was obliged to begin at the first and so the readings continued throughout.

After that he never read me any thing save a small portion of The Lady of the Lake. His fame became so firmly established that he grew quite careless about the previous opinion of his literary friends. But he said to me one evening "I am going to adventure a poem of quite a different nature on the public from my two last. Perfectly different in its theme stile and measure" I have sometimes thought since that it was not so very different. But these were his very words and after that he read me the tour of the fiery cross and the battle of the Trossacks and these were the last unpublished things of his which I ever heard read.

But the first thing he ever read to me from M.S was a review of a sporting tour in the Highlands I do not know where it was published or whether ever it was published or not. It was full of sterling humour He set out with the assertion and proof that the patriarch Job was a reviewer and knew the art and its effects perfectly well which he inferred from the fervent exclamation from Job "O that mine enemy had written a book!" The idea was so ludicrous that I was like to die of laughing at it and Scott joined me for he set out on the same principles with Col. Thornton which Job wanted to do

The success which that poem had was beyond all example in modern days. I confess it is my favourite but I have heard men of more judgement than me assert that Marmion was superior and I believe that that there are some descriptions in Marmion unequalled in any part of his writings. But in these simple anecdotes I cannot enter into any review of his works else the amount would be endless. I merely want to exhibit my illustrious friend as he was among his daily acquaintances.

There was one day I met him on the North Bridge as he was coming from the Parliament house on which he took my arm saying "Come along with me Hogg I want to have some chat with you and to introduce you to The Brownie of Bodsbeck. At least he is *my*

Brownie and does a great deal of work for which the government is pleased to pay me very liberally" I went with him into an apartment of the Register Office where a little very good looking fellow (his deputy clerk I suppose) produced papers bunch after bunch to the amount I am sure of some hundreds all of which Sir Walter signed with *W. Scott* laughing and cracking with me all the while. I went home with him to dinner where I met with Terry and Ballantyne.

There cannot be a better trait given of Sir Walter's character than that all who knew him intimately loved him Nay they almost worshipped him. The affection of the two Ballantynes to him quite surpasses description. They were masters of all his secrets and all his transactions and faithful to the last and he reposed the most implicit confidence in them and had he taken some of James's advices I know well he never would have been involved as he was. John he likewise loved as a brother but had not such reliance on his word for he said to me one day (and perhaps it is not very fair to tell this) I was telling him something about the author of some literary article I have forgot what it was But he said "I doubt that Mr Hogg. I guessed from the stile that the author was a different person altogether. Indeed I am almost sure of it.

"No no ye're wrang Mr Scott" said I "for Johny Ballantyne tauld me an' he coudna but ken."

"Ay but you should hae tried to find out whether it was leeing Johny or true Johny that told you that story for they are two as different persons as exist on the face of the earth. But you may always depend upon James" he added "James never diverges from the line of downright truth.

As Mr Southey once told me the same thing I think I am at liberty to publish the sentiments of two such eminent men But in fact the affection of Sir Walters subordinate friends excelled all that I ever saw or ever knew. Constable once took a tyrravy at him but all the rest of his life save that half year he was actually a worshipper, Scott's word or reccomendation was supreme with him. Scott was very shy of his name. In fact he would not grant it to any body either to a great man or a great publisher but his purse was always open as far as he was able to every man in distress especially to literary men. I could state a hundred instances of his generosity in this way but a number of his protegees are still living (though Mr A Campbell and the two Irvings are no more who all for some time depended on his bounty for their daily bread. There was one day when I was chatting with Ballantyne in his printing office where I was generally a daily stranger I chanced to say to him "I never knew a man like Scott. Do you know that he is actually lending assistance at this time to every poor author in this country and the best thing of all he never lets his left hand know what his right hand is doing."

Ballantyne's face glowed with delight and the tears stood in his eyes. "I am glad" said he that you so justly appreciate the merits of our noble our invaluable friend. Look here" and turning up his day-book he said "Some word had reached Mr Scott that Matturin the Irish poet was lying in prison for a small debt and here have I by Scott's orders been obliged to transmit him a bill of exchange for £60 and the best of all is that Matturin is never to know from whence it came" I have said it oft and say it again that "those who knew Scott only by the few thousands of volumes he has published knew only half of the man and that not the best half neither He was a sterling friend and one whose advices were worth a thousand of others and laying his strenous denials of the Novels aside which he denied not only to the King and the Duke of Buccleuch with the most fervent asseverations but to every body: I have heard him deny them a hundred times with the most perfect ease and indifference, he was the most upright man I ever knew Yet he loved to talk of his early prose works. I remember one fine spring day before dinner of be-ing walking round and round the top of the Calton Hill with him when his whole conversation was about Guy Mannering. He laughed most heartily at some of its scenes and told me where he weened the author had succeeded and where failed until we met with Peter Robertson who turned with us and marred the theme with his non-sense, which made Sir Walter laugh as he had been tickled. (At that time I really believed that Sir Walter was not the author of those inimitable scenes as Johny Ballantyne had fairly sworn me out of my belief.)

He was the best formed man I ever saw and laying his weak limb out of the question a perfect model of a man for gigantic strength The muscles of his arms were beyond belief. There was a gentle-man once told me that he walked in one morning just as the footman was showing another gentleman out and that walking into Sir Walter's study he found him stripped with his shirt sleeves rolled up to his shoulders and his face very red. "Good God Scott what is the mat-ter?" said he "Pray may I ask an explanation of this?"

"Why the truth is that I have just been giving your friend Mr. Martin a devil of a drubbing" said Scott laughing "The scoundrel dared me to touch him but with one of my fingers at my peril; but if I have not given him a complete basting he knows himself. He is the most impudent and arrant knave I ever knew but it will be a while

before he attempts to impose upon me again." This Mr Martin the
gentleman said was some great picture-dealer. But as I never once
heard Sir Walter allude to this adventure in his hours of hilarity I
suspect the truth of it very much. As he says himself

> "I cannot tell how the truth may be
> I say the tale as 'twas said to me"

I could multiply such reminscences of my honoured and regretted friend to the extent of volumes but I have written enough to let
the world know what manner of man he was in his every-day clothes.
I knew him intimately for upwards of thirty years and he was always the friend that I applied to for advice and assistance in every
emergency and they never were denied me. I think he told his mind
and his opinions as frankly to me as any man in the world with the
exception of James Ballantyne and William Laidlaw. The former is
no more but he was the man who ought to have left some anecdotes
of Sir Walter He was as one may say his bosom friend to whom he
entrusted every transaction of his life. James was an affected, pomp-
ous, but honest and worthy man and possessed of a heart too affectionate and feeling for this evil world. Is it not a singular circumstance that all connected with these mighty works have as it were
been hurled into Eternity together? The author the publisher and
the printers are all gone one shortly after another and no one remains to tell the little secrets of that community of rash and specula-
tive friends.

There is no man now living who knows so much of Scott as
William Laidlaw does. Although a subordinate he was his daily associate for twenty years and the conductor of all his plans and improvements. What a pity it is that Laidlaw should ever leave the
estate of Abbotsford for it appears to me that without him the estate
will be like a carcass without a head. Laidlaw knows the value of
every acre of land there and of every tree in the forest and without
his superintendence that dear bought and classical estate must go to
wreck. Sir Walter said to me one day when we were walking out
about Abbotslee. I was so much interested in the speech that I think
I can indite it word by word.

"Was it not an extraordinary luck for me that threw Laidlaw into
my hands? Without Laidlaw's head I could have done nothing; and
to him alone I am indebted for all those improvements" And he
added "I never found a mind so inexhaustible as Laidlaw's. With
the worst of all manners of expression the resources of his mind are
without end. I have met with some of the greatest men of our coun-

try but found that after I had sounded them on one or two subjects there their information terminated But every day, every hour Laidlaw has some new idea and he sometimes abuses me like a tinker because I don't pay proper attention to his insinuations."

As long as he was able to take his customary walks Sir Walter popped in upon Laidlaw or Mrs Laidlaw every day. I remember of his coming in twice to breakfast when I was there and he sat down and took his salt herring and his tea with us with the greatest freedom and good humour. Another day he got a cut of a bull trout which he enjoyed and commended greatly. He was rather late in coming in that day and I noticed that Mrs Laidlaw regarded him so much as a door neighbour that she did not even put new tea in the tea-pot at which I was rather vexed but did not like to say any thing.

Another day he said to me "I once reccommended Laidlaw to the Earl of Mansfield as his factor but repented it; for in the first place I was afraid that his precarious health would unfit him for such a responsible situation. And more than that I found that I *could not* live without him and was obliged maugre all misfortunes to bring him back to his old situation."

Laidlaw wrote sundry of the Novels from Scott's diction when the latter could but seldom rise from the sofa. I wish it could be so arranged that Laidlaw should not be seperated from Abbotsford for though my own brother has long had and still has a high responsibility there as chief shepherd and superintendant of the inclosures I cannot see how the management of Abbotsford can go on without Laidlaw. I say still that it is a carcass without a head.

But to put an end to these trivial anecdotes for trivial they are were they not about so extraordinary a man. The greatest man in the world while he lived and must long be remembered as such now that he is gone What are kings or emperors compared with Sir Walter Scott? Dust and Sand! The most part of their names regarded with detestation. But here is a name that next to that of William Shakespere's will descend with rapt admiration to all the ages of futurity. And is it not a proud boast for an old shepherd that he could call this man FRIEND and could associate with him every day and every hour that he chose?

Yes! It is my highest pride and boast. Sir Walter first attached himself to me without my knowing any thing about him and though I sometimes took the pet and even insulted him his interest in my welfare never subsided for one moment; although he let me know that I behoved to depend entirely on myself for my success in life At the same time he always assured me that I had talents to ensure that success if those talents were properly used.

He had a clear head a benevolent heart was a good man an anxiously kind husband an indulgent parent and a sincere and foregiving friend. He was chary of his name or interest as I have said before but always ready with his purse or with some friendly advice which was often of far greater value. He was a punctual correspondent a just judge and a shrewd and judicious observer of every thing in nature. He knew mankind well. He knew the w[ay] to their hearts. And he certainly had the art of leading the taste of an empire. I m[ay] almost say of the world above all men that ever existed. As long as Sir Walter Scott wrote poetry there was no man or woman ever thought of reading or writing any thing but poetry. But the instant that he gave over writing poetry there was neither man nor woman ever read it more. All turned to tales and novels which I among others was obliged to do. Such is the man we have lost and such a man we shall never again see in our day. As to the monuments so much talked of let his generous countrymen take a shepherd's word that next to his immortal works Abbotsford will always be the earthly monument which succeeding generations will croud to see. It is a thing altogether of his own creation; armoury, hall, library, garden, forest and every thing about it. In short it has been changed from The Clarty Hole into Abbotsford and where shall we find any thing like it. Every tree in the lower wood at least has to my certain knowledge been pruned by his own hand and with his own little axe.

He once showed me a little grove I think west of the mansion-house which he called Joanna Baillie's. He made her sit in the middle of it on a chair until he planted a circle of trees around her with his own hand gave it her name and dedicated it to her. If this little grove is not rendered sacred to genius what in this world can b[e] Either times will greatly alter to the worse else many hundred of years hence a splice of wood from that little grove will be regarded as a most precious relic and one of inestimable value. Let Abbotsford therefore be secured to his lineal descendants in the first place, and then all is well; as nothing more can be effected to preserve the remembrance of one whose name and fame are immortal. That first; and as many monuments as they like afterwards. Blessed be his memory! he was a great and a good man!

*Familiar Anecdotes of*
# Sir Walter Scott

*By the Ettrick Shepherd*

# Lines to Sir Walter Scott, Bart.

SOUND, my old Harp, thy boldest key
To strain of high festivity!
Can'st thou be silent in the brake,
Loitering by Altrive's mountain lake,
When he who gave the hand its sway
That now has tuned thee many a day,
Has gained the honours, trulier won
Than e'er by sword of Albyn's son?
High guerdon of a soul refined,
The meed of an exalted mind!

  Well suits such wreath thy loyal head,
My counsellor, and friend in deed.
Though hard through life I've pressed my way
For many a chill and joyless day,
Since I have lived enrapt to hail
My sovereign's worth, my friend's avail,
And see what more I prize than gain,
Our Forest harp the bays obtain,
I'll ween I have not lived in vain.

  Ah! could I dream when first we met,
When by the scanty ingle set,
Beyond the moors where curlews wheel
In Ettrick's bleakest, loneliest sheil,
Conning old songs of other times,
Most uncouth chants and crabbed rhymes;–
Could I e'er dream that wayward wight,
Of roguish joke, and heart so light,
In whose oft-changing eye I gazed,
Not without dread the head was crazed,
Should e'er, by genius' force alone,
Skim o'er an ocean sailed by none,
All the hid shoals of envy miss,
And gain such noble port as this?

  I could not: but I cherish still
Mirth at the scene, and ever will;

When o'er the fells we took our way,
('Tis twenty years, even to a day,
Since we two sought the fabled urn
Of marble blue by Rankleburn):
No tomb appeared; but oft we traced
Towns, camps, and battle-lines effaced,
Which never were, nor could remain,
Save in the bold enthusiast's brain:
The same to us,—it turned our lays
To chiefs and tales of ancient days.
One broken pot alone was found
Deep in the rubbish under ground,
In middle of the ancient fane,
"A gallant helmet split in twain!"
The truth was obvious; but in faith
On you all words were waste of breath;
You only looked demure and sly,
And sore the brow fell o'er the eye;
You could not bear that you should ride
O'er pathless waste and forest wide,
Only to say that you had been
*To see that nought was to be seen.*

The evenings came; more social mirth
Ne'er flowed around the cottage hearth:
When Maitland's song first met your ear,
How the furled visage up did clear,
Beaming delight! though now a shade
Of doubt would darken into dread
That some unskilled presumptuous arm
Had marred tradition's mighty charm.

Scarce grew thy lurking dread the less
Till she, the ancient Minstreless,
With fervid voice, and kindling eye,
And withered arms waving on high,
Sung forth these words in eldritch shriek,
While tears stood on thy nut-brown cheek—

"Na, we are nane o' the lads o' France,
   Nor e'er pretend to be;
We be three lads of fair Scotland,
   Auld Maitland's sons, a' three!"

Thy fist made all the table ring,—
"By —, Sir, but that is the thing!"

Yes, twenty years have come and fled
Since we two met, and time has shed
His riming honours o'er each brow—
My state the same, how changed art thou!
But every year yet overpast
I've loved thee dearer than the last;
For all the volumes thou hast wrote,
Those that are owned, and that are not,
Let these be conned, even to a grain,
I've said it, and will say't again,—
Who knows thee but by these alone,
The better half is still unknown.

I know thee well—no kinder breast
Beats for the woes of the distrest,
Bleeds for the wounds it cannot heal,
Or yearns more o'er thy country's weal:
Thy love embraces Britain o'er,
And spreads and radiates with her shore;
Scarce fading on her ocean's foam,
But still 'tis brightest nearest home,
Till those within its central rays,
Rejoicing, bask within the blaze.

Blessed be the act of sovereign grace
That raised thee 'bove the rhyming race;
Blessed be the heart and head elate,
The noble generous estimate
That marked thy worth, and owned the hand
Resistless in its native land.
Bootless the waste of empty words,
Thy pen is worth ten thousand swords.

Long brook thy honours, gallant Knight,
So firm of soul, so staunch of right,
For had thy form but reached its prime,
Free from mischance in early time,
No stouter sturdier arm of weir
Had wielded sword or battle spear!

For war thy boardly frame was born,
For battle shout, and bugle-horn;
Thy boyish feats, thy youthful dream—
How thy muse kindles at the theme!
Chance marred the path, or Heaven's decree;
How blessed for Scotland and for me!

Scarce sounds thy name as 't did before,—
Walter the Abbot now no more:
Well, let it be, I'll not repine,
But love the title since 'tis thine.
Long brook thy honours, firm to stand
As Eildon rock; and that thy land,
The first e'er won by dint of rhyme,
May bear thy name till latest time;
And stretch from bourn of Abbot's-lea
To Philhope Cross, and Eildon Tree,
Is the heart's wish of one who's still
Thy grateful Shepherd of the Hill!

ALTRIVE LAKE,
*April* 24, 1820.

# Familiar Anecdotes of Sir Walter Scott

In the following miscellaneous narrative, I do not pretend to give a life of my illustrious and regretted friend. That has been done by half-a-dozen already and will ultimately be given by his son in law fully and clearly, the only man who is thoroughly qualified for the task and is in possession of the necessary documents. The whole that I presume to do is after an intimate acquaintance of thirty years to give a few simple and personal anecdotes which no man can give but myself. It is well known what Sir Walter was in his study but these are to show what he was in the parlour in his family and among his acquaintances and in giving them I shall in nothing extenuate or set down aught through partiality and as for malice that is out of the question.

The first time I ever saw Sir Walter was one fine day in the summer of 1801. I was busily engaged working in the field at Ettrickhouse, when old Wat Shiel came posting over the water to me and told me that I boud to gang away down to the Ramsey-cleuch as fast as my feet could carry me, for there were some gentlemen there who wanted to see me directly.

"Wha can be at the Ramsey-cleuch that want to see me, Wat."

"I coudna say, for it wasna me they spake to i' the bygangin', but I'm thinking it's the SHIRRA an' some o' his gang."

I was rejoiced to hear this, for I had seen the first volumes of the "Minstrelsy of the Border," and had copied a number of ballads from my mother's recital, or chaunt rather, and sent them to the editor preparatory to the publication of a third volume. I accordingly flung down my hoe and hasted away home to put on my Sunday clothes, but before reaching it I met the SHIRRA and Mr. William Laidlaw, coming to visit me. They alighted, and remained in our cottage a considerable time, perhaps, nearly two hours, and we were friends on the very first exchange of sentiments. It could not be otherwise, for Scott had no duplicity about him, he always said as he thought. My mother chaunted the ballad of Old Maitlan' to him, with which he was highly delighted, and asked her if she thought it ever had been in print? And her answer was, "O na, na, sir, it never was printed i' the world, for my brothers an' me learned it an' many mae frae auld Andrew Moor, and he learned it frae auld Baby Mettlin, wha was housekeeper to the first laird of Tushilaw. She was said to hae been another nor a gude ane, an' there are many queer stories about hersel', but O, she had been a grand singer o' auld songs an' ballads."

"The first laird of Tushilaw, Margaret?" said he, "then that must be a very old story indeed?"

"Ay, it is that, sir! It is an auld story! But mair nor that, excepting George Warton an' James Stewart, there war never ane o' my sangs prentit till ye prentit them yoursel', an' ye hae spoilt them awthegither. They were made for singing an' no for reading; but ye hae broken the charm now, an' they'll never be sung mair. An' the worst thing of a', they're nouther right spell'd nor right setten down."

"Take ye that, Mr. Scott," said Laidlaw.

Scott answered with a hearty laugh, and the quotation of a stanza from Wordsworth, on which my mother gave him a hearty rap on the knee with her open hand, and said, "Ye'll find, however, that it is a' true that I'm tellin' ye." My mother has been too true a prophetess, for from that day to this, these songs, which were the amusement of every winter evening, have never been sung more.

We were all to dine at Ramsey-cleuch with the Messrs. Brydon, but Scott and Laidlaw went away to look at some monuments in Ettrick church-yard, and some other old thing, I have forgot what, and I was to follow. On going into the stable-yard at Ramsey-cleuch I met with Mr. Scott's groom, a greater original than his master, at whom I asked if the SHIRRA was come?

"Oo ay, lad, the Shirra's come," said he. "Are ye the chap that mak's the auld ballads, an' sings them sae weel?"

I said, I fancied I was he that he meant, though I could not say that I had ever made ony very auld ballads.

"Ay, then, lad, gang your ways into the house, and speir for the Shirra. They'll let ye see where he is, an' he'll be very glad to see ye, that I'll assure ye o'."

During the sociality of the evening, the discourse ran very much on the different breeds of sheep, that everlasting drawback on the community of Ettrick Forest. The original black-faced forest breed being always denominated the *short sheep*, and the Cheviot breed the *long sheep*. The disputes at that time ran very high about the practicable profits of each. Mr. Scott, who had come into that remote district to visit a bard of Nature's own making and preserve what little fragments remained of the country's legendary lore, felt himself rather bored with the everlasting question of the long and short sheep. So, at length, putting on his most serious calculating face, he turned to Mr. Walter Brydon, and said, "I am rather at a loss regarding the merits of this *very* important question. How long must a sheep actually measure to come under the denomination of *a long sheep*?"

Mr. Brydon, who, in the simplicity of his heart, neither perceived the quiz nor the reproof, fell to answer with great sincerity, "It's the woo', sir; it's the woo' that mak's the difference, the lang sheep hae the short woo' an' the short sheep hae the lang thing, an' these are just kind o' names we gie them, ye see."

Laidlaw got up a great guffaw, on which Scott could not preserve his face of strict calculation any longer; it went gradually awry, and a hearty laugh followed. When I saw the very same words repeated near the beginning of the Black Dwarf, how could I be mistaken of the author? It is true that Johnie Ballantyne swore me into a nominal acquiescence to the contrary for several years, but in my own mind I could never get the better of that and several other similar coincidences.

The next day we went off, five in number, to visit the wilds of Rankleburn, to see if, on the farms of Buccleuch and Mount Comyn, the original possession of the Scotts, there were any relics of antiquity which could mark out the original residence of the chiefs whose distinction it was to become the proprietors of the greater part of the border districts. We found no remains of either tower or fortalice, save an old chapel and church-yard, and the remnants of a kiln-mill and mill-dam, where corn never grew, but where, as old Satchells very appropriately says:

> "Had heather bells been corn o' the best,
> The Buccleuch mill would have had a noble grist."

It must have been used for grinding the chief's black mails, which it is well known were all paid to him in kind; and an immense deal of victual is still paid to him in the same way, the origin of which no man knows.

Besides having been mentioned by Satchells, the most fabulous historian that ever wrote, there was a remaining tradition in the country that there was a font-stone of blue marble, out of which the ancient heirs of Buccleuch were baptized, covered up among the ruins of the old church. Mr. Scott was curious to see if we could discover it, but on going among the ruins where the altar was known to have been, we found the rubbish at that spot dug out to the foundation, we knew not by whom, but it was manifest that the font had either been taken away, or that there was none there. I never heard since that it had ever been discovered by any one.

As there appeared, however, to have been a sort of recess in the eastern gable, we fell a turning over some loose stones, to see if the baptismal font was not there, when we came to one-half of a small pot encrusted thick with rust. Mr. Scott's eyes brightened and he swore it was part of an ancient consecrated helmet. Laidlaw, however, fell a picking and scratching with great patience until at last he came to a layer of pitch inside, and then, with a malicious sneer, he said, "The truth is, Mr. Scott, it's nouther mair nor less than an auld tar-pot, that some of the farmers hae been buisting their sheep out o' i' the kirk lang syne." Sir Walter's shaggy eye-brows dipped deep over his eyes, and, suppressing a smile, he turned and strode away as fast as he could, saying, that "we had just rode all the way to see that there was nothing to *be* seen."

He was, at that time, a capital horseman, and was riding on a terribly high-spirited grey nag, which had the perilous fancy of leaping every drain, rivulet, and ditch that came in our way. The consequence was, that he was everlastingly bogging himself, while sometimes the rider kept his seat in spite of the animals' plunging, and at other times he was obliged to extricate himself the best way he could. In coming through a place called the Milsey Bog, I said to him, "Mr. Scott, that's the maddest de'il of a beast I ever saw. Can you no gar him tak' a wee mair time? he's just out o' ae lair intil another wi' ye."

"Ay," said he, "he and I have been very often like the Pechs (*Picts*) these two days past, we could stand straight up and tie the latchets of our shoes." I did not understand the allusion, nor do I yet, but those were his words.

We visited the old castles of Tushilaw and Thirlstane, dined and spent the afternoon and the night with Mr. Brydon of Crosslee. Sir Walter was all the while in the highest good humour, and seemed to enjoy the range of mountain solitude which we traversed, exceedingly. Indeed, I never saw him otherwise in the fields. On the rugged mountains, and even toiling in the Tweed to the waist, I have seen his glee surpass that of all other men. His memory, or, perhaps I should say, his recollection, was so capacious, so sterling, and minute, that a description of what I have witnessed regarding it would not gain credit. When in Edinburgh, and even at Abbotsford, I was often obliged to apply to him for references in my historical tales, that so I might relate nothing of noblemen and gentlemen named that was not strictly true. I never found him at fault. In that great library, he not only went uniformly straight to the book, but ere ever he stirred from the spot, turned up the page which contained the information I wanted. I saw a pleasant instance of this retentiveness of memory recorded lately of him, regarding Campbell's PLEASURES OF HOPE, but I think I can relate a more extraordinary one.

He, and Skene of Rubislaw, and I were out one night about midnight, leistering kippers in Tweed, about the end of January, not long after the opening of the river for fishing, which was then on the tenth, and Scott having a great range of the river himself, we went up to the side of the Rough haugh of Elibank; but when we came to kindle our light, behold our peat was gone out. This was a terrible disappointment, but to think of giving up our sport was out of the question, so we had no other shift save to send Rob Fletcher all the way through the darkness, the distance of two miles, for another fiery peat.

The night was mild, calm, and as dark as pitch, and while Fletcher was absent we three sat down on the brink of the river, on a little green sward which I never will forget, and Scott desired me to sing them my ballad of "Gilman's-cleuch." Now, be it remembered, that this ballad had never been printed, I had merely composed it by rote, and, on finishing it three years before, had sung it once over to Sir Walter. I began it, at his request, but at the eighth or ninth stanza I stuck in it, and could not get on with another verse, on which he began it again and recited it every word from beginning to end. It being a very long ballad, consisting of eighty-eight stanzas, I testified my astonishment, knowing that he had never heard it but once, and even then did not appear to be paying particular attention. He said he had been out with a pleasure party as far as the opening of the Frith of Forth, and, to amuse the company, he had recited both that ballad and one of Southey's, (The Abbot of Aberbrothock,) both of which ballads he had only heard once from their respective authors, and he believed he recited them both without misplacing a word.

Rob Fletcher came at last, and old Mr. Laidlaw of the Peel with him, carrying a lantern, and into the river we plunged in a frail bark which had suffered some deadly damage in bringing up. We had a fine blazing light, and the salmon began to appear in plenty, "turning up sides like swine;" but wo be to us, our boat began instantly to manifest a disposition to sink, and in a few minutes we reached Gleddie's Weal, the deepest pool in all that part of Tweed. When Scott saw the terror that his neighbour old Peel was in, he laughed till the tears blinded his eyes. Always the more mischief the better sport for him. "For God's sake, push her to the side!" roared Peel. "Oh, she goes fine," said Scott.

" 'An' gin the boat war bottomless,
An' seven miles to row.' "

A verse of an old song; and during the very time he was reciting
these lines, down went the boat to the bottom, plunging us all into
Tweed, over head and ears. It was no sport to me, at all, for I had no
change of raiment at Ashiesteel, but that was a glorious night for
Scott, and the next day was no worse.

I remember leaving my own cottage here one morning with him,
accompanied by my dear friend, William Laidlaw, and Sir Adam
Ferguson, to visit the tremendous solitudes of Loch-Skene and the
Grey-mare's-tail. I conducted them through that wild region by a
path, which, if not rode by Clavers, as reported, never was rode by
another gentleman. Sir Adam rode inadvertantly into a gulf and got
a sad fright, but Sir Walter, in the very worst paths, never dis-
mounted, save at Loch-Skene to take some dinner. We went to Moffat
that night, where we met with Lady Scott and Sophia, and such a
day and night of glee I never witnessed. Our very perils were to
him matter of infinite merriment; and then there was a short tempered boot-boy at the inn, who wanted to pick a quarrel with him
for some of his sharp retorts, at which Scott laughed till the water
ran over his cheeks.

I was disappointed in never seeing some incident in his subsequent works laid in a scene resembling the rugged solitude around
Loch-Skene, for I never saw him survey any with so much attention. A single serious look at a scene generally filled his mind with
it, and he seldom took another. But, here, he took the names of all
the hills, their altitudes, and relative situations with regard to one
another, and made me repeat all these several times. Such a scene
may occur in some of his works which I have not seen, and I think it
will, for he has rarely ever been known to interest himself either in
a scene or a character, which did not appear afterwards in all its
most striking peculiarities.

There are not above three people now living, who, I think, knew
Sir Walter better and who understood his character better than I
did, and I once declared that if I outlived him, I should draw a mental and familiar portrait of him, the likeness of which to the original
could not be disputed. In the meantime, this is only a reminiscence,
in my own homely way, of an illustrious friend among the mountains. That revered friend is now gone, and the following pages are
all that I deem myself at liberty to publish concerning him.

The enthusiasm with which he recited and spoke of our ancient
ballads, during that first tour through the Forest, inspired me with a

determination immediately to begin and imitate them, which I did, and soon grew tolerably good at it. I dedicated "The Mountain Bard," to him:

> Bless'd be his generous heart, for aye,
> He told me where the relic lay,
> Pointed my way with ready will,
> Afar on Ettrick's wildest hill;
> Watch'd my first notes with curious eye,
> And wonder'd at my minstrelsy:
> He little ween'd a parent's tongue
> Such strains had o'er my cradle sung.

The only foible I ever could discover in the character of Sir Walter was a too strong leaning to the old aristocracy of the country. His devotion for titled rank was prodigious and in such an illustrious character altogether out of place. It amounted almost to adoration and not to mention the numerous nobility whom I have met at his own house and in his company I shall give a few instances of that sort of feeling in him to which I allude.

Although he of course acknowledged Buccleuch as the head and chief of the whole clan of Scott yet he always acknowledged Harden as his immediate chieftain and head of that powerful and numerous sept of the name and Sir Walter was wont often to relate how he and his father before him and his grandfather before that always kept their Christmas with Harden in acknowledgment of their vasselage. This he used to tell with a degree of exultation which I always thought must have been astounding to every one who heard it as if his illustrious name did not throw a blaze of glory on the house of Harden a hundred times more than that van of old Border barbarians however brave could throw over him.

He was likewise descended from the chiefs of Haliburton and Rutherford on the maternal side and to the circumstance of his descent from these three houses he adverted so often mingling their arms in his escutcheon that to me who alas to this day could never be brought to discern any distinction in ranks save what was constituted by talents or moral worth it appeared perfectly ludicrous thinking as no man could help thinking of the halo which his genius shed over those families while he only valued himself as a dependant of their's.

I may mention one other instance at which I was both pleased and mortified. We chanced to meet at a great festival at Bowhill when Duke Charles was living and in good health. The company being

very numerous there were two tables set in the dining room one
along and one across. They were nearly of the same length but at
the one along the middle of the room all the ladies were seated
mixed alternately with gentlemen and at this table all were noble
save if I remember aright Sir Adam Ferguson whose everlasting
good humour insures him a passport into every company. But I
having had some chat with the ladies before dinner and always rather
a flattered pet with them imagined they could not possibly dine without me and placed myself among them. But I had a friend at the
cross table at the head of the room who saw better. Sir Walter who
presided there arose and addressing the Duke of Buccleuch requested
of him as a particular favour and obligation that he would allow Mr
Hogg to come to his table for that in fact he could not do without him
and moreover he added

> If ye reave the Hoggs o Fauldshope
> Ye herry Harden's gear.

I of course got permission and retired to Sir Walter's table when
he placed me on the right hand of the gentleman on his right hand
who of course was Scott of Harden. And yet notwithstand[ing] the
broad insinuation about the Hoggs of Fauldshope I sat beside that
esteemed gentleman the whole night and all the while took him for
an English clergyman! I knew there were some two or three clergy-
men of rank there connected with the family and I took Harden for
one of them and though I was mistaken I still say he ought to have
been one. I was dumfoundered next day when the Duke told me
that my divine whom I thought so much of was Scott of Harden for
I would have liked so well to have talked with him about old matters my forefathers having been vassals under that house on the
lands of Fauldshope for more than two centuries and were only
obliged to change masters with the change of proprietors. It was
doubtless owing to this connection that my father had instilled into
my youthful mind so many traditions relating to the house of Harden
of which I have made considerable use.

But the anecdote which I intended to relate before my ruling passion of egotism came across me was this. When the dinner came to
be served Sir Walter refused to let a dish be set on our table which
had not been first presented to the Duke and the nobility "No no!"
said he "This is literally a meeting of the Clan and its adherents and
we shall have one dinner in the feudal stile. It may be but for once in
our lives."

Assoon as the Duke percieved this whim he admitted of it although I believe the dishes were merely set down and lifted again. In the mean time the venison and beef stood on the side-board which was free to all so that we were all alike busy from the beginning.

At the end of our libations and before we parted some time in the course of the morning the Duke set his one foot on the table and the other on his chair requesting us all to do the same with which every man complied and in that position he sung "Johnie Cope are ye wauking yet" while all joined in the chorus. Sir Walter set his weak foot on the table and kept his position steadily apparently more firm than when he stood on the floor joining in the chorus with his straight forward bass voice with great glee and enjoying the whole scene exceedingly as he did every scene of hilarity that I ever saw. But though a more social companion never was born he never filled himself drunk. He took always his wine after dinner and at least for upwards of twenty years a little gin toddy after supper but he was uniformly moderate in eating and drinking. He liked a good breakfast but often confessed that he never knew what a good breakfast was till he came to my cottage but he should never want it again and he kept steadily to his resolution.

He was a most extraordinary being. How or when he composed his voluminous works no man could tell. When in Edin$^r$ he was bound to the parliament house all the forenoon. He never was denied to any living neither lady nor gentleman poor nor rich and he never seemed discomposed when intruded on but always good humoured and kind. Many a time have I been sorry for him for I have remained in his study in Castle Street in hopes to get a quiet word of him and witnessed the admission of ten intruders foreby myself. Noblemen Gentlemen painters poets and players all crouded to Sir Walter not to mention booksellers and printers who were never absent but these spoke to him privately. When at Abbotsford for a number of years his house was almost constantly filled with company for there was a correspondence carried on and always as one freight went away another came. It was impossible not to be sorry for the time of such a man thus broken in upon. I felt it exceedingly and once when I went down by particular invitation to stay a fortnight I had not the heart to stay any longer than three days and that space was generally the length of my visits. But Sir Walter never was discomposed. He was ready assoon as breakfast was over to accompany his guests wherever they chose to go to stroll in the wood or take a drive up to Yarrow or down to Melrose or Dryburgh where his sacred ashes now repose. He was never out of humour when well but when ill he was very cross he being subject to a billious complaint of the most dreadful and severe nature accompanied by pangs most excrutiating; and when under the influence of that malady it was not easy to speak to him and I found it always the best plan to keep a due distance. But then his sufferings had been most intense for he told me one day when he was sitting as yellow as a primrose that roasted salt had been prescribed to lay on the pit of his stomach which was applied and the next day it was discovered that his breast was all in a blister and the bosom of his shirt burnt to an izel and yet he never felt it!

But to return to our feast at Bowhill from which I have strangely wandered although the best of the fun is yet to come. When the Duke retired to the drawing-room he deputed Sir Alex$^r$ Don who sat next him to his chair. We had long before been all at one table. Sir Alex$^r$ instantly requested a bumper out of champaign glasses to the Duke's health with all the honours. It was instantly complied with and every one drank it to the bottom. Don then proposed the following of so good an example as His Grace had set us and accordingly we were obliged all to mount our chairs again and setting one foot on the table sing Johny Cope over again. Every one at least attempted it and Sir Alex$^r$ sung the song in most capital stile. The Scotts and the Elliotts and some Taits now began to fall with terrible thuds on the floor but Sir Walter still kept his station as steady as a rock and laughed immoderately. But this was too good fun to be given up. The Marquis of Queensberry who was acting as Croupier said that such a loyal and social Border Clan could never separate without singing "God Save the King" and that though we had drunk to his health at the beginning we behoved to do it again and join in the Anthem. We were obliged to mount our chairs again and in the same ticklish position sing The King's Anthem. Down we went one after another. Nay they actually fell in heaps above each other. I fell off and took a devil of a run to one corner of the room against which I fell which created great merriment. There was not above six stood the test this time out of from thirty to forty. Sir Walter did and he took all the latter bumpers off to the brim. He had a good head more ways than one.

There was no man who ever testified more admiration and even astonishment than he did at my poetical productions both songs and poems and sometimes in very high terms before his most intimate friends. It was somewhat different with regard to my prose works with which he uniformly found fault and always with the disagreeable adjunction "how good they might have been made with a little pains." When THE THREE PERILS OF MAN was first put to press he requested to see the proof-slips Ballantyne having been telling him something about the work. They were sent to him on the instant and on reading them he sent expressly for me as he wanted to see and speak with me about my forthcoming work. We being both at that time residing in Edin[r] I attended directly and I think I remember every word that passed. Indeed so implicit was my dependance on his friendship his good taste and judgement that I never forgot a sentence nor a word that he said to me about my own works but treasured them up in my heart.

"Well Mr Hogg I have read over your proofs with a great deal of pleasure and I confess with some little portion of dread. In the first place the meeting of the two princesses at Castle-Weiry is excellent. I have not seen any modern thing more truly dramatic. The characters are all strongly marked old Peter Chisholm's in particular. Ah man what you might have made of that with a little more refinement care and patience! But it is always the same with you just hurrying on from one vagary to another without consistency or proper arrangement."

"Dear Mr Scott a man canna do the thing that he canna do."

"Yes but you *can* do it. Witness your poems where the arrangements are all perfect and complete but in your prose works with the exception of some short tales you seem to write merely by random without once considering what you are going to write about."

"You are not often wrong Mr Scott and you were never righter in your life than you are now for when I write the first line of a tale or novel I know not what the second is to be and it is the same way in every sentence throughout. When my tale is traditionary the work is easy as I then see my way before me though the tradition be ever so short but in all my prose works of imagination knowing little of the world I sail on without star or compass."

"I am sorry to say that is often but too apparent. But in the next place and it was on that account I sent for you. Do you not think there is some little danger in making Sir Walter Scott of Buccleuch the hero of this wild extravagant tale?"

"The devil a bit."

"Well I think differently. The present chief is your patron your sincere friend and your enthusiastic admirer. Would it not then be a subject of regret not only to yourself and me but to all Scotland should you by any rash adventure forfeit the countenance and friendship of so good and so great a man?"

"There's nae fears o' that ata' Mr Scott. The Sir Walter o' my tale is a complete hero throughout and is never made to do a thing or say a thing of which his descendant our present chief winna be proud."

"I am not quite sure of that. Do you not think you have made him a rather too selfish character?"

"Oo ay but ye ken they were a' a little gi'en that gate else how could they hae gotten haud o' a' the south o' Scotland nae body kens how?"

Sir Walter then took to himself a hearty laugh and then pronounced these very words: "Well Hogg you appear to me just now like a man dancing upon a rope or wire at a great height. If he is successful and finishes his dance in safety he has accomplished no great matter but if he makes a slip he gets a devil of a fall."

"Never say another word about it Mr Scott. I'm satisfied, the designation shall be changed throughout before I either eat or sleep" and I kept my word.

I went when in Edin$^r$ at his particular request two or three days every week to breakfast with him as I was then always sure of an hour's conversation with him before he went to the parliament house and I often went for many days successively as I soon found it was impossible to be in his company without gaining advantage. But there was one Sunday morning I found him in very bad humour indeed. He was sitting at his desk in his study at Castle-Street and when I went in he looked up to me with a visage as stern as that of a judge going to pronounce sentence on a malefactor and at the same time he neither rose nor saluted me which was always his wont and the first words that he addressed to me were these "Mr Hogg I am very angry with you. I tell you it plainly; and I think I have a right to be so. I demand Sir an explanation of a sentence in your SPY of yesterday."

Knowing perfectly well to what sentence he alluded my peasant blood began to boil and I found it rushing to my head and face most violently as I judged myself by far the most aggrieved. "Then I must first demand an explanation from you Mr Scott" said I. "Were you the author of the article alluded to in my paper which places you at the head and me at the tail nay as the very dregs of all the poets of Britain?"

"What right had you Sir to suppose that I was the author of it" said he in a perfect rage.

"Nay what right had *you* to suppose that you were the author of it that you are taking it so keenly to yourself" said I. "The truth is that when I wrote the remarks I neither knew nor cared who was the author of the article alluded to but before the paper went to press I believed it to have been Mr Southey for Johny Ballantyne told me so and swore to it. But if the feather suits your cap you are perfectly welcome to it."

"Very well Hogg" said he. "That is spoken like a man and like yourself. I am satisfied. I thought it was meant as personal to me in particular. But never mind. We are friends again as usual. Sit down and we will go to our breakfast together immediately and it shall never more be mentioned between us."

Mr Southey long afterwards told me that he was not the author of that article and that he believed it to have been written by Scott. If it was it was rather too bad of him but he never said it was not his. It was a review of modern literature in the Edin^r Annual Register. As some readers of these anecdotes may be curious to see the offensive passage in THE SPY I shall here extract it that work being long ago extinct and only occassionally mentioned by myself as a parent will sometimes mention the name of a dear unfortunate lost child who has been forgotten by all the world beside.

"The papers which have given the greatest personal offence are those of Mr Shuffleton which popular clamour obliged the editor reluctantly to discontinue. Of all the poets and poetesses whose works are there emblematically introduced one gentleman alone stood the test and his firmness was even by himself attributed to foregiveness. All the rest male and female tossed up their noses and pronounced the writer an ignorant and incorr[ig]ible barbarian. THE SPY hereby acknowledges himself the author of these papers and adheres to the figurative characters he has there given of the poetical works of those authors. He knows that in a future edition it is expected that they are all to be altered or obliterated–They never shall! Though the intreaties of respected friends prevailed on him to relinquish a topic which was his favourite one what he has published he has published and no private consideration shall induce him to an act of such manifest servility as that of making a renounciation. Those who are so grossly ignorant as to suppose the figurative characteristics of the poetry as having the smallest reference to the personal characters of the authors are below reasoning with. And since it has of late become fashionable with some great poets to give an estimate of their great powers in periodical works of distinction surely others have an equal right to give likewise their estimates of the works of such bards. It is truly amusing to see how artfully a gentleman at the head of a school of poetry and one who is perhaps his superior at the tail of it. How he can make himself to appear as the greatest genius that ever existed. With what address he can paint his failings as beauties and depict his greatest excellencies as slight defects finding fault only with those parts which every one must admire. The design is certainly an original though not a very creditable one. Great authors cannot remain always concealed let them be as cautious as they will the smallest incident often assisting curiosity in the discovery." SPY *for August 24ᵗʰ 1811.*

This last sentence supposing Sir Walter to have been the author which I now suspect he was certainly contained rather too broad and too insolent a charge to be passed over with impunity. When I wrote it I believed he was but had I continued to believe so I would not have called on him the next morning after the publication of the paper. Luckily before putting the paper to press I waited on Mr John Ballantyne and asked him who was the author of that insolent paper in his Annual Register which placed me as the dregs of all the poets in Britain.

"O the paper was sent to our office by Southey" said he. "You know [he] is editor and part proprietor of the work and we never think of objecting to any thing that he sends us. Neither my brother James nor I ever read the article until it was published and we both thought it a good one."

Now this was a story beside the truth for I found out afterwards that Mr James Ballantyne had read the paper from M.S. in a literary [     ] long before its publication where it was applauded in the highest terms I however implicitly believed it as I have done every body all my life. At that period the whole of the aristocracy and literature of our country were set against me and determined to keep me down nay to crush me to a nonentity; thanks be to God I have lived to see the sentiments of my countrymen completely changed.

There was once more and only once that I found Sir Walter in the same querulous humour with me. It was the day after the publication of my BROWNIE OF BODSBECK. I called on him after his return from the parliament House on pretence of asking his advice about some very important advice but in fact to hear his sentiments of my new work. His shaggy eyebrows were hanging very sore down, a bad prelude, which I knew too well.

"I have read through your new work Mr Hogg" said he "and must tell you downright and plainly as I always do that I like it very ill—very ill indeed."

"What for Mr Scott?"

"Because it is a false and unfair picture of the times and the existing characters altogether An exhaggerated and unfair picture!"

"I dinna ken Mr Scott. It is the picture I hae been bred up in the belief o' sin' ever I was born and I had it frae them whom I was most bound to honour and believe. An' mair nor that there is not one single incident in the tale–not one–which I cannot prove from history to be literally and positively true. I was obliged sometimes to change the situations to make one part coalesce with another but in no one instance have I related a story of a cruelty or a murder which is not literally true. An' that's a great deal mair than you can say for your tale o' Auld Mortality."

"You are over shooting the mark now Mr Hogg. I wish it were my tale. But it is *not* with regard to that, that I find fault with your tale at all but merely because it is an unfair and partial picture of the age in which it is laid."

"Na, I shoudna hae said it was *your* tale for ye hae said to your best friends that it was not an' there I was wrang. Ye may hinder a man to speak but ye canna hinder him to think an' I can yerk at the thinking. But whoever wrote Auld Mortality kenning what I ken an' what ye ken I wadna wonder at you being ill-pleased with my tale if ye thought it written as a counter-poise to that but ye ken weel it was written lang afore the other was heard of."

"Yes I know that a part of it was in M.S. last year but I suspect it has been greatly exhaggerated since."

"As I am an honest man Sir there has not been a line altered or added that I remember of. The original copy was printed. Mr Blackwood was the only man beside yourself who saw it. He read it painfully which I now know you did not and I appeal to him."

"Well well. As to its running counter to Old Mortality I have nothing to say. Nothing in the world: I only tell you that with the exception of Old Nanny the crop-eared Covenanter who is by far the best character you ever drew in your life I dislike the tale exceedingly and assure you it is a distorted a prejudiced and untrue picture of the Royal party."

"It is a devilish deal truer than your's though; and on that ground I make my appeal to my country" And with that I rose and was going off in a great huff.

"No no! stop" cried he "You are not to go and leave me again in bad humour. You ought not to be offended at me for telling you my mind freely."

"Why to be sure it is the greatest folly in the world for me to be sae. But ane's beuks are like his bairns he disna like to hear them spoken ill o' especially when he is concious that they dinna deserve it."

Sir Walter then after his customary short good humoured laugh repeated a proverb about the Gordons which was exceedingly *apropos* to my feelings at the time but all that I can do I cannot remember it though I generally remembered every [word] that he said of any import. He then added "I wish you to take your dinner with me to day. There will be no body with us but James Ballantyne who will read you something new and I wanted to ask you particularly about something which has escaped me at this moment. Ay it was this. Pray had you any tradition on which you founded that ridiculous story about the Hunt of Eildon."

"Yes I had" said I "as far as the two white hounds are concerned and of the one pulling the poisoned cup twice out of the Kings hand when it was at his lips."

"That is very extraordinary" said he "for the very first time I read it it struck me I had heard something of the same nature before but how or where I cannot comprehend. I think it must have been when I was on the nurse's knee or lying in the cradle yet I was sure I had heard it. It is a very ridiculous story that Mr Hogg The most ridiculous of any modern story I ever read. What a pity it is that you are not master of your own capabilities for that tale might have been made a good one."

It was always the same on the publication of any of my prose works. When The Three Perils of Man appeared he read me a long lecture on my extravagance in demonology and assured me I had ruined one of the best tales in the world. It is manifest however that the tale had made no ordinary impression on him as he subsequently copied the whole of the main plot into his tale of Castle Dangerous.

Sir Walter's conversation was always amusing always interesting. There was a conciseness a candour and judiciousness in it which never was equalled. His anecdotes were without end and I am almost certain they were all made off hand for I never heard one of them either before or after. His were no Joe Miller jokes. The only time ever his conversation was to me perfectly uninteresting was with Mr John Murray of Albemarl Street London. Their whole conversation was about noblemen parliamenters and literary men of all grades none of which I had ever heard of or cared about; but every one of which Mr Murray seemed to know with all their characters society and propensities. This information Sir Walter seemed to drink in with as much zest as I did his whisky toddy and this conversation was carried on for two days and two nights with the exception of a few sleeping hours and there I sat beside them all the while like a perfect stump; a sheep who never got in a word not even a bleat. I wish I had the same opportunity again.

I first met with Sir Walter at my own cottage in the wilds of Ettrick Forest as above narrated and I then spent two days and two nights in his company. When we parted he shook my hand most heartily and invited me to his cottage on the banks of the North Esk above Lasswade. "By all means come and see me" said he "and I will there introduce you to my wife. She is a foreigner. As dark as a black-berry and does not speak the broad Scots so well as you and me. Of course I don't expect you to admire her much but I shall ensure you of a hearty welcome."

I went and visited him the first time I had occassion to be in Edin$^r$ expecting to see Mrs Scott a kind of half blackamore whom our Sherrif had married for a great deal of money. I knew nothing about her and had never heard of her save from his own description but the words "as dark as a blackberry" had fixed her colour indelibly on my mind. Judge of my astonishment when I was introduced to one of the most beautiful and handsome creatures as Mrs Scott whom I had ever seen in my life. A brunnette certainly with raven hair and large black eyes but in my estimation a perfect beauty. I found her quite affable and she spoke English very well save that she put al-ways the $d$ for the th and left the aspiration of the h out altogether. She called me all her life Mr Og. I understood perfectly well what she said but for many years I could not make her understand what I said. She had frequently to ask an explanation from her husband. And I must say this of Lady Scott though it was well known how jealous she was of the rank of Sir Walter's visitors yet I was all my life recieved with the same kindness as if I had been a relation or one of the family although one of the most homely of his daily asso-ciates! But there were many others both poets and play-actors whom she recieved with no very pleasant countenance. Jeffery and his sattelites she could not endure and there was none whom she dis-liked more than Brougham for what reason I do not know but I have heard her misca' him terribly as well as "dat body Jeffery". It might be owing to some reviews which I did not know about. After the review of Marmion appeared she never would speak to Jeffery again for though not a lady who possessed great depth of penetra-tion she knew how to appreciate the great powers of her lord from the beginning and despised all those who ventured to depreciate them.

I have heard Sir Walter tell an anecdote of this review of Marmion. As he and Jeffery Southey Curwin and some other body I have forgot who were sailing on Derwent Water at Keswick in Cumberland one fine day Mr Jeffery to amuse the party took from his pocket the

M.S. of the Review of Marmion and read it throughout. This I think was honest in Jeffery but the rest of the company were astonished at his insolence and at some passages did not know where to look. When he had finished he said "Well Scott! What think you of it? What shall be done about it?"

"At all events I have taken *my* resolution what to do" said Scott. "I'll just sink the boat" The Review was a little modified after that.

But to return to lady Scott she is cradled on my remembrance and ever shall as a sweet kind and affectionate creature. When any of the cottagers or retainers about Abbotsford grew ill they durst not tell her as it generally made her worse than the sufferers and I have heard of her groaning and occassionally weeping for a whole day and a good part of the night for an old tailor who was dying and leaving a small helpless family behind him. Her daughter Anne is very like her in the contour and expression of her countenance.

Who was lady Scott originally? I really wish any body would tell me for surely somebody must know. There is a veil of mystery hung over that dear lady's birth and parentage which I have been unable to see through or lift up; and there have been more lies told to me about it and even published in all the papers of Britain by those who *ought* to have known than ever was told about those of any woman that ever was born. I have however a few cogent reasons for believing that the present Sir Walter's grandfather was a nobleman of very high rank.

Like other young authors Sir Walter was rather vain of his early productions and liked to make them the subject of conversation. He recited Glen-Finlas one day to me on horseback long before its publication. He read me also the Lay of the Last Minstrel from M.S. at least he and William Erskine (lord Kineder) and James Ballantyne read it Canto about. He always preferred their readings to his own. Not so with me. I could always take both the poetry and the story along with me better from his reading than any other body's whatsoever. Even with his deep-toned bass voice and his Berwick burr he was a far better reader than he was sensible of. Every thing that he read was like his discourse it always made an impression.

He likewise read me Marmion before it was published but I think it was then in the press for part of it at least was read from proof slips and sheets with corrections on the margin. The Marmion M.S. was a great curiosity. I wonder what became of it. It was all written off-hand in post letters from Ashiesteel, Mainsforth, Rokeby and London.

The readings of Marmion began on his own part. I had newly

gone to Edin' and knew nothing about the work—had never heard of it. But the next morning after my arrival on going to breakfast with him he sought out a proof sheet and read me his description of my beloved St. Mary's Lake in one of his introductions I think to canto second to ask my opinion as he said of its correctness as he had never seen the scene but once. I said there never was any thing more graphic written in this world and I still adhere to the assertion so it was no flattery; and I being perfectly mad about poetry then begged of him to let me hear the canto that followed that vivid description expecting to hear something more about my native mountains. He was then to humour me obliged to begin at the beginning of the poem and that day he read me the two first books.

That night my friends Grieve and Morison who were as great enthusiasts as myself expressed themselves so bitterly at my advantage over them that the next morning I took them both with me and they heard him read the two middle cantos which I am sure neither of them will ever forget. When we came to the door Morison said "For God's sake Hogg don't ring."

"What for?" said I.

"Because I know there will be something so terribly gruff about him I dare not for my soul go in" said he.

"You never were so far mistaken in your life" said I "Sir Walter's manner is just kindness personified" and rung the bell.

When the Lady of the lake was mostly or at least partly in M.S. he said to me one evening "I am going to adventure a poem on the public quite different from my two last perfectly different in its theme stile and measure" on which he took the M.S. from his desk and read me the course of The Fiery Cross and The Battle of the Trossachs. I said "I could not percieve any difference at all between the stile of that and his former poems, save that because it was quite new to me I thought it rather better." He was not quite well pleased with the remark and was just saying I would think differently when I had time to peruse the whole poem when Sir John Hope came in and I heard no more.

After that he never read any thing more to me before publishing save one ghost story. His fame became so firmly established that he cared not a fig for the opinions of his literary friends before hand. But there was one fore-noon he said to me in his study. "I have never durst venture upon a real ghost story Mr Hogg but you have published some such thrilling ones of late that I have been this very day employed in writing one. I assure you "it's no little that gars auld Donald pegh" but yon Lewis stories of your's frighted me so much that I could not sleep and now I have been trying my hand on one and here it is." He read it; but it did not make a great impression on me for I do not know at this moment not having his works by me where it is published. It was about the ghost of a lady and I think appeared in the Abbot or Monastry. He read me also a humorous poem in M.S. which has never been published that I know of. It was something about finding out the happiest man and making him a present of a new holland shirt. Paddy got it who had never known the good of a shirt. Mr Scott asked me what I thought of it. I said the characters of the various nations were exquisitely hit off but I thought the winding up was not so effective as it might have been made. He said he believed I was perfectly right. I never heard what became of that poem or whether it was ever published or not for living in the wilderness as I have done for the last twenty years I know very little of what is going on in the literary world. One of Sir Walter's representatives has taken it upon him to assert that Sir Walter always held me in the lowest contempt! He never was farther wrong in his life but Sir Walter would still have been farther wrong if he had done so. Of that posterity will judge; but I assure that individual that there never was a gentleman in the world who paid more respect or attention to a friend than Sir Walter did to me for the space of the thirty years that we were acquainted. True he sometimes found fault with me but in that there was more kindness than all the rest.

I must confess that before people of high rank he did not much encourage my speeches and stories. He did not hang down his brows then as when he was ill pleased with me but he raised them up and glowred and put his upper lip far over the under one seeming to be always terrified at what was to come out next and then he generally cut me short by some droll anecdote to the same purport of what I was saying. In this he did not give me fair justice for in my own broad hamely way I am a very good speaker and teller of a story too.

Mrs Hogg was a favourite of his. He paid always the greatest deference and attention to her. When we were married I of course took her down to Abbotsford and introduced her and though the company was numerous he did her the honour of leading her into the dining-room and placing her by his side. When the ladies retired, he before all our mutual friends present testified himself highly pleased with my choice and added that he wondered how I had the good sense and prudence to make such a one. "I dinna thank ye ata' for the compliment Sir Walter" said I.

As for her poor woman she perfectly adored him. There was one day when he was dining with us at Mount-Benger on going away he snatched up my little daughter Margaret Laidlaw and kissed her and then laying his hand on her head said "God Almighty bless you my dear child!" on which my wife burst into tears. On my coming back from seeing him into the carriage that stood at the base of the hill I said "What ailed you Margaret."

"O" said she "I thought if he had but just done the same to them all I do not know what in the world I would not have given!"

There was another year previous to that when he was dining with me at the same place he took a great deal of notice of my only son James trying to find out what was in him by a number of simple questions not one of which James would answer. He then asked me anent the boy's capabilities. I said he was a very amiable and affectionate boy but I was afraid he would never be the Cooper of Fogo for he seemed to be blest with a very thick head. "Why but Mr Hogg you know it is not fair to lay the saddle upon a foal" said he "I for my part never liked precocity of genius all my life and can venture to predict that James will yet turn out an honour to you and all your kin" I was gratified by the prediction and lost not a word of it.

The boy had at that time taken a particular passion for knives particularly for large ones and to amuse him Sir Walter showed him a very large gardener's knife which he had in his pocket which contained a saw but I never regarded it and would not have known it the next day. James However never forgot it and never has to this day and I should like very well if that knife is still to be found that James should have it as a keepsake of his father's warmest and most esteemed friend. Col. Ferguson percieving the boy's ruling passion made him a present of a handsome two bladed knife. But that made no impression on James. Col. Ferguson he forgot the next day but Sir Walter he never forgot till he came back again always denominating him "The man wi' the gude knife."

The last time Margt saw him was at his own house in Maitland-Street a very short time before he finally left it. We were passing from Charlotte Square to make a call in Lawrieston when I said "see yon is Sir Walter's house at yon red lamp" "O let me go in and see him once more!" said she.

"No no Margt" said I "you know how little time we have and it would be too bad to intrude on his hours of quiet and study at this time of the day." "O but I must go in!" said she "and get a shake of his kind honest hand once more. I cannot go bye" So I knowing that

> "Nought's to be won at woman's hand
> Unless ye gie her a' the plea"

Was obliged to comply. So in we went and were recieved with all the affection of old friends but his whole discourse was addressed to my wife while I was left to shift for myself among books and newspapers. He talked to her of our family and of our prospects of being able to give them a good education which he reccommended at every risk and at every sacrifice. He talked to her of his own family one by one and of Mr Lockhart's family giving her a melancholly account of little Hugh John Lockhart (now the celebrated Hugh Little-John) who was a great favourite of his but whom as he said that day he despaired of ever seeing reach manhood.

The only exchange of words I got with him during that short visit which did not extend to the space of an hour was of a very important nature indeed. In order to attract his attention from my wife to one who I thought as well deserved it I went close up to him with a scrutinizing look and said "Gudeness guide us Sir Walter but ye hae gotten a braw gown!" On which he laughed and said "I got it made for me in Paris (such a year) when certain great personages chose to call on me of a morning and I never thought of putting it on since until the day before yesterday on finding that my every-day one had been sent to Abbotsford. But I shall always think the more highly of my braw gown Mr Hogg for your notice of it." I think it was made of black twilled satin and lined.

But to return to some general anecdotes with which I could fill volumes. When I first projected my literary paper THE SPY I went and consulted him as I generally did in every thing regarding literature. He shook his head and let fall his heavy eye-brows but said nothing. The upper lip came particularly far down. I did not like these prognostics at all; so I was obliged to broach the subject again without having recieved one word in answer.

"Do you not think it rather dangerous ground to take after Addison Johnson and Henry M,Kenzie?" said he.

"No a bit!" said I "I'm no the least feared for that. My papers may no be sae yelegant as their's but I expect to make them mair original."

"Yes they will certainly be original enough with a vengeance" said he.

I asked him if he thought threepence would be a remunerating price? He answered with very heavy brows that "taking the extent of the sale into proper calculation he suspected she must be a fourpenny cut." He said this with a sneer which I never could forget. I asked if he would lend me his assistance in it? He said he would first see how I came on and if he saw the least prospect of my success he would support me and with this answer I was obliged to be content. He only sent me one letter for the work inclosing two poems of Leyden's. He was however right in discouraging it and I was wrong in adventuring it.

I never knew him wrong in any of his calculations or inhibitions but once and there I am sure my countrymen will join with me in saying that he was wrong. He wrote to me once when I was living in Nithsdale informing me that he was going to purchase the estate of Broadmeadows on Yarrow. That he was the highest offerer and was he believed sure of getting it and that he had offered half and more on my account that I might be his chief Shepherd and manager of all his rural affairs. The plan misgave. Mr Boyd overbid him and became the purchaser on which Sir Walter was so vexed on my account I having kept myself out of a place depending upon his that he actually engaged me to Lord Porchester as his chief Shepherd where I was to have a handsome house a good horse a small pendicle rent free and twenty pounds a year. I approved of the conditions as more than I expected or was entitled to only they were given with this *proviso* that "I was to put my poetical talent under lock and key for ever!" I have the letter. Does any body think Sir Walter was right there? I can't believe it and I am sure my friend the present Lord Porchester would have been the last man to have exacted such a stipulation. I spurned the terms and refused to implement the bargain. This is the circumstance alluded to in the Queen's wake as a reflection on Walter the Abbot which I think it proper to copy here to save researches for an extract where it may be impossible to find it. It alludes to the magic harp of Ettrick banks and Yarrow Braes.

> "The day arrived blest be the day
> Walter the Abbot came that way
> The sacred relic met his view
> Ah! Well the pledge of heaven he knew!
> He screwed the chords he tried a strain
> 'Twas wild–He tuned and tried again
> Then poured the numbers bold and free
> The ancient magic melody
>     The land was charmed to list his lays
> It knew the harp of ancient days
> The Border Chiefs that long had been
> In sepulchres unhearsed and green
> Pass'd from their mouldy vaults away
> In armour red and stern array
> And by their moonlight halls were seen

In visor helm and habergeon
Even fairies sought our land again
So powerful was the magic strain
    Blest be his generous heart for aye
He told me where the relic lay
Pointed my way with ready will
Afar on Ettrick's wildest hill
Watched my first notes with curious eye
And wonder'd at my minstrelsy
He little weened a parent's tongue
Such strains had o'er my cradle sung
    O could the Bard I loved so long
Repprove my fond aspiring song!
Or could his tongue of candour say
That I should throw my harp away?
Just when her notes began with skill
To sound beneath the southern hill
And twine around my bosom's core
How could we part for evermore?
'Twas kindness all. I cannot blame
For bootless is the minstrel flame
But sure a bard might well have known
Another's feelings by his own

Queen's Wake sixth edition p. 336-7

I never knew any gentleman so shy and chary of his name and interest as Sir Walter was and though I know Allan Cunningham and Captain J. G. Burns will not join me in this "Let every man roose the ford as he finds it" he never would do any thing for me in that save by the honour of his undeviating friendship and genuine good advices both of which were of great value to me the one insuring me a welcome among all the genteel company of the kingdom and the other tending greatly to guide my path in a sphere with which I was entirely unacquainted and these I set a high value on. But he would never bring me forward in any way by the shortest literary remark in any periodical. Never would review any of my works although he once promised to do it. No he did not promise he only said before several friends to whom he had been speaking very highly of the work that he was thinking of doing it. But seeing I suppose that the poem did not take so well as he had anticipated he never accomplished his kind intent. I asked him the following year why he had not fulfilled his promise to me.

"Why the truth is Hogg" said he "that I began the thing and took a number of notes marking extracts but I found that to give a proper view of your poetical progress and character I was under the necessity of beginning with the ballads and following through THE WAKE and all the rest and upon the whole I felt that we were so much of the same school that if I had said of you as I wished to say I would have been thought by the world to be applauding myself."

I cannot aver that these were Sir Walter's very words but they were precisely to that purport. But I like other dissapointed men not being by half quite satisfied with the answer said "Dear Sir Walter ye can never suppose that I belang to your school o' chivalry? Ye are the king o' that school but I'm the king o' the mountain an' fairy school which is a far higher ane nor yours."

He rather hung down his brows and said "The higher the attempt to ascend the greater might be the fall" and changed the subject by quoting the saying of some old English Baronet in a fox chase.

He paid two high compliments to me without knowing of either and although some other person should have related these rather than me I cannot refrain from it. One of them was derogatory to himself too, a thing which a young poet is not very apt to publish. He was he said quarter-master to the Edin^r gentlemen cavalry and composed a song for the corps got a friend to learn it and sing it at the Mess but it did not take very well. At length a Mr Robertson got up and said "Come come. That's but a drool of a sang. Let us have Donald M,Donald." On which Donald M,Donald was struck up and was joined in with such glee that all the Mess got up joined hands and danced round the table and added Scott "I joined the ring too and danced as well as I could and there were four chaps all of the Clan-Donachie who got so elevated that they got upon the top of the table and danced a highland reel to the song". He did not know it was mine until after he had told the anecdote when I said "Dear man that sang's mine an' was written sax or seven years bygane. I wonder ye didna ken that."

There was another day as we were walking round the north side of St. Andrew's Square to call on Sir C. Sharpe in York Place he said to me laughing very heartily "I found Ballantyne in a fine quandary yesterday as I called on leaving the Parliament House. He was standing behind his desk actually staring and his mouth quite open. I am glad you have come in Mr Scott said he to tell me if you think I am in my right senses to day or that I am in a dream? O it is quite manifest from the question that you are not in your right senses said I What is the matter? Here is a poem sent me by Mr Gillies to publish in a work of his said he It is in his own hand writing and the gradation of the ascent is so regular and well managed that I am bound to believe it is his. Well before you came in I read and read on in these two proofs until at last I said to myself Good lord is this the poetry of Mr Gillies that I am reading! I must be asleep and dreaming and then I bit my little finger to prove if I was not asleep and I thought I was not. But sit down and judge for yourself.

So James read the poem to me from beginning to end continued he and then said Now what think you of this. The only thing that I can say said I is that the former part of the poem is very like the writing of an eunuch and the latter part like that of a man. The stile is altogether unknown to me but Mr Gillies's it cannot be" (I was sorry I durst not inform him it was mine for it had been previously agreed between Mr Gillies and me that no one should know. It was a blank verse poem but I have entirely forgot what it is about. The latter half only was mine.)

"So you say that poetry is *not* the composition of Mr Gillies?" said James.

"Yes I do positively. The thing is impossible."

"Well sir I can take your word for that; and I have *not* lost my senses nor am I dreaming at all."

There was one day I met with him on the North Bridge on his return from the Court of Session when he took my arm and said "come along with me Hogg I want to introduce you to a real brownie one who does a great deal of work for me for which I am paid rather liberally." I accompanied him in an [apartment] of the Register Office where a good looking little spruce fellow his deputy clerk I suppose produced papers bunch after bunch to the amount of some hundreds all of which he signed with W. SCOTT laughing and chatting with me all the while. We then took a walk round the Calton Hill till dinner time when I went home with him and met Ballantyne and Terry. I think it was on that day for it was during a walk round the Calton Hill and I never enjoyed that pleasure with him but twice in my life that we were discussing the merits of his several poems. THE LADY OF LAKE had had an unprecedented run previous to that and as it was really my favourite I was extolling it highly assured that I was going on safe ground but I found that he preferred Marmion and said something to the following effect that THE LADY OF THE LAKE would always be the favourite with ladies and people who read merely for amusement but that Marmion would have the preference by real judges of poetry. I have heard people of the first discernment express the same opinion since. For me I think in the LADY

OF THE LAKE he reached his acme in poetry for in fact the whole both of his poetry and prose have always appeared to me as two splendid arches of which the LADY OF THE LAKE is the keystone of the one and Guy Mannering and Old Mortality the joint keystones of the other. I should like very well to write a review of his whole works but that lies quite out of my way at present.

The only other walk I ever got with him round and round the Calton hill was several years subsequent to that. At that time I did not believe that he was the author of the celebrated novels for Johny Ballantyne had fairly sworn me out of my original fixed belief so I began about them very freely and he did the same laughing heartily at some of the jokes and often standing still or sitting down and telling me where he thought the author had succeeded best and where least and there were some places where he did not scruple to say he had failed altogether. He never tried to defend any passage when it was attacked but generally laughed at the remarks.

There cannot be a better trait of Sir Walter's character than this. That all who knew him intimately loved him nay many of them almost worshipped him. The affection and subservience of the two Messrs Ballantyne far surpassed description. They were entrusted with all his secrets and all his transactions and faithful to the last and I know that had he taken some most serious advices which James gave him he never would have been involved as he was. In James he always reposed the most implicit confidence. John he likewise trusted with every thing and loved him as a wayward brother but he often broke a joke at his expense. There was one day I was telling the Sherrif some great secret about the author of a certain work or article I have quite forgot what it was when he said "I suspect you are widely misinformed there Mr Hogg for I think I know the author to be a very different person."

"Na na Mr Scott you are clean wrang" said I "For Johny Ballantyne tauld me an' he coudna but ken."

"Ay but ye should hae ascertained whether it was leeing Johny or true Johny who told you that before you avouched it; for they are two as different persons as exist on the face of the earth" said he. "Had James told you so you might have aver'd it for James never diverges from the right forward truth." As Mr Southey once told me the very same thing I think I am at liberty to publish the sentiments of two such eminent men of the amiable deceased. James was a man of pomp and circumstance but he had a good and affectionate heart. It was too good and too kind for this world and the loss first of his lady and then of his great patron and friend broke it and he followed him instantly to the land of forgetfulness. How strange it is that all connected with those celebrated Novels have been hurled off the stage of time as it were together! The publisher the author the two printers and last of all the corrector of the press the honest and indefatigable Daniel M,Corkindale. All gone! And none to tell the secrets of that faithful and devoted little community.

There was no man knew Scott so well as James Ballantyne and I certainly never knew a man admire and revere a friend and patron so much. If any person ventured to compare other modern productions with those of Scott he stared with astonishment and took it as a personal insult to himself. There was one time that in my usual rash forward way I said that Miss Ferrier's novels were better than Sir Walter's. James drew himself up. I wish any reader of this had seen his looks of utter astonishment for he was always a sort of actor James. "What do I hear? What do I hear?" cried he with prodigious emphasis "Is it possible Sir that I hear such a sentiment drop from *your* lips?" I was obliged to burst out a laughing and run away.

Sir Walter's attached and devoted friends were without number but William Erskine and James Ballantyne were his constant and daily associates. It is a pity that Ballantyne had not left a written character of him for he could and would have done him justice. But the interesting part of their correspondence will soon all come to light in Lockhart's life of his illustrious father-in-law. He was the only man I ever knew whom no man either poor or rich held at ill will. I was the only exception myself that ever came to my knowledge but that was only for a short season and all the while it never lessened his interest in my welfare. I found that he went uniformly on one system. If he could do good to any man he would do it but he would do harm to no man. He never resented a literary attack however virulent of which there were some at first but always laughed at them. This showed a superiority of mind and greatness of soul which no other young author is capable of. He never retaliated but trusted to his genius to overcome all and it was not on a bruised reed that he leaned.

Although so shy of his name and literary assistance which indeed he would not grant to any one on any account save to Lockhart yet to poor men of literary merit his purse strings were always open as far as it was in his power to assist them. I actually knew several unsuccessful authors who for years depended on his bounty for their daily bread. And then there was a delicacy in his way of doing it which was quite admirable. He gave them some old papers or old ballads to copy for him pretending to be greatly interested in them for which he sent them a supply every week making them believe that they were reaping the genuine fruit of their own labours.

There was one day when I was chatting with Ballantyne in his office where I was generally a daily visitor as well as my illustrious friend I chanced to say that I never in my life knew a man like Scott for that I knew to a certainty he was at that time feeling himself a successful author lending pecuniary assistance to very many unsuccessful ones and the best thing of all he never let his left hand know what his right hand was doing.

Ballantyne's face glowed with delight and the tear stood in his eye. "You never were more right in your life" said he "You never were more right in your life! And I am glad that you know and so duly appreciate the merits of our noble our invaluable friend. Look here" And with that he turned up his daybook and added "Some word it seems had reached Scott that Matturin the Irish poet was lying in prison for a small debt and here have I by Mr Scott's orders been obliged to transmit him a bill of exchange for £60 and Matturin is never to know from whom or whence it came." I have said it oft and now say it again for the last time that those who knew Scott only from the few hundreds or I might say hundreds of thousands of volumes to which he has given birth and circulation through the world knew only one half of the man and that not the best half neither. As a friend he was sometimes stern but always candid and sincere and I always found his counsels of the highest value if I could have followed them. I was indebted to him for the most happy and splendid piece of humorous ballad poetry which I ever wrote. He said to me one day after dinner "It was but very lately Mr Hogg that I was drawn by our friend Kirkpatrick Sharpe to note the merits of your ballad The Witch of Fife. There never was such a thing written for genuine and ludicrous humour but why in the name of wonder did you suffer the gude auld man to be burnt skin and bone by the English at Carlisle (for in the first and second editions that was the issue). I never saw a piece of such bad taste in all my life. What had the poor old carl done to deserve such a fate? Only taken a drappy o' drink too much at another man's expense which you and I have done often. It is a *finale* which I cannot bear and you *must* bring of[f] the old man by some means or other no matter how extravagant or ridiculous in such a ballad as yon but by all means bring off the fine old fellow for the present termination of the ballad is one which I cannot brook." I went home and certainly brought off the old man with flying colours which is by far the best part of the ballad. I never adopted a suggestion of his either in prose or verse

which did not improve the subject. He knew mankind well. He knew
the way to the human heart and he certainly had the art of leading
the taste of an empire I may say of a world above all men that ever
existed. As long as Sir Walter Scott wrote poetry there was neither
man nor woman ever thought of either reading or writing any thing
but poetry. But the instant that he gave over writing poetry there
was neither man nor woman ever read it more! All turned to tales
and novels which I among others was reluctantly obliged to do. Yes
I was obliged from the tide the irresistible current that followed him
to forego the talent which God had given me at my birth and enter
into a new sphere with which I had no acquaintance. The world of
imagination had been opened wide to me but of the world of real
life I knew nothing. Sir Walter knew it in all its shades and grada-
tions and could appreciate any singular character at once. He had a
clear head as well as a benevolent heart; was a good man; an anxiously kind husband an indulgent parent and a sincere foregiving
friend; a just judge and a punctual correspondent. I believe that he
answered every letter sent to him either from rich or poor and generally not very shortly. Such is the man we have lost and such a
man we shall never see again. He was truly an extraordinary man;
the greatest man in the world. What are kings or Emperors compared with him? Dust and sand! And unless when connected with
literary men the greater part of their names either not remembered
at all or only remembered with detestation. But here is a name who
next to that of William Shakespeare will descend with rapt admiration to all the ages of futurity. And is it not a proud boast for an old
shepherd that for thirty years he could call this man friend and associate with him every day and hour that he chose?

Yes it is my proudest boast. Sir Walter sought me out in the wilderness and attached himself to me before I had ever seen him and
although I took cross fits with him his interest in me never subsided
for one day or one moment. He never scrupled to let me know that
I behoved to depend entirely on myself for my success in life but at
the same time always assured me that I had talents to ensure that
success if properly applied and not suffered to run to waste. I was
always recieved in his house like a brother and he visited me on the
same familiar footing. I never went into the inner house of Parliament where he sat on which he did not rise and come to me and
conduct me to a seat in some corner of the outer house where he
would only sit with me two or three minutes. I am sorry to think
that any of his relations should entertain an idea that Sir Walter
undervalued me for of all men I ever met with not excepting the

noblemen and gentlemen in London there never was a gentleman paid more deference to me than Sir Walter and although many of my anecdotes are homely and common place ones I am sure there is not a man in Scotland who appreciates his value more highly or reveres his memory more.

With regard to his family I have not much to say for I know but little. Sophia was a baby when I first visited him about two or three months old and I have watched her progress ever since. By the time she had passed beyond the years of infancy I percieved that she was formed to be the darling of such a father's heart and so it proved. She was a pure child of nature without the smallest particle of sophistication in her whole composition. And then she loved her father so. O how dearly she loved him! I shall never forget the looks of affection that she would throw up to him as he stood leaning on his crutch and hanging over her at the harp as she chaunted to him his favourite old Border Ballads or his own wild highland gatherings. Whenever he came into a room where she was her countenance altered and she often could not refrain from involuntary laughter. She is long ago a wife and mother herself but I am certain she will always cherish the memory of the most affectionate of fathers.

Walter is a fine manly gentlemanly fellow without pride or affectation but without the least spark of his father's genius that I ever could discern and for all the literary company that he mixed with daily in his youth he seemed always to hold literature and poetry in particular in very low estimation. He was terribly cast down at his father's death. I never saw a face of such misery and dejection and though I liked to see it yet I could not help shedding tears on contemplating his features thinking of the jewel that had fallen from his crown.

I always considered Anne as the cleverest of the family; shrewd, sensible, and discerning but I believe a little of a satyrist for I know that when she was a mere girl her associates were terrified for her. Charles is a queer chap and will either make a spoon or spoil a good horn.

Of Lockhart's genius and capabilities Sir Walter always spoke with the greatest enthusiasm more than I thought he deserved for I knew him a great deal better than Sir Walter did and whatever Lockhart may pretend I knew Sir Walter a thousand times better than he did. There is no man now living who knows Scott's character so thoroughly in all its bearings as William Laidlaw does. He was his land steward his amanuensis and managed the whole of his rural concerns and improvements for the period of twenty years and sorry am I that the present Sir Walter did not find it meet to keep Laidlaw on the estate for without him that dear-bought and classical property will be like a carcass without a head. Laidlaw's head made it. He knows the value of every acre of land on it to a tithe and of every tree in the forest with the characters of all the neighbours and retainers. He was to be sure a subordinate but Sir Walter always treated him as a friend inviting Mrs Laidlaw and him down to every party where there was any body he thought Laidlaw would like to meet and Sir Walter called on Mrs Laidlaw once or twice every good day when he was in the country. I have seen him often pop in to his breakfast and take his salt herring and tea with us there with as much ease and good humour as if he had come into his brother's house. He once said to me as we were walking out about Abbotslee and I was so much interested in the speech that I am sure I can indite it word by word for Laidlaw was one of my earliest and dearest friends.

"Was it not an extraordinary chance for me that threw Laidlaw into my hands? Without Laidlaw's head I could have done nothing and to him alone I am indebted for all those improvements. I never found a mind so inexhaustible as Laidlaw's. I have met with many of the greatest men of our country but uniformly found that after sounding them on one or two subjects there their information terminated. But with the worst of all manners of expression Laidlaw's mind is inexhaustible. Its resources seem to be without end. Every day every hour he has something new either of theory or experiment and he sometimes abuses me like a tinkler because I refuse to follow up his insinuations."

Another day he said to me "You know I reccommend your friend Laidlaw last year to Lord Mansfield as his factor but was obliged to withdraw my reccomendation and give his lordship a hint to relinquish his choice. For in the first place I was afraid that Laidlaw's precarious health might unfit him for such a responsible situation and more than that I found that I could not live without him and was obliged maugre all misfortunes to replace him in his old situation." I therefore wish from my heart and soul that matters could have been so arranged that Laidlaw should not have been separated from Abbotsford for though my own brother has long had and still has a high responsibility as shepherd and superintendent of the inclosures I cannot see how the management of the estate can go on without Laidlaw. Under the law agents it will both cost more and go to ruin and I say again Without Laidlaw that grand classical estate is a carcass without a head.

Whenever Sir Walter spoke of any of his two sons which he frequently did it was always in a jocular way to raise a laugh at their expense. His description of Walter when he led in Mrs Lockhart a bride with his false mustachios and whiskers was a source of endless amusement to him. He was likewise wont often to quote some of Charles's wise sayings which in the way that he told them never failed to set the table in a roar of laughter.

Sir Walter had his caprices like other men and when in poor health was particularly cross but I always found his heart in the right place and that he had all the native feelings and generosity of a man of true genius. I am ashamed to confess that his feelings for individual misfortune were far more intense than my own. There was one day that I went in to breakfast with him as usual when he said to me with eyes perfectly staring "Good God Hogg have you heard what has happened?"

"Na no that I ken o'. What is it that ye allude to Mr Scott?"

"That our poor friend Irving has cut his throat last night or this morning and is dead."

"Oo ay! I heard o' that" said I with a coldness that displeased him. "But I never heedit it for the truth is that Irving was joost like the Englishman's fiddle the warst faut that he had he was useless. Irving could never have done any good either for himself his family or ony other leevin creature."

"I don't know Mr Hogg what that poor fellow might have done with encouragement. This you must at least acknowledge that if he did not write genuine poetry he came the nearest to it of any man that ever failed." These were Sir Walter's very words and I record them in memory of the hapless victim of despair and dissapointed literary ambition. He farther added "For me his melancholly fate has impressed me so deeply and deranged me so much that it will be long before I can attend to any thing again."

He abhorred all sorts of low vices and blackguardism with a perfect detestation. There was one Sunday when he was riding down Yarrow in his carriage attended by several gentlemen on horseback and I being among them went up to the carriage door and he being our sherriff I stated to him with the deepest concern that there was at that moment a cry of *murder* from the Broadmeadows wood and that Will Watherston was murdering Davie Brunton. "Never you regard that Hogg" said he with rather a stern air and without a smile on his countenance. "If Will Watherston murder Davie Brunton and be hanged for the crime it is the best thing that can befal to the parish. Drive on Peter."

He was no great favorer of religion and seldom or never went to church He was a complete and finished aristocrate and the prosperity of the state was his great concern which prosperity he deemed lost unless both example and precept flowed by regular gradation from the highest to the lowest. He dreaded religion as a machine by which the good government of the country might be deranged if not uprooted. There was one evening when he and Morrit of Rokeby some of the Fergusons and I were sitting over our wine that he said "There is nothing that I dread so much as a very religious woman. She is not only a dangerous person but a perfect shower-bath on all social convivivality. The enthusiasm of our Scottish ladies has now grown to such a height that I am almost certain it will lead to some dangerous revolution in the state. And then to try to check it would only make the evil worse. If you ever chuse a wife Hogg for God's sake as you value your own happiness don't chuse a *very* religious one."

He had a settled impression on his mind that a revolution was impending over this country even worse than that we have experienced and he was always keeping a sharp look out on the progress of enthusiasm in religion as a dangerous neighbour. There was one day that he and Laidlaw were walking in the garden at Abbotsford during the time that the western portion of the mansionhouse was a building. The architects name I think was Mr Paterson.

"Well, do you [know] Laidlaw" said Scott "that I think Paterson one of the best-natured shrewd sensible fellows that I ever met with. I am quite delighted with him for he is a fund of continual amusement to me. If you heard but how I torment him! I attack him every day on the fundamental principles of his own art. I take a position which I know to be false and persist in maintaining it and it [is] truly amazing with what good sense and good nature he supports his principles. I really like Paterson exceedingly."

"O he's verra fine fallow" said Laidlaw. "An extrodnar fine fallow an' has a great deal o' comings an' gangings in him. But dinna ye think Mr Scott that it's a great pity he should hae been a preacher?"

"A preacher?" said Scott staring at him "Good lord! What do you mean?"

"Aha! It's a' that ye ken about it!" said Laidlaw "I assure you he's a preacher an' a capital preacher too. He's reckoned the best baptist preacher in a' Galashiels an' preaches every Sunday to a great community o' low kind o' fo'ks."

On hearing this Sir Walter (then Mr Scott) wheeled about and halted off with a swiftness Laidlaw had never seen him exercise before exclaiming vehemently to himself "Preaches! G– d– him!" From that time forth his delightful colloquoys with Mr Paterson ceased.

There was another time at Abbotsford when some of the Sutherland family (for I dont remember the English title) and many others were there that we were talking of the Earl of Buchan's ornamental improvements at Dryburgh and among other things of the collossal statue of Wallace which I rather liked and admired but which Sir Walter perfectly abhorred he said these very words. "If I live to see the day when the men of Scotland like the children of Israel shall every one do that which is right in his own eyes *which I am certain either I or my immediate successors will see* I have settled in my own mind long ago what I shall do first. I'll go down and blow up the statue of Wallace with gun powder. Yes I shall blow it up in such stile that there shall not be one fragment of it left! the horrible monster!"

He had a great veneration for the character of Sir William Wallace and I have often heard him eulogize it. He said to me one morning long ago when Miss Porter's work The Scottish Chiefs first appeared "I am grieved about this work of Miss Porters! I cannot describe to you how much I am dissapointed. I wished to think so well of it; and I do think highly of it as a work of genius. But lord help her! Her Wallace is no more our Wallace than Lord Peter is or than King Henry's messenger to Piercy Hotspur. It is not safe meddling with the hero of a country and of all others I cannot endure to see the character of Wallace frittered away to that of a fine gentleman."

Sir Walter was the best formed man I ever saw and laying his weak limb out of the question a perfect model of a man for gigantic strength. The muscles of his arms were prodigious. I remember of one day long ago I think it was at some national dinner in Oman's Hotel that at a certain time of the night a number of the young heros differed prodigiously with regard to their various degrees of muscular strength. A general measurement took place around the shoulders and chest and I as a particular judge in these matters was fixed on as the measurer and umpire. Scott who never threw cold water on any fun submitted to be measured with the rest. He measured most round the chest and to their great chagrin I was next to him and very little short. But when I came to examine the arms! Sir Walter's had double the muscular power of mine and very nearly so of every man's who was there. I declare that from the elbow to the shoulder they felt as if he had the strength of an ox.

There was a gentleman once told me that he walked into Sir

Walter's house in Castle street just as the footman was showing another gentleman out and that being an intimate acquaintance he walked straight into Sir Walter's study where he found him stripped with his shirt sleeves rolled up to his shoulders and his face very red "Good God Scott what is the matter?" said the intruder. "Pray may I ask an explanation of this?"

"Why the truth is that I have just been giving your friend Mr Martin a complete drubbing" said Scott laughing. "The scoundrel dared me to touch him but with one of my fingers; but if I have not given him a thorough basting he knows himself. He is the most impudent and arrant knave I ever knew! But I think it will be a while before he attempts to impose again upon me." This Mr Martin the gentleman said was some great picture dealer. But as I never heard Sir Walter mention the feat in his hours of hilarity I am rather disposed to discredit the story. He was always so reasonable and so prudent that I hardly think he would fall on and baste even a knavish picture-dealer black and blue in his own study. The gentleman who told me is alive and well and may answer for himself in this matter.

Sir Walter in his study and in his seat in the Parliament House had rather a dull heavy appearance but in company his countenance was always lighted up and Chauntry has given the likeness of him then precisely. In his family he was kind condescending and attentive but highly imperative. No one of them durst for a moment disobey his orders and if he began to hang down his eyebrows a single hint was enough. In every feature of his face decision was strongly marked. He was exactly what I concieve an old Border Baron to have been with his green jacket his blue bonnet his snow-white locks muscular frame and shaggy eyebrows.

He was said to be a very careless composer yet I have seen a great number of his M.S.S. corrected and enlarged on the white page which he alternatly left a plan which I never tried in my life. He once undertook to correct the press for a work of mine "The Three Perils of women" when I was living in the country and when I gave the M.S. to Ballantyne I said "Now you must send the proofs to Sir Walter he is to correct them for me."

"He correct them for you!" exclaimed Ballantyne "L–d help you and him both! I assure you if he had no body to correct after him there would be a bonny sang through the country. He is the most careless and incorrect writer that ever was born of a voluminous and popular writer and as for sending a proof-sheet to him we may as well keep it in the office. He never heeds it. No no you must trust the correction of the press to my men and me I shall answer for them and if I am in a difficulty at any time I'll apply to Lockhart. He is a very different man and has the best eye for a corrector of any gentleman corrector I ever saw. He often sends me an article written off hand like your own with[out] the interlineation of a word or the necessity of correcting one afterwards. But as for Sir Walter he will never look at either your proofs or his own unless it be for a few minutes amusement."

The Whig ascendancy in the British cabinet killed Sir Walter. Yes I say and aver it was that which broke his heart deranged his whole constitution and murdered him. As I have shown before a dread of revolution had long preyed on his mind; he withstood it to the last; he fled from it but it affected his brain and killed him. From the moment he percieved the veto of a democracy prevailing he lost all hope of the prosperity and ascendancy of the British empire. He not only lost hope of the realm but of every individual pertaining to it as my last anecdote of him will show for though I could multiply these anecdotes and remarks to volumes yet I must draw them to a conclusion. They are trivial in the last degree did they not relate to so great and so good a man. I have depicted him exactly as he was as he always appeared to me and was reported by others and I revere his memory as that of an elder brother.

The last time I saw his loved and honoured face was at the little inn on my own farm in the Autumn of 1830. He sent me word that he was to pass on such a day on his way from Drumlanrig Castle to Abbotsford but he was sorry he could not call at Altrive to see Mrs Hogg and the bairns it being so far off the way. I accordingly waited at the inn and handed him out of the carriage. His daughter was with him but we left her at the inn and walked slowly down the way as far as Mountbenger-Burn. He then walked very ill indeed for the weak limb had become almost completely useless but he leaned on my shoulder all the way and did me the honour of saying that he never leaned on a firmer or a surer.

We talked of many things past present and to come but both his memory and onward calculation appeared to me then to be considerably decayed. I cannot tell what it was but there was something in his manner that distressed me. He often changed the subject very abruptly and never laughed. He expressed the deepest concern for my welfare and success in life more than I had ever heard him do before and all mixed with sorrow for my worldly misfortunes. There is little doubt that his own were then preying on his vitals. He told me that which I never knew nor suspected before that a certain gamekeeper on whom he bestowed his maledictions without reserve had prejudiced my best friend the young Duke of Buccleuch against me by a story which though he himself knew it to be an invidious and malicious lie yet seeing his Grace so much irritated he durst not open his lips on the subject farther than by saying. "But my lord Duke you must always remember that Hogg is no ordinary man although he may have shot a stray moorcock." And then turning to me he said "Before you had venture[d] to give any saucy language to a low scoundrel of an English gamekeeper you should have thought of Fielding's tale of Black George."

"I never saw that tale" said I "an' dinna ken ought about it. But never trouble your head about that matter Sir Walter for it is awthegither out o' nature for our young chief to entertain ony animosity against me. The thing will never mair be heard of an' the chap that tauld the lees on me will gang to hell that's aye some comfort."

I wanted to make him laugh but I could not even make him smile. "You are still the old man Hogg careless and improvident as ever" said he with a countenance as gruff and demure as could be.

Before we parted I mentioned to him my plan of trusting an edition of my prose tales in twenty volumes to Lockhart's editing. He dissaproved of the plan decidedly and said "I would not for any thing in the world that Lockhart should enter on such a responsibility for taking your ram-stam way of writing into account the responsibility would be a very heavy one. Ay and a dangerous one too!" Then turning half round leaning on his crutch and fixing his eyes on the ground for a long space he said "You have written a great deal that might be made available Hogg with proper attention. And I am sure that one day or other it will be made available to you or your family. But in my opinion this is not the proper season. I wish you could drive off the experiment until the affairs of the nation are in better keeping for at present all things and literature in particular are going straight down hill to destruction and ruin." And then he mumbled something to himself which I took to be an inward curse. I say again and I am certain of it that the democratic ascendancy and the grievious and shameful insults he recieved from the populace of his own country broke the heart and killed the greatest man that ever that country contained.

When I handed him into the coach that day he said something to me which in the confusion of parting I forgot and though I tried to reccollect the words the next minute I could not and never could again. It was something to the purport that it was likely it would be long ere [he] leaned as far on my shoulder again but there was an expression in it conveying his affection for me or his interest in me which has escaped my memory for ever.

This is my last anecdote of my most sincere and esteemed friend. After this I never saw him again. I called twice at Abbotsford during his last ilness but they would not let me see him and I did not at all regret it for he was then reduced to the very lowest state of degradation to which poor prostrate humanity could be subjected. He was described to me by one who saw him often as exactly in the same state with a man mortally drunk who could in nowise own or assist himself the pressure of the abcess on the brain having apparently had the same effect as the fumes of drunkenness. He could at short intervals distinguish individuals and pronounce a few intelligible words but these lucid glimpses were of short duration the sunken eye soon ceased again from distinguishing objects and the powerless tongue became unable to utter a syllable though constantly attempting it which made the sound the most revolting that can be concieved.

I am sure Heaven will bless Lockhart for his attentions to the illustrious sufferer. The toil and watching that he patiently endured one would have thought was beyond human nature to have stood and yet I never saw him look better or healthier all the while. He will not miss his reward. I followed my friend's sacred remains to his last narrow house remained the last man at the grave and even then left it with reluctance.

> *Omnes eodem cogimur omnium*
> *Versatur urna serius ocyus*
> *Sors exitura.*

# Appendix:
# War Songs by Hogg and Scott

Hogg and Scott wrote the two war songs mentioned in *Anecdotes of Scott* (pp. 23–24, 61) at a time when Britain was bracing itself for an expected invasion by the forces of Napoleon. Scott's song is reprinted below from the *Scots Magazine*, 65 (October 1803), 725–26.

## War Song,
## for the Edinburgh Cavalry Association.
### By Mr Walter Scott.

The reader will peruse with much satisfaction the following admirable effusion of the warlike and animated muse of this ingenious author. It is calculated to produce every effect which a British patriot can desire; and although it may not have the impressive variety which other poems of a similar strain possess, yet it has that exquisite flow of the imagination which is adapted to excite the performance of heroic deeds.

> To horse! to horse! the standard flies,
>     The bugles sound the call;
> The Gallic Navy stem the seas,
> The voice of battle's on the breeze,
>     Arouse ye one and all!
>
> From high Dunedin's towers we come,
>     A band of brothers true;
> Our casques the leopard's spoils surround,
> With Scotland's hardy thistle crown'd,
>     We boast the red and blue.
>
> Though tamely crouch, to Gallia's frown,
>     Dull Holland's hardy train.
> Their ravish'd toys, though Romans mourn,
> Though gallant Switzers vainly spurn,
>     And foaming gnaw the chain:

Oh! had they mark'd the avenging call,
  Their Brethren's murder gave,
Disunion ne'er their ranks had mown,
Nor Patriot valour, desperate grown,
  Sought freedom in the grave.

Shall we, too, bend the stubborn head,
  In Freedom's Temple born;
Dress our pale cheek in timid smile,
To hail a Master in our isle,
  Or brook a Victor's scorn?

No, tho' destruction o'er the land
  Come pouring as a flood—
The Sun, that sees our falling day,
Shall mark our sabre's deadly sway,
  And set that night in blood.

For gold let Gallia's legions fight,
  Or plunder's bloody gain;
Unbrib'd, unbought, our swords we draw,
To guard our King, to fence our Law;
  Nor shall their edge be vain.

If ever breath of British gale
  Shall fan the tri-colour;
Or footstep of Invader rude,
With rapine foul and red with blood,
  Pollute our happy shore—

Then, farewell Hope, and farewell Friends!
  Adieu each tender tie;
Resolved we mingle in the tide,
Where charging squadrons furious ride,
  To conquer or to die!

To horse! to horse! the sabres gleam,
  High sounds our bugles call;
Combin'd by honour's sacred tie,
Our word is, *"Laws and Liberty!"*—
  March forward, one and all!

In his *Memoir of the Author's Life* Hogg writes that his song 'Donald M'Donald' was composed in 1800 'on the threatened invasion by Buonaparte', and published as a broadside by John Hamilton of Edinburgh (*Memoir of the Author's Life* and *Familiar Anecdotes of Sir Walter Scott*, ed. by D. S. Mack (Edinburgh: Scottish Academic Press, 1972), p. 14). This rare broadside is reproduced in facsimile overleaf from the copy in Stirling University Library, by kind permission of the Librarian. The broadside is undated, but the sheet of paper on which this copy is printed carries the watermark date 1801.

# DONALD M'DONALD,

### A Favorite New Scots Song,

SET FOR THE

## *Voice, Piano-Forte, and Ger. Flute.*

### WRITTEN BY JAMES HOG.

PRICE 6d.

*Printed and Sold by J. Hamilton, No 24, North Bridge Street.*

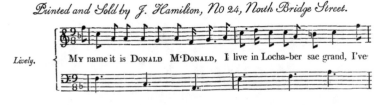

*Lively.* My name it is DONALD M'DONALD, I live in Locha-ber sae grand, I've

follow'd our banner, an' will do, Wherev-er my maker has land ; When rankit a-

mang the blue bannets, Nae danger can fear me a-va', I ken that my brethren a-roun' me, Are

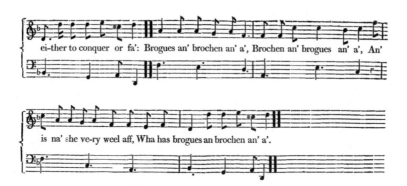

ei-ther to conquer or fa': Brogues an' brochen an' a', Brochen an' brogues an' a', An'

is na' she ve-ry weel aff, Wha has brogues an brochen an' a'.

Last year we were wonderfu' canty,
    Our frien's an' our country to see;
But since the proud Consul's grown vantie,
    We'll meet him by land or by sea.
Whenever a clan is disloyal,
    Wherever our king has a foe,
He'll quickly see Donald M'Donald,
    Wi's highlandmen a' in a row.
Guns an' pistols an a',
    Pistols an' guns an' a',
He'll quickly see Donald M'Donald,
    Wi' guns an' pistols an'a'.

What tho' we befriendit young Charley,
    To tell it I dinna think shame,
Poor lad he came to us but barely,
    And reckon'd our mountains his hame;
'Tis true that our reason forbade us,
    But tenderness carry'd the day,
Had Geordy come friendless amang us,
    Wi' him wi' had a' gane away.
Sword an' buckler an' a',
    Buckler an' sword an' a';
For George we'll encounter the devil,
    Wi' sword an' buckler an'a'.

An' O I wad eagerly press him,
    The keys o' the East to retain;
For sude he gie up the possession,
    We'll soon hae to force them again.
Than yield up ae inch wi' dishonour,
    Tho' it were my finishing blow,

He ay may depend on M'Donald,
    Wi's highlandmen a' in a row.
Knees an' elba's an' a'
    Elba's an' knees an' a',
Depend upon Donald M'Donald,
    His knees an' elba's an' a',

If Bonaparte land at Fort William,
    Auld Europe nae langer sal grane,
I laugh when I think how we'll gall him,
    Wi' bullet, wi' steel, an' wi' stane.
Wi' rocks o' the Nevis an' Gairy,
    We'll rattle him aff frae our shore;
Or lull him asleep in a cairney,
    An' sing him Lochaber no more.
Stanes an' bullets an' a',
    Bullets an' stanes an' a',
We'll batter the Corsican callan,
    Wi' stanes an' bullets an' a'.

The Gordon is gude in a hurry,
    An' Campbell is steel to the bane,
An'Grant, an M'Kenzie, an'Murray,
    An' Cameron will hurkle to nane.
The Stuart is sturdy and wannel,
    An' sae is M'Leod an' M'Kay,
An' I, their gude-brither M'Donald,
    Sal ne'er be the last in the fray.
Brogues an' brochen an' a',
    Brochen an' brogues an' a',
An' up wi' the bonny blue bannet,
    The kilt, an' the feather, an' a'.

# Note on the Texts

The text of the *Anecdotes of Sir W. Scott* endeavours to reproduce the manuscript as faithfully as possible. Hogg initially wrote this version for use by John M'Crone and never intended it for publication under his own name. After Lockhart's strenuous objections, Hogg withdrew the *Anecdotes*, determined that 'they shall not [see the light] as long as I live'. (See the Note on the Genesis of the Texts, pp. xxxvi–xl.) A verbatim transcript, therefore, reflects the informal nature of this manuscript and the fact that it was never published in Hogg's time.

In the case of the *Familiar Anecdotes of Sir Walter Scott*, however, slight editorial interventions acknowledge Hogg's different intention for this manuscript, and its consequently more formal nature. (See Note on the Genesis of the Texts, p. l.) These silent interventions have been limited to the insertion of periods where necessary and of inverted commas where speech marks are either absent or incomplete. Words or parts of words not present in the manuscript which have been inserted to clarify meaning are enclosed in square brackets and noted.

There are two passages in the present text of *Familiar Anecdotes of Sir Walter Scott* which are not present in Hogg's manuscript. After the first paragraph of the manuscript Hogg inserted the following parenthetical instruction: '(then copy the whole of the Reminiscences of him in The Altrive Tales)', referring to his *Altrive Tales* (London: James Cochrane, 1832), pp. cx–cxxi. This passage extends through the verse extract on page 43 of the present edition, and perhaps explains why that reappears in the longer verse extract on pages 59–60. The producers of the first edition of 1834 duly inserted the passage according to Hogg's request, but there are significant textual differences between the version of that edition and the original passage in *Altrive Tales*. The most likely explanation is that Hogg's manuscript was accompanied in its passage to America by a copy of *Altrive Tales* in which he had marked various changes and other corrections in the relevant passage. Therefore this section has been reprinted from *Familiar Anecdotes of Sir Walter Scott* (New York: Harper and Brothers, 1834), pp. 122–41.

Hogg's letter to De Witt Bloodgood of 22 June 1833 (accompanying his manuscript) is cited in the Note on the Genesis of the Texts, pp. xlviii–xlix. In this letter Hogg expressed a desire that one of his poems 'written about 1820 and addressed to Sir Walter on first hearing that he was made a baronet' should be added to the work if possible. Presumably his American publishers were not able to locate the poem, but the present edition fulfills his wish by reprinting the poem on pp. 33–36 from Hogg's *Poetical Works*, 4 vols (Edinburgh: Constable and Co., 1822), IV, 131–40.

The present edition of *Anecdotes of Scott* also includes an Appendix reprinting Scott's 'War Song, for the Edinburgh Cavalry Association' from the *Scots Magazine*, 65 (October 1803), 725–26. Although this is not a part of either version of Hogg's anecdotes it is referred to in both, and in a footnote to the manuscript of *Anecdotes of Sir W. Scott* (reproduced on p. 23 of the present edition) Hogg wrote (presumably for M'Crone's benefit), 'If you can find this song give a copy'. The Appendix accordingly attempts to fulfill this instruction. Hogg compares Scott's song with his own 'Donald M'Donald', and the Appendix also gives a facsimile reprint of the broadside in which, around 1800, 'Donald M'Donald' was first published.

The following principles of correction apply to both versions of Hogg's manuscript texts:

1. Hogg indicates a new paragraph with a + sign. These have all been deleted and a period and indentation inserted in their place.
2. In the manuscript it is often difficult to distinguish Hogg's upper-case and lower-case p from one another and his upper-case and lower-case s. In these instances of ambiguity, and only in these, correct capitalisation has been employed. In all other places, manuscript capitalisation has been retained.
3. Proper names have been capitalised where necessary.
4. Double underlining in the manuscript has been indicated by small capitals in the printed text.
5. Hogg occasionally repeats words, frequently at the end of one page and the beginning of the next line or page. Where such doublings are obvious errors, they have been corrected and noted.
6. Hogg's deletions are indicated in the manuscripts by a straight line through the word or phrase, and these words or phrases have been deleted from the printed text. Passages with other changes, not clearly attributable to Hogg, have been restored to their original form.

## Textual Notes on *Anecdotes of Sir W. Scott*

The manuscript (Hogg, James. Papers. f MS-Papers-0042-01) belongs to the Alexander Turnbull Library, National Library of New Zealand, Wellington, with whose permission it is here published. Included with the manuscript is a handwritten note: 'MS.S. Of Memories of Sir Walter Scott. It had been better had it never been published'. The note is signed 'M. G. G.', the initials of Hogg's youngest daughter Mary Gray Garden, and dated 1876. Her sister Harriet emigrated to New Zealand in 1879, and the large collection of Hogg papers there was donated to the National Library by Harriet's descendants.

In the lists below, deletions in the manuscript are enclosed between angle brackets < thus >, additions are printed bold type **thus,** [eop] signifies [end of page], and [eol] signifies [end of line]. The references are to page and line numbers.

| | |
|---|---|
| p.3, l. 1 | In the manuscript, '(or we)' is written in above the 'I'. The 'I' here signifies John McCrone, for whose use Hogg originally composed the *Anecdotes*. After the first sentence of the second paragraph, however, Hogg drops the pretence of a persona. |
| p.3, l. 11 | manuscript: that I < could > ever < say I > discerned |
| p.5, l. 2 | manuscript: my youth [eop] youthful mind |
| p.6, l. 19 | manuscript: < But > with regard to |
| p.6, l. 38 | manuscript: and < also > there was also |
| p.7, ll. 3–4 | manuscript: remarking with [eop] with apparently |
| p.7, l. 4 | manuscript: and < apparent > determination |
| p.7, ll. 19–20 | manuscript: its tower and its < bastions > bartizans |
| p.7, l. 21 | manuscript: the < archichects > architects |
| p.7, l. 22 | manuscript: the family took < took > |
| p.7, l. 23 | manuscript: < then > raging then |
| p.7, l. 26 | manuscript: < we are > gaining |
| p.7, l. 42 | manuscript: £2000= |
| p.8, l. 11 | manuscript: I < once > got a letter |
| p.8, l. 20 | manuscript: £20= |
| p.9, l. 6 | manuscript: I'm < in > |
| p.9, l. 6 | manuscript: the mountain and < and > |
| p.9, l. 8 | manuscript: the greater < the greater > |
| p.11, l. 25 | manuscript: which he < said > had once lost |
| p.12, ll. 32–33 | manuscript: You< r > are certainly |
| p.13, l. 34 | manuscript: < he > was very cross |
| p.14, l. 30 | In the manuscript, 'lad' is struck through, but it does not appear to be Hogg's deletion. |

p.14, l. 42      manuscript: < is > has now grown

p.15, ll. 2–3    manuscript: only make the< m > evil

p.16, l. 9       In the manuscript, the second 'to' is struck through with a dou-
                 ble line, but it does not appear to be Hogg's deletion.

p.16, l. 16      manuscript: well if [eop] if that knife

p.16, l. 17      At the top of this page, just above 'keepsake' in the manuscript,
                 Hogg has written the instruction 'A new line at every +'.

p.17, l. 39      manuscript: till < that > that day

p.18, l. 6       In the manuscript, 'I have forgot what*' is struck through. At
                 the bottom of the page, separated from the text, Hogg has
                 written '*If you know what he alluded to mention the place or
                 copy it'. The corrector has inserted 'Black George'.

p.18, l. 32      manuscript: on the ground < and on my cottage alternately >

p.20, l. 40      manuscript: He knows < that > it is expected

p.21, l. 9       manuscript: likewise [eop] likewise

p.22, ll. 10–11  manuscript: not one in the < the > whole

p.22, l. 34      manuscript: < Yo > said he "You

p.23, l. 33      In the manuscript at the bottom of the page, separated from
                 the text, Hogg has written '*If you can find this song give a
                 copy'.

p.23, l. 38      manuscript: the < name > **clan** of M,Donald

p.24, l. 14      In the manuscript, the n in 'noblemen' is written in lower-case
                 with double underlining.

p.24, l. 17      manuscript: as I < did > did

p.24, l. 25      manuscript: < end > **beginning** to end.

p.24, l. 29      manuscript: I could always < I could always >

p.25, l. 21      After 'read*' in the manuscript, Hogg inserts this instruction:
                 '(The paragraph on the other page here)'. He refers to the next
                 paragraph, which is written on the final leaf of the manuscript,
                 which also serves as a wrapper.

p.26, l. 7       manuscript: him to <my> dinner

p.26, ll. 40–41  manuscript: one day when I was < **one day** >

p.26, l. 42      manuscript: daily stranger < when >

p.27, l. 3       manuscript: his < right > left hand

p.27, l. 10      manuscript: £60=

p.27, l. 16      In the manuscript, the k in 'king' is written in lower-case with
                 double underlining.

p.27, ll. 19–20  manuscript: his early < ones > prose works

p.28, l. 21      manuscript: been < bundled > **hurled**

p.28, l. 37      In the manuscript, the l in 'laidlaw's' is written in lower-case
                 with double underlining.

p.29, l. 5       manuscript: walks < he > **Sir Walter**

p.29, l. 23      manuscript: high< ly >

p.29, l. 40      manuscript: he < always > let me know

p.30, ll. 8, 10  and   w[ay] [...] m[ay]: The manuscript is torn here, but the equivalent passage in *Familiar Anecdotes of Sir Walter Scott* (p. 66) supports the conjectural readings.

p.30, l. 20      manuscript: < from > armoury,

p.30, ll. 27–28 manuscript: sit < on > in the middle

p.30, l. 30      b[e]: The manuscript is torn at this point, so the reading must remain conjectural.

## Textual Notes on *Familiar Anecdotes of Sir Walter Scott*

The manuscript (MA 192 fol.) of this edition belongs to the Pierpont Morgan Library, New York, with whose permission it is here published. It was first published·in 1834 in Albany, New York by Harper and Brothers as *Familiar Anecdotes of Sir Walter Scott. By James Hogg the Etrick Shepherd. With A Sketch of the Life of the Shepherd, By S. DeWitt Bloodgood*. It appeared in a pirated edition shortly thereafter in Glasgow ( John Reid & Co.), Edinburgh (Oliver and Boyd), and London (Black, Young, and Young; Whittaker, Treacher, & Co.; and various imprints) under the title of *The Domestic Manners and Private Life of Sir Walter Scott*, by James Hogg, with a memoir of the author, notes, etc.

p.37, ll. 11–12  After 'out of the question', Hogg writes in the manuscript '(then copy the whole of the Reminiscences of him in The Altrive Tales)'. From this point until p. 43, l. 11 (after the excerpt from *The Queen's Wake*), the text is taken from the section on Scott in Hogg's *Memoir of the Author's Life* as modified for the edition of the *Familiar Anecdotes* published in Albany in 1834.

p.37, l. 22      1834: "I was rejoiced

p.43, l. 33      manuscript: that to me who alas < who > to this day

p.44, ll. 19–20 manuscript: and yet notwithstand the broad

p.44, l. 32      manuscript: house of harden

p.45, ll. 15–16 manuscript: he was < always > **uniformly** moderate

p.45, l. 26      manuscript: Castle street

p.46, ll. 33–34 manuscript: he took < off > all the latter bumpers off to the brim

p.47, l. 28      In the manuscript, XX appears above 'me'; these are most likely not Hogg's marks.

p.48, l. 11      manuscript: if he < gets > makes a slip

p.48, ll. 30–31 manuscript: and < my > face most violently

p.49, l. 21     manuscript: test and his firmness < and his firmness >

p.49, l. 23     manuscript: an ignorant and incorrible barbarian

p.50, l. 13     In the manuscript, the a in 'Annual Register' is written in lower-case with two lines inserted under it, probably by a corrector.

p.50, l. 16     manuscript: know is editor

p.50, l. 21     The manuscript has crossed-out inverted commas before 'Mr'.

p.50, l. 22     manuscript: in a literary long before   [Hogg clearly left out a noun, but his intention is not apparent.]

p.51, l. 2      manuscript: mair < na > nor that

p.51, l.13      manuscript: Na, I < I > shoudna

p.51, ll. 15–16 manuscript: at the the thinking

p.52, ll. 3–4   manuscript: every that he said of any import.

p.53, ll. 19–20 manuscript: put always the <u>d</u> for the < the > th

p.54, l. 14     manuscript: a small helpless family [eol] family behind him

p.55, l. 19     In the manuscript, the w in '"What for?"' is written in lower-case with two lines inserted under it, probably by a corrector.

p.59, l. 10     manuscript: sure of getting it it

p.59, ll. 26–27 In the manuscript, there is a + struck through after 'find it.' Hogg may have originally intended to begin the quoted passage at this point and then decided to add one more sentence.

p.59, l. 39     The two words 'sepulchres unhearsed' are hard to make out in Hogg's hand, and the corrector has written them in superscript, perhaps after consulting the printed edition of *The Queen's Wake*.

p.60, l. 12     manuscript: O < cl > could

p.60, ll. 28–29 manuscript: any thing for me < at > in that

p.60, l. 33     manuscript: un[eop] unacquainted

p.61, ll. 6–7   manuscript: if < he > I had said of < me > **you** as < he > I wished to say < he > I would have been thought by the world to be applauding < himself > **myself**.

p.62, l.1       manuscript: his < round > own hand writing

p.62, ll. 12–16 (I was [...] was mine). The brackets are not present in the manuscript. They have been added to separate the comment of the narrative voice from the direct account of the conversation here recorded.

p.62, ll. 26–27 manuscript: I accompanied him in an of the Register Office

p.62, l. 29     In the manuscript 'W. Scott' is double-underlined.

p.63, l. 4      manuscript: and Old Mortality < as > the joint

p.63, l. 16     manuscript: generally laughed at the [eop] the remarks

p.63, ll. 19–20 manuscript: the two Messrs Ballantyne'< s >

p.63, l. 24     manuscript: the most < and > implicit confidence

p.63, l. 28     manuscript: I suspect< ed >

p.64, l. 6      manuscript: the < little > secrets

p.65, l. 17     manuscript: £60=

p.65, l. 37       manuscript: bring of the old man

p.66, l. 24       manuscript: with < dest > detestation.

p.68, l. 6        manuscript: he was [eol] was to be sure

p.70, l. 24       manuscript: "Well, do you Laidlaw"

p.70, l. 29       manuscript: and it truly amazing

p.70, l. 41       manuscript: < fl > fo'ks."

p.71, l. 32       manuscript: their < different > **various** degrees

p.71, l. 34       manuscript: in these < sporttin >[?] matters

p.72, l. 23       manuscript: he was < always > kind

p.72, l. 28       manuscript: his blue bonnet < and > his snow-white locks

p.72, ll. 30–31   manuscript: a great number< s >

p.72, l. 39       manuscript: bonny sang through< t >

p.73, l. 5        Hogg probably intended to write 'without' rather than 'with'.

p.74, l. 8        manuscript: had venture to

p.74, l. 23       manuscript: enter on < any > such **a**

p.74, l. 26       manuscript: leaning on his < chuth > crutch

p.74, l. 30       manuscript: family < some day or other >.

p.74, l. 31       manuscript: the affairs of the nation < were > **are**

p.75, l. 1        manuscript: long ere leaned

# Notes

In the Notes which follow, page references include a letter enclosed in brackets: (a) indicates that the passage concerned is to be found in the first quarter of the page, while (b) refers to the second quarter, (c) to the third quarter, and (d) to the final quarter. The Bible is referred to in the Authorised King James version familiar to Hogg and his contemporaries. For references to plays by Shakespeare the edition used has been *The Complete Works: Compact Edition*, ed. by Stanley Wells and Gary Taylor (Oxford: Clarendon Press, 1988). Parenthetical citations refer to the following:

**Carruthers**: Robert Carruthers, 'Abbotsford Notanda; or, Sir Walter Scott and His Factor', in Robert Chambers, *Life of Sir Walter Scott* (London: W. & R. Chambers, 1871)

**Grierson**: *The Letters of Sir Walter Scott*, ed. by H. J. C. Grierson, 12 vols (London: Constable, 1932–37)

**Mrs. Hughes**: Mary Ann Watts Hughes, *Letters and Recollections of Sir Walter Scott*, ed. by Horace G. Hutchinson (London: Smith and Elder, 1904)

**Journal**: *The Journal of Sir Walter Scott*, ed. by W. E. K. Anderson (Oxford: Clarendon Press, 1972)

**Lockhart**: John Gibson Lockhart, *Memoirs of the Life of Sir Walter Scott, Bart.*, 7 vols. (Edinburgh: Cadell, 1837–38)

**NLS**: National Library of Scotland

## Anecdotes of Sir W. Scott

3(a) **When I was in Scotland** Hogg quickly drops the pretence of a persona. This manuscript was originally submitted to John M'Crone, who visited Hogg in the autumn of 1832. M'Crone hoped to write a biography of Scott and requested Hogg's reminiscences. However, it is not clear exactly whom Hogg had in mind as the author of record. After the second paragraph, he either intentionally removes or forgets the voice of the intermediary and speaks to the reader *in propria persona*. Hogg's dealings with M'Crone are discussed in the Note on the Genesis of the Texts, pp. xxxvi–xlviii.

3(a) **The Shepherd** Hogg's *nom de plume* for his contributions to *Blackwood's Edinburgh Magazine* was 'The Ettrick Shepherd', and his character in the *Noctes Ambrosianae* was so called. The pen name often accompanied his own; there was no intention to preserve anonymity.

3(c) **Dr Hughes** the Rev. Thomas Hughes (1756–1833), Vicar of Uffington and Canon of St Paul's. Scott met him and his wife in London in 1809. They visited Edinburgh and Abbotsford in the spring of 1824 and in the summer of 1828. In 1827 Scott suggested that Mrs. Hughes ('such a resolute bustler') might help Hogg's candidacy for the Royal Literary Society (Grierson, x, 208).

3(c) **Dominie Sampson** a character in Scott's *Guy Mannering* (1815), thought to be largely modelled on George Thomson (1792–1838), tutor at Abbotsford from 1812 to 1820. Scott cherished his eccentricities. Lockhart describes him as follows:

[This was] Mr George Thomson, son of the minister of Melrose, who, when the house afforded better accommodation, was and continued for many years to be domesticated at Abbotsford. Scott had always a particular tenderness towards persons afflicted with any bodily misfortune; and Thomson, whose leg had been amputated in consequence of a rough casualty in boyhood, had a special share in his favour from the high spirit with which he refused at the time to betray the name of the companion that had occasioned the mishap, and continued ever afterwards to struggle against its disadvantages. Tall, vigorous, athletic, a dauntless horseman, and expert at the singlestick, George formed a valuable as well as picturesque addition to the *tail* of the new laird, who often said, "In the Dominie, like myself, accident has spoiled a capital lifeguardsman." His many oddities and eccentricities in no degree interfered with the respect due to his amiable feelings, upright principles, and sound learning; nor did *Dominie Thamson* at all quarrel in after times with the universal credence of the neighbourhood that he had furnished many features for the inimitable personage whose designation so nearly resembled his own; and if he has not yet "wagged his head" in a "pulpit o' his ain," he well knows it has not been so for want of earnest and long-continued intercession on the part of the author of Guy Mannering. (Lockhart, III, 8–9.)

**3(c) Dr Rutherford of Yarrow** John Rutherford (1641–1710) was Scott's maternal great-grandfather. He served as minister of Yarrow from 1691 until his death. Hogg is mistaken that Scott neglected his descent from Dr Rutherford. When planning the decoration of the ceiling shields at Abbotsford, he took great pains to clarify his maternal line. See his letter of 25 May 1823 to Thomas Shortreed (Grierson, VIII, 6–8).

**3(d) Buccleuch [...] Harden** Charles William Henry Scott, 4th Duke of Buccleuch (1772–1819), succeeded to the title in 1812. Walter Francis Montagu Douglas Scott, 5th Duke of Buccleuch (1806–84), succeeded to the title in 1819. Hugh Hepbourne-Scott (1758–1841) became 12th Laird of Harden in 1793 and 6th Baron Polwarth in 1835.

**4(a) Bowhill** seat of the Duke of Buccleuch, near Selkirk. The 'great festival' probably took place on 4 December 1815 after a celebrated football match at Carterhaugh between the men of Selkirk and Yarrow.

**4(b) Sir Adam Ferguson** Ferguson (1770–1855) was a friend of Scott's from his days at Edinburgh University. In 1816 he retired from the army and the next year rented the house and small farm of Totfield (renamed Huntlyburn) on the grounds of Abbotsford. Scott's influence led to Ferguson's being awarded the office of Keeper of the Regalia of Scotland, and George IV knighted him during the Royal Visit to Edinburgh in 1822. Their friendship lasted until Scott's death.

**4(b) placed myself among them** Lockhart's version of this incident differs from Hogg's:

Who can read this, and not be reminded of Sancho Panza and the Duchess? And, after all, he quite mistook what Scott had said to him; for certainly there was, neither on this, nor on any similar occasion at Bowhill, any *high table for the nobility*, though there was a *side-table for the children*, at which when the Shepherd of Ettrick was about to seat himself, his friend probably whispered that it was reserved for the "*little* lords and ladies, and their playmates." This blunder may seem undeserving of any explanation; but it is often in small matters that the strongest feelings are most strikingly betrayed—and this story is, in exact proportion to its silliness, indicative of the jealous feeling which mars and distorts so many of Hogg's representations of Scott's conduct and demeanour. (Lockhart, III, 398.)

4(c) **"If ye reave the Hoggs o Fauldshope / Ye herry Harden's gear"** *reave* and *herry* mean 'to plunder'; *gear* means 'property'. Hogg quotes these lines in a note to 'The Fray of Elibank' in *The Mountain Bard* (Edinburgh: Constable, 1807), pp. 66–67.

The author's progenitors possessed the lands of Fauldshop, under the Scotts of Harden, for ages; until the extravagance of John Scott occasioned the family to part with them. They now form part of the extensive estates of Buccleugh. Several of their wives were supposed to be rank witches; and it is probable that the famous witch of Fauldshop was one of them, who so terribly hectored Mr Michael Scott, by turning him into a hare, and hunting him with his own dogs, until forced to take shelter in his own jaw-hole. The cruel retaliation which he made in showing his art to her, is also well known. It appears also, that some of the Hoggs had been poets before now, as there is still a part of an old song extant relating much to them. Observe how elegantly it flows on:—

     \*   \*   \*   \*   \*   \*

    And the rough Hoggs of Fauldshop,
      That wear both wool and hair;
    There's nae sic Hoggs as Fauldshop's,
      In all Saint Boswell's fair.

And afterwards, near the end:—

    But the hardy Hoggs of Fauldshop,
      For courage, blood, and bane;
    For the Wild Boar of Fauldshop,
      Like him was never nane.
    If ye reave the Hoggs of Fauldshop,
      Ye herry Harden's gear;
    But the poor Hoggs of Fauldshop
      Have had a stormy year.

The Brydens, too, have long been a numerous and respectable clan in Ettrick forest and its vicinity.

5(a) **as Burns says** Hogg quotes from 'A Dedication to Gavin Hamilton, Esq.' (1786):

    But when Divinity comes cross me,
    My readers still are sure to lose me. (ll. 80–81)

5(c) **"Johny Cope are ye wauking yet"** a Jacobite song which commemorates the defeat at Prestonpans in 1745 of the Hanoverian forces under General Sir John Cope. Hogg includes the words and melody of this song in his collection of *Jacobite Relics*, second series (Edinburgh: Blackwood, 1821), pp. 111–15.

5(d) **Sir Alexander Don** Scott's neighbour and friend (1780–1826); he succeeded in

1815 as 6th Baronet of Newton Don. On his death in April 1826 Scott recalls his character:

> His habits were those of a gay man, much connected with the turf; but he possessed strong natural parts, and in particular few men could speak better in public when he chose. He had tact, with power of sarcasm, and that indescribable something which marks the gentleman. His manners in society were extremely pleasing, and as he had a taste for literature and the fine arts, there were few more agreeable companions, besides being a highly-spirited, steady, and honourable man. His indolence prevented his turning these good parts towards acquiring the distinction he might have attained. He was among the *detenus* whom Buonaparte's iniquitous commands confined so long in France; and coming into possession of a large estate in right of his mother, the heiress of the Glencairn family, he had the means of being very expensive, and probably then acquired those gay habits which rendered him averse to serious business. (Lockhart, VI, 289.)

**6(a) the chiefs of Haliburton and Rutherford** ancestors on Scott's maternal side. On the conferral of his baronetcy, Scott expresses an ironic attitude to his ancestors in a letter of 15 February 1820 to Lord Melville:

> I expect to be in London immediatly when our Court rises and I suppose I may reckon on the honour so long destined for me being conferd and I have had a hint from the Herald Office vice Sir Geo: Nailor that I must prepare my escutcheon. Now this was easy enough my ancestors for 300 years before the union of the Kingdoms having murderd stolen and robbd like other border gentlemen and from James reign to the Revolution having held commissions in Gods own parliamentary army canted prayd & so forth persecuted others and been persecuted themselves during the reigns of the last Stuarts hunted drunk claret rebelld & fought duels down to the times of my father and grandfather. And to the great surprize of the Herald office I made them look with some attention to the proofs of all these doughty doings. (Grierson, VI, 133–34.)

**6(b) his house in Castle Street** 39 North Castle Street, Scott's house in Edinburgh, was eventually sold as part of the bankruptcy proceedings in 1826.

**6(c) Abbotsford** Scott's estate on the Tweed, purchased in 1811 from the Rev. Dr Douglas of Galashiels. Until his financial difficulties, Scott repeatedly expanded the estate through purchases of adjoining land and built and furnished his mansion, regarding it as the realisation of a vision, 'a sort of romance in Architecture' (Grierson, VIII, 129).

**6(d) "Clarty Hole!"** the farmhouse and its outbuildings, actually called 'Cartley Hole', were located in a hollow so muddy that it was sarcastically nicknamed 'Clarty (dirty, miry) Hole'.

**6(d) the Rev^d Dr. Douglas** Robert Douglas (1747–1820) served as minister of Galashiels from 1770 until his death. In the spring of 1812, he sold Scott 110 acres of land on the Tweed which Scott renamed Abbotsford. This 'shrewd and unbigoted Dr Douglas of Galashiels' was the model for his 'minister of the Gospel' in *Paul's Letters to his Kinsfolk* (Lockhart, III, 352).

**7(d) the French in Sarragossa** in 1809 the French captured Saragossa in Spain, but only after prolonged and heroic resistance by the defenders of the city.

**7(d) Johny Ballantyne** John Ballantyne (1774–1821) was managing partner of John

Ballantyne and Co., the publishing house in which Scott became a secret partner in 1809. The firm failed in 1816. John Ballantyne thereafter worked as an auctioneer and Scott's literary agent and advisor. They remained close friends until Ballantyne's death from consumption.

7(d) **a legacy of £2000** John Ballantyne died on 16 June 1821. He left Scott £2,000 for the library at Abbotsford, but the sum was life-rented to Mrs. Ballantyne; i.e., the proceeds allocated to her use until she died. She lived until 1854, so Scott never received any money from John Ballantyne's estate. Lockhart comments:

> I am sorry to take leave of John Ballantyne with the remark, that his last will was a document of the same class with too many of his *states* and *calendars*. So far from having £2000 to bequeath to Sir Walter, he died as he had lived, ignorant of the situation of his affairs, and deep in debt. (Lockhart, v, 78.)

8(b) **in Nithsdale** Hogg lived in Nithsdale in south-west Scotland, first as a shepherd and later as a farmer, from 1804 to 1809.

8(b) **Broadmeadows** a house and farm in Selkirkshire. Carruthers quotes Laidlaw on Scott's passion for acquiring land:

> 'I have more than once–such was his modesty'–said Laidlaw, 'heard Sir Walter assert that had his father left him an estate of £500 or £600 a year, he would have spent his time in miscellaneous reading, not writing. This, to a certain extent, might have been the case; and had he purchased the property of Broadmeadows, in Yarrow, as he at one time was very anxious to do, and when the neighbourhood was in the possession of independent proprietors, the effect might have been the same. At Abbotsford, surrounded by little lairds, most of them ready to sell their lands as soon as he had money to advance, the impulse to exertion was incessant; for the desire to possess and to add increased with every new acquisition, until it became a passion of no small power. Then came the hope to be a large landed proprietor, and to found a family.' (Carruthers, p. 139.)

8(b) **Lord Porchester** Henry Herbert, Lord Porchester of Highclere and Earl of Carnarvon (1741–1811). This incident apparently took place in the first half of 1804, before Hogg's ill-fated trip to Harris and subsequent removal to Nithsdale. Lockhart's version (II, 9) differs substantially.

8(c) **the present Lord Porchester** Henry John George Herbert (1800–49), himself a poet (*The Moor*, 1825), playwright (*Don Pedro*, 1828), travel writer and conservative member of the House of Lords. Scott describes him in 1825 as 'nephew to Mrs Scott of Harden, a young man who lies on the carpet and looks poetical and dandyish–fine lad too' (*Journal*, p. 10).

8(c) **The Queen's Wake** this poem (1813) was very well received and established Hogg's literary reputation in Edinburgh. It is structured as a frame narrative enclosing a series of seventeen legends and stories, each sung by a different regional bard in a great contest of minstrels (a 'wake') to celebrate the return of Queen Mary to Scotland in 1561. Many of the minstrels at the queen's wake are thinly-disguised portraits of Scottish poets of Hogg's own period. *The Queen's Wake* includes several of Hogg's best-known poems such as 'The Witch of Fife' and 'Kilmeny'.

8(c) **Walter the Abbot** the 'Conclusion' of *The Queen's Wake* (Edinburgh: Goldie, 1813) tells of the ancient harp which is the Scottish poetic tradition. Through the generations, many people have attempted to play this harp; and Hogg himself was shown the way to it by 'Walter the Abbot' (that is, Walter Scott, who had moved to Abbotsford in 1812). Hogg quotes the lines in question (using the sixth edition (1819) of *The Queen's Wake*) in *Familiar Anecdotes* at pp. 59–60.

**8(d) Queen Hynde** Hogg's epic poem (1824), which offers an alternative version of the kind of traditional narrative material that underpins James Macpherson's *Ossian* epics.

**8(d) THE MOUNTAIN BARD** Hogg's collection of poems and ballads appeared in 1807. It includes the first version of his autobiographical *Memoir of the Author's Life*. Scott helped to convince Constable to publish it, and Hogg actually turned a modest profit from its sales.

**9(b) *The three perils of Man*** Hogg's novel published in 1822 has a medieval setting and relates the rise to power of the Scotts of Buccleuch.

**10(b) as narrated somewhere else** in Hogg's *Memoir of the Author's Life*, his autobiographical sketch first published with *The Mountain Bard* in 1807, revised and brought up to date for the new edition in 1821, revised and brought up to date again and published in *Altrive Tales* in 1832. This last version was again revised, either by Hogg or his American editor Bloodgood, and incorporated into the published edition of the *Anecdotes* in 1834.

**10(b) his cottage on the North Esk a little above Laswade** Scott rented this rural retreat, six miles from Edinburgh, in the summer of 1798. He and his family spent the long vacations there until the move to Ashestiel in 1804. Much of the work on the *Minstrelsy of the Scottish Border* was done at Lasswade cottage.

**10(b) the Sherrif as we called him** in 1799 Scott was appointed Sheriff-Depute of Selkirkshire, a patronage position worth £300; nevertheless, Scott took his duties seriously and regularly presided at court in Selkirk when the Court of Session in Edinburgh was in recess.

**10(d) Jeffery and his sept** Francis Jeffrey (1773–1850) was a Scottish advocate and judge and editor of the Whig *Edinburgh Review*. Despite their political and literary differences, he and Scott respected each other.

**10(d)–11(a) She was subjected [...] for curing it** in the manuscript, this passage is deleted with two strokes, although it is not clear by whom. The ink is darker than the text, but it resembles other deletions. Lockhart may have struck out this passage when he saw the manuscript in London. Or Hogg may have had second thoughts about it. No reference to Lady Scott's drug dependency appears in either of the published editions of 1834.

**11(a) Sophia [...] Anne [...] Charles** Hogg here mentions three of Scott's four children. Sophia (1799–1837) married John Gibson Lockhart in 1820; they had four children, two of whom died in infancy or childhood. Walter (1801–47), 2nd Baronet, married Jane Jobson in 1825; he joined the army in 1819 and rose to the rank of Lieutenant-Colonel. Anne (1803–33) lived with her father until his death. After her mother's death, she kept house for Scott and travelled with him. Charles (1805–41) was educated at Oxford and joined the Foreign Office; he served as attaché at Naples.

**11(c) the anonymous novels** *Waverley* (1814) was published anonymously, and the subsequent novels were attributed on their title pages either to a fictive persona or to 'the Author of Waverley'. For the frame material, Scott employed various personae, including Jedidiah Cleishbotham, Laurence Templeton, Captain Clutterbuck, and Chrystal Croftangry. Although he did not formally acknowledge his authorship until 1826, Hogg suspected it from the beginning.

**11(d) Lady Scott was [...] the daughter of a Mr John Carpenter** Scott's family pressured him for information on Charlotte's background, but the truth remains elusive. She was legally the daughter of Jean Charpentier, civil servant in Lyons, and his wife Élie. After her father's death, she became the ward of Lord Downshire. The precise nature of the relationships between the two men and between Lord Downshire and Mme. Charpentier are not known. For details see Edgar Johnson, *Sir Walter Scott: The Great Unknown*, 2 vols (New York: Macmillan, 1970), I, 144–48 and John Sutherland, *The Life of Walter Scott* (Oxford: Blackwell, 1995) pp. 58–62. Hogg's sanitised version of this passage in the *Familiar Anecdotes* appears on p. 54.

**12(b) prouder of Lockhart than any of his other sons** John Gibson Lockhart (1794–1854) married Scott's daughter Sophia in 1820. He was part of the original 'Blackwood's Group' involved in the elaborate (and sometimes vicious) literary jokes, hoaxes, reviews and feuds of *Blackwood's Edinburgh Magazine*. In 1825 he and his family moved to London, where Lockhart became editor of the *Quarterly Review*. He was Scott's literary executor and authorised biographer. Carruthers quotes a letter from Scott to Mrs. Stewart Mackenzie of Seaforth:

> Mr Lockhart, to whom Sophia is now married, is the husband of her choice. He is a man of excellent talents, master of his pen and of his pencil, handsome in person, and well-mannered, though wanting that ease which the *usage du monde* alone can give. I like him very much; for having no son who promises to take a literary turn, it is of importance to me, both in point of comfort and otherwise, to have some such intimate friend and relation, whose pursuits and habits are similar to my own—so that, upon the whole, I trust I have gained a son instead of losing a daughter. (Carruthers, p. 157.)

**12(b) knowing him a great deal better** Hogg and Lockhart were both regular contributors to *Blackwood's Edinburgh Magazine*. Along with John Wilson, they collaborated on the infamous 'Chaldee Manuscript'.

**12(c) Ashiesteel** from 1804 until 1811 Scott rented the house and farm of Ashestiel from James Russell. It was located on the Tweed near Clovenfords, six miles from Selkirk. Since his appointment as Sheriff-Depute in 1799, Scott had been under pressure from Lord Napier, Lord Lieutenant of the County, to establish residence in Selkirkshire.

**12(d) the court of Session** Scott was appointed Clerk of the Court of Session in 1806, a post which freed him from the necessity to plead cases for clients.

**13(a) Chantry** Sir Francis Chantrey (1782–1841), English sculptor. Scott sat for the famous bust during his visit to London in 1820, when he was knighted by George IV.

**13(b) our poor friend Irving** William Scott Irving, unsuccessful and impecunious poet and teacher.

**14(a) Peter drive on** Scott's coachman was Peter Matheson (1768–1852).

**14(a) he wrote two very indifferent moral sermons** Scott wrote them in 1824 for his amanuensis, George Huntly Gordon, who was afflicted by writer's block. Scott intended Gordon to present them as his own work in order to obtain a clerical appointment, but Gordon did not use them. In 1827 he asked Scott's permission to publish the sermons, under Scott's name, in order to extricate himself from debt. Scott assented reluctantly, and they were published by Colbourne in 1828 under the title *Religious Discourses By a Layman*.

**14(b) Laidlaw** William Laidlaw (1780–1845), son of Hogg's employer at Blackhouse (1790–1800) and Hogg's lifelong friend. He helped with the collection of ballads for the *Minstrelsy* and later managed Scott's estate at Abbotsford. Through Scott's influence, he became a contributor to *Blackwood's*. Laidlaw also served Scott as occasional amanuensis. In 1817 Scott invited him to come and live on the Abbotsford estate, and Lockhart provides the following rather patronising character:

> Though possessed of a lively and searching sagacity as to things in general, he had always been as to his own worldly interests simple as a child. His tastes and habits were all modest; and when he looked forward to spending the remainder of what had not hitherto been a successful life, under the shadow of the genius that he had worshipped almost from boyhood, his gentle heart was all happiness. He surveyed with glistening eyes the humble cottage in which his friend proposed to lodge him, his wife, and his little ones, and said to himself that he should write no more sad songs on *Forest Flittings*. (Lockhart, IV, 63.)

**14(b) Mr Paterson** William Paterson was a mason and a partner in the building firm of Sanderson and Paterson of Galashiels. This firm worked at Abbotsford from 1812 to 1819. Carruthers's version of the incident is somewhat more restrained:

> One day Sir Walter was loud in praise of one of the workmen engaged at Abbotsford, a native of the neighbouring village of Darnick. 'Yes,' added Laidlaw; 'and do you know, Sir Walter, he is an excellent Burgher preacher.' 'A preacher, d—n him!' exclaimed Scott jocularly, and wheeling round as if to whistle the Burgher preacher down the wind. (Carruthers, p. 179.)

**14(d) Mr Morritt** John Bacon Sawrey Morritt (1771–1843), classical scholar and Member of Parliament, was one of Scott's best friends and most astute critics. His estate in Yorkshire is the scene of Scott's *Rokeby* (1813).

**15(a) the forenoon service from the liturgy** Hogg implies that Scott's family worship was Episcopalian rather than Presbyterian.

**15(a) that dread alone which made him quit the country** Scott left Britain for Malta and Italy on 29 October 1831 in a vain attempt to mend his health in a warm climate. After the House of Lords voted down the Reform Bill on 8 October, widespread protests occurred in London and the North.

> Ill-health and political agitation brought darker days to Abbotsford. The Reform Bill was Sir Walter's *bête noire*. The neighbouring Tory lairds, proud of his co-operation, induced him to join in their local movement against the bill, and this still further aggravated his morbid feeling. In March 1831, he was present at a meeting of the freeholders of Roxburgh, held at Jedburgh, to pass resolutions against the Reform Bill. He was dragged to the meeting by the young Duke of Buccleuch and Mr Henry Scott of Harden, contrary to his prior resolution, and his promise to Miss Scott; for his health was then much shattered. 'He made a confused imaginative speech,' says Laidlaw, 'which was full of evil forebodings and mistaken views. The people who were auditors, in proportion to their love and reverence for him, felt disappointed and sore, and, like himself, were carried away by their temporary chagrin, to the great regret of the country around.' At the election in Jedburgh, Sir Walter was hooted at, and hissed, and saluted with cries of

'Burke Sir Walter!' Laidlaw adds: 'The same people, a few weeks afterwards, when Mr Oliver, the sheriff of Roxburgh, was foolishly swearing in constables at Melrose, said boldly they need not bring them to fight against reform, for they would fight for it; but if any one meddled with Sir Walter Scott, they would fight for him.' (Carruthers, p. 178.)

**15(b) lord Buchans statue of Wallace** the following passage is quoted from Grose's *Antiquities of Scotland* in 'Description of Dryburgh Abbey', appended to 'Funeral of Sir Walter Scott, Bart. of Abbotsford' in *Views of Dryburgh Abbey*, (n.a., 1832), p. 9n.

This name (the Celtic Darach-Bruach, "the bank of the sacred grove of oaks, or, the settlement of the Druids") would apply to the hill behind Dryburgh, on the brow of which the late Earl of Buchan, with patriotic taste, erected a colossal statue of Wallace, which will remind those who have travelled in Italy of the magnificent bronze statue of that eminently virtuous prelate, Carlo Borromeo, archbishop of Milan, which stands in a commanding situation on the banks of the Lago Maggiore, near Arona. The statue of the Scottish hero was cut by a native artist, of reddish stone, taken from the same quarry which supplied materials for the abbey.

David Stewart Erskine, Earl of Buchan, purchased the house of Newmains and the Abbey in 1786. It was presented to the nation in 1919.

**15(b) every one do that which is right in his own eyes** 'In those days there was no king in Israel, but every man did that which was right in his own eyes.' ( Judges 17.6 and 21.25.)

**15(c) Miss Porter's work** THE SCOTTISH CHIEFS *The Scottish Chiefs* by Jane Porter (1776–1850) was published in 1810.

**15(d) *yaup*** hungry.

**16(a) Mount-Benger** Hogg's farm in the Yarrow valley in Ettrick Forest. See also note for 16(d).

**16(a) the Cooper of Fogo** 'Fogo is a small, and now almost extinct village in the Merse. It is locally famous for a certain succession of coopers of old times, whereof the second was so decided an improvement upon the first, that he gave rise to a proverb, "Father's better, the cooper of Fogo". A rhyme expresses the particulars:

> He's father's better, cooper o' Fogo,
> At girding a barrel, and making a cogie,
> Taming a stoup, or kissing a roguie.

This proverb is equivalent to an English one—Filling a father's shoes; or, as we more energetically express it in Scotland, Riving his bonnet.": Robert Chambers, *Popular Rhymes of Scotland* (London and Edinburgh: W. and R. Chambers, 1870), p. 211.

**16(b) Col Ferguson** James Ferguson, brother of Sir Adam and Colonel in the 23rd Bengal Native Infantry, returned from India in 1823. Sir Adam Ferguson is discussed in a note for 4(b).

**16(c) Mrs Hogg** Hogg married Margaret Phillips in April 1820.

**16(d) Mount-Benger** shortly after his marriage, in expectation of financial help from his father-in law, Hogg signed a nine-year lease for the farm of Mount Benger. But the assistance was not forthcoming, and the venture turned into a financial disaster. Hogg left when the lease expired and returned to the farm at Altrive.

**16(d) his own house in Maitland-street** after Scott's bankruptcy forced the sale of his Castle Street house in the winter of 1826, he rented a furnished house in nearby Walker Street for himself and his daughter Anne. In November 1827, he took a four-month lease of a house at No 6 Shandwick Place belonging to Mrs. Jobson, the mother of his daughter-in-law Jane, who was spending the winter in Canterbury. Shandwick Place comprises the part of Maitland Street directly to the west of Princes Street, and the Lothian Road extends south from the west end of Princes Street.

17(b) **Hugh John Lockhart** John Hugh Lockhart (1821–1831), the elder son of Scott's daughter Sophia and John Gibson Lockhart, was sickly and frail throughout his short life. Scott wrote *Tales of a Grandfather* for 'Hugh Littlejohn'.

17(b) **a braw gown [...] made for me in Paris** Scott visited Brussels and Paris in the summer of 1815, shortly after the Battle of Waterloo. He returned to Paris in the autumn of 1826.

17(c) **the little inn on my own farm** the Gordon Arms, which still flourishes.

17(c) **Altrive** in 1815 the Duke of Buccleuch granted to Hogg lifetime rent-free tenancy of the farm of Altrive Lake in Ettrick Forest.

> One day, after Hogg had been in London—and 'The Hogg,' as Lockhart said, 'was the lion of the season'—Allan Cunningham chanced to meet James Smith of the *Rejected Addresses* at the table of the great bibliopole, John Murray. 'How,' said Smith, aloud, to Allan, 'how does Hogg like Scotland's small cheer after the luxury of London?' 'Small cheer!' echoed Allan; 'he has the finest trout in the Yarrow, the finest lambs on its braes, the finest grouse on its hills, and, besides, he as good as keeps a *sma' still'* [smuggled whisky]. 'Pray, what better luxury can London offer?' All these sumptuosities the Shepherd cheerfully shared with the wayfarers who flocked to Altrive Cottage. (Carruthers, p. 150.)

17(c) **His daughter was with him** Blackwood reports Lockhart's version:

> Hogg details to McC at great length an interview he had with Sir Walter on his last return from Drumlanrig, when, he says, Sir Walter called on him with Miss Scott. He makes Sir Walter pay him the most extravagant compliments, and exalt him far above any poet of the age. And this is all pure fiction, except that Sir Walter did call, and Mr. Lockhart was with him, not Miss Scott. (Letter of 19 April 1833, NLS, MS 4035, fols 51–54; reprinted slightly changed in Mrs. [Margaret] Oliphant, *William Blackwood and His Sons*, 2 vols (Edinburgh: Blackwood, 1897), II, 120.)

18(a) **Fielding's tale** in *Tom Jones*, III, ii, Fielding tells the story of a poaching incident and the subsequent bravery of young Tom, who endures a beating from Mr Thwackum rather than reveal the identity of his accomplice, a selfish and cowardly gamekeeper.

18(a) **paetrick** partridge.

18(b) **auld Tam Whitson** possibly Tam Hudson, formerly gamekeeper at Bowhill.

18(d)–19(a) **the Whig ascendancy in the British cabinet** the Wellington ministry fell in November 1830 and was replaced by a moderately reformist Whig administration under Earl Grey.

19(a) **his last illness** after a long and painful journey, Scott returned from Italy to Abbotsford on 11 July 1832. He died there on 21 September.

19(d) **two poems of Leyden's** John Leyden (1775–1811) was an early friend of Scott who, before he left Scotland in 1803 for an appointment as a physician in India, showed great promise as a writer and editor. He became a scholar of Asian languages and cultures and died of fever in Java on 28 August 1811. The two poems are 'The Battle of Assaye', *The Spy* no. 9 (27 October 1810), p. 72 (included in Leyden's *Poetical Remains* (London: Longman, 1819) with the note 'written in 1803': in *The Spy*, the introductory letter from a 'Constant Reader' is by Scott); and 'Song of Wallace', *The Spy* no. 21 (19 January 1811), p. 168.

20(a) **the greater part of the third vol. of The Border Minstrelsy** this is an overstatement, but Hogg did contribute significantly to volume III and subsequent editions of the *Minstrelsy*, first through William Laidlaw and then directly. 'Auld Maitland', 'The Lament of the Border Widow', and 'Otterburn' all came through Hogg, although the degree to which he tampered with them remains questionable.

20(b) **Mr Southey** the poet Robert Southey (1774–1843) wrote the 'History of Europe' for the *Edinburgh Annual Register* from 1809 to 1813.

20(c) **a review of modern literature in the Edin$^r$ Annual Register** 'Of the Living Poets of Great Britain' appeared in the *Edinburgh Annual Register* in volume I part ii, pp. 417–43, dated 1808 but published in 1810. It has been reprinted by Kenneth Curry in *Sir Walter Scott's Edinburgh Annual Register* (Knoxville: University of Tennessee Press, 1977), pp. 60–98. In this essay, generally attributed to Scott, the author mocks the fashion for uneducated poets. Although he distinguishes Hogg as the most worthy of this group for public attention, he condemns Hogg's poetry for its 'vulgarity of conception and expression'. Scott relegates him and those of this category to 'the van and rear of the class of occasional poets'. Scott seems to have regarded his article with some irony. In an 1810 letter to Robert Southey he writes of the *Register*, 'I know not where they have picked up their poetical critic who is a dashing fellow but lets I think his tongue run a little before his wits; a common fault in his trade'. (Grierson, II, 283.)

20(c) **THE SPY** a largely satirical periodical primarily written by Hogg which ran for a year from September 1810. The quoted passage is extracted with a few alterations from 'The Spy's Farewell to His Readers', no. 52, pp. 409–15 (pp. 411–12). Hogg supplies the correct date (24 August 1811), but the narrative misleads the reader into supposing that the events took place in fairly rapid sequence. In reality, at least eight months must have elapsed between the appearance of Scott's article in 1810 and Hogg's rejoinder.

20(d) **Mr Shuffleton** a continuing character in *The Spy* whose magic mirror serves as Hogg's vehicle for literary criticism. 'Mr Shuffleton's Allegorical Survey of the Scottish Poets of the Present Day' appeared in nos 2 (8 September 1810), 5 (29 September 1810) and 10 (3 November 1810), pp. 9–15, 33–39, 73–79.

21(d) **James Ballantyne** James Ballantyne (1772–1833) was Scott's printer and a close friend from early school days in Kelso. He was John Ballantyne's brother and Scott's business partner in the publishing house of John Ballantyne and Company. See note for 7(d).

21(d) **The Brownie of Bodsbeck** Hogg's first novel strongly sympathised with the persecuted Covenanters and presented Claverhouse as an unmitigated villain. It was published in 1818, although Hogg claims to have written almost all of it before the publication of *Old Mortality* at the end of 1816. He cites as his sources local tradition and Robert Wodrow's *History of the Sufferings of the Church of Scotland* (Edinburgh, 1771–72). Hogg's version of the timing of the two novels appears in his *Memoir of the Author's Life*:

That same year I published "The Brownie of Bodsbeck," and other Tales, in two volumes. I suffered unjustly in the eyes of the world with regard to that tale, which was looked on as an imitation of the tale of "Old Mortality," and a counterpart to that; whereas it was written long ere the tale of "Old Mortality" was heard of, and I well remember my chagrin on finding the ground, which I thought clear, pre-occupied before I could appear publicly on it, and that by such a redoubted champion. It was wholly owing to Mr. Blackwood that this tale was not published a year sooner, which would effectually have freed me from the stigma of being an imitator, and brought in the author of the "Tales of My Landlord" as an imitator of me. That was the only ill turn that ever Mr. Blackwood did me; and it ought to be a warning to authors never to intrust booksellers with their manuscripts. (Hogg, *Memoir of the Author's Life* and *Familiar Anecdotes of Sir Walter Scott*, ed. by Douglas S. Mack (Edinburgh: Scottish Academic Press, 1972), pp. 44–45).

Carruthers's version differs significantly from Hogg's:

It is never too late to do justice. In one of these magazine missives, written in January 1818, Blackwood refers to the Ettrick Shepherd. 'If you see Hogg, I hope you will press him to send me instantly his *Shepherd's Dog*, and anything else. I received his *Andrew Gemmells*; but the editor is not going to insert it in this number. [...] I expected to have received from him the conclusion of the *Brownie of Bodsbeck*; there are six sheets of it already printed'.

Now, the latter part of this extract seems distinctly to disprove a charge which Hogg thoughtlessly brought against Mr Blackwood. His novel, the *Brownie of Bodsbeck*, was published in 1818, and he suffered unjustly, as he states in his autobiography, with regard to that tale, as it was looked upon as an imitation of Scott's *Old Mortality*. It was wholly owing to Blackwood, he asserts, that his story was not published a year sooner; and he relates the case as a warning to authors never to intrust booksellers with their manuscripts. But the fact is, *Old Mortality* was published in December 1816; and we have Blackwood, in the above letter to Laidlaw, stating that he had not, in January 1818–more than a twelvemonth afterwards–received the whole of the 'copy' of the *Brownie of Bodsbeck*. How could he go to press with an unfinished story? How make bricks without straw? The accusation is altogether a myth, or, to use one of the Shepherd's own expressions, 'a mere shimmera' [chimera] 'of the brain.' (Carruthers, pp. 146–47.)

The letter from Blackwood to Laidlaw also appears in Alan Lang Strout, *Life and Letters of James Hogg Volume 1 (1770–1825)* (Lubbock: Texas Tech Press, 1946), p. 146. The Introduction to Douglas Mack's edition of *The Brownie of Bodsbeck* (Edinburgh: Scottish Academic Press, 1976) cites evidence (pp. xiv–xvii) to support Hogg's version of events. This includes a discussion of the watermark dates in the paper on which Hogg's manuscript was written; and Mack argues that these dates indicate that the opening section of Hogg's manuscript (containing the first six chapters of the novel) may have been in existence in or before 1813. Mack presents other evidence which suggests that the later sections of Hogg's surviving manuscript were probably transcripts of an earlier manuscript. Two letters of January 1818 from Hogg to Blackwood indicate that the material, or 'copy', for which Blackwood was waiting was actually a transcript of an earlier manuscript. Hogg repeatedly complained about Blackwood's failure to return manuscripts; his insistence on making a copy of this one is quite understandable. Carruthers's account of Blackwood's plight in January of 1818, therefore, need not invalidate Hogg's claim to have written the novel before the publication of *Old Mortality*. See also the note to Chapter XVII on pp. 194–95 of Mack's edition.

**22(b) your tale o' Auld Mortality** Scott's fourth work of fiction was published anonymously at the end of 1816. It represents the Covenanters as destructive religious fanatics and treats Claverhouse with some sympathy.

**22(b) yerk** to snatch, tug or pull.

**22(c) Mr Blackwood** publisher of *The Brownie of Bodsbeck*; see note for 21(d).

**23(a) Eildon [...] white hounds** 'The Hunt of Eildon' was published along with *The Brownie of Bodsbeck* and 'The Wool-Gatherer' in two volumes in 1818. Each of the three narratives deals with Hogg's native Ettrick at a different stage of its development; 'The Hunt of Eildon' is set in Ettrick during its days as a medieval royal hunting forest; *The Brownie of Bodsbeck* deals with Ettrick in the civil wars of the late seventeenth century; and 'The Wool-Gatherer' is a modern Ettrick love story.

**23(b) Sindbad the Sailor** 'Es-Sindibád of the Sea' from *The Arabian Nights' Entertainments, or, The Thousand and One Nights.*

**23(c) his correspondence with Miss Seward and Lord Byron** Anna Seward (1747– 1809), 'the Swan of Lichfield', poet, correspondent, and friend of Scott, left her collected poetry to his reluctant literary executorship when she died. At Scott's urging, she reviewed Hogg's *Mountain Bard* in the *Critical Review*, 12 (1807), 237– 44. The review is patronising and objects to Hogg's transgression of everything from class barriers to literary rules. It ranks him a sorry fourth in the list of poets of 'high though unschooled pretensions'; i.e., after Chatterton, Burns and Bloomfield, 'this mountain bard not unworthily brings up the rear'. In a letter to Byron of 6 November 1813, Scott writes of Hogg in a more generous but somewhat similar tone of patronising admiration:

> The author of the Queen's Wake will be delighted with your approbation. He is a wonderful creature for his opportunities, which were far inferior to those of the generality of Scottish peasants. Burns, for instance—(not that their extent of talents is to be compared for an instant)—had an education not much worse than the sons of many gentlemen in Scotland. But poor Hogg literally could neither read nor write till a very late period of his life; and when he first distinguished himself by his poetical talent, could neither spell nor write grammar. When I first knew him, he used to send me his poetry, and was both indignant and horrified when I pointed out to him parallel passages in authors whom he had never read, but whom all the world would have sworn he had copied. An evil fate has hitherto attended him, and baffled every attempt that has been made to place him in a road to independence. But I trust he may be more fortunate in future. (Grierson, III, 373.)

**23(c) a song for the corps** 'To horse! to horse! the standard flies', Scott's 'War-Song, for the Edinburgh Cavalry Association', written in 1802, was first published in the *Scots Magazine*, 65 (October 1803), 725–26, and is reprinted in the Appendix to the present edition (pp. 77–78).

23(d) **drool** a low, mournful note.

23(d) **Donald M,Donald** Hogg claims that he composed this song in 1800 (Hogg, *Memoir of the Author's Life* and *Familiar Anecdotes of Sir Walter Scott*, ed. by Douglas S. Mack (Edinburgh: Scottish Academic Press, 1972), p. 14); and he also claims that he wrote it as 'a barefooted lad herding lambs on the Blackhouse Heights, in utter indignation at the threatened invasion from France' (*Songs by the Ettrick Shepherd* (Edinburgh: Blackwood, 1831), p. 1). In 1800, however, Hogg would have been 'a lad' of 29 years. Hogg's song was first published (as an engraved broadsheet) by John Hamilton of Edinburgh in 1800 or 1801: a copy survives in Stirling University Library, and this copy is reproduced in facsimile in the Appendix to the present edition (pp. 80–81). This song was later included in *The Mountain Bard* of 1807. Hogg observed several times thereafter that he never received credit for the composition, even though it became enormously popular. Compare this to the *Familiar Anecdotes* version (p. 61), where Hogg says he himself told Scott of his authorship.

23(d) **I danced the best way I could** Scott suffered from polio at the age of eighteen months. The disease left him with a badly disabled right leg.

24(a) **Tom Gillespie and John Wilson** Thomas Gillespie (1777–1844); clergyman in Fife, Professor of Humanity at St Andrews University, and contributor to *Blackwood's Edinburgh Magazine*. Hogg published Gillespie's 'The Scots Tutor' in *The Spy* no. 38 (18 May 1811), no. 42 (15 June 1811), and no. 46 (13 July 1811), pp. 297–303, 328–36, 361–67. John Wilson (1785–1854); the 'Christopher North' of *Blackwood's*; appointed as Professor of Moral Philosophy at Edinburgh University in 1820. Largely responsible for the *Noctes Ambrosianae*, he also contributed a great deal of straightforward but strongly partisan critical and religious writing.

24(b) **Mr Murray of Albemarle Street** John Murray (1778–1843) was the powerful and prosperous London publisher of the works of Byron and the *Quarterly Review*. He visited Scott at Abbotsford in the autumn of 1814 and again in September of 1818. Of the latter visit Hogg wrote to William Blackwood on 12 October:

> I was vexed that I got so little cracking with Murray Scott and he had so many people to crack about whom no body knows aught about but themslves that they monopolized the whole conversation. (NLS, MS 4003, fols 99–100.)

24(c) **Glenfinlas** Scott's ballad composed in 1798.

24(c) **William Erskine (Lord Kineder)** Erskine (1768–1822) was a fellow-advocate and Scott's long-time friend. He served as Sheriff-Depute of Orkney from 1809 and accompanied Scott on his 1814 tour to the Hebrides. In 1822 he was elevated to the bench as Lord Kinedder. Scott dedicated to him the Introduction to Canto Third of *Marmion*.

24(d) **Mr Morison** John Morrison (1782–1853) was a land surveyor and friend of Hogg. His account of this meeting occurs in the first instalment (10 (September 1843), 572–73) of his 'Random Reminiscences of Sir Walter Scott, of the Ettrick Shepherd, Sir Henry Raeburn, etc.' in *Tait's Edinburgh Magazine*, 10–11 (September 1843 to January 1844).

25(a) **St. Mary's Loch** lake in Selkirkshire. Hogg's monument gazes down upon St Mary's Loch from a nearby hillside. Scott describes the scene in the Introduction to Canto Second of *Marmion*:

> Oft in my mind such thoughts awake,
> By lone St Mary's silent lake;

Thou know'st it well,—nor fen, nor sedge,
Pollute the pure lake's crystal edge;
Abrupt and sheer, the mountains sink
At once upon the level brink;
And just a trace of silver sand
Marks where the water meets the land.
Far in the mirror, bright and blue,
Each hill's huge outline you may view;
Shaggy with heath, but lonely bare,
Nor tree, nor bush, nor brake is there,
Save where, of land, yon slender line
Bears thwart the lake the scattered pine.
Yet even this nakedness has power,
And aids the feeling of the hour:
Nor thicket, dell, nor copse you spy,
Where living thing concealed might lie;
Nor point, retiring, hides a dell,
Where swain, or woodman lone, might dwell;
There's nothing left to fancy's guess,
You see that all is loneliness:
And silence aids—though the steep hills
Send to the lake a thousand rills;
In summer tide, so soft they weep,
The sound but lulls the ear asleep;
Your horse's hoof-tread sounds too rude,
So stilly is the solitude.

**25(c) a review of a sporting tour in the Highlands** in the *Edinburgh Review* for January 1805 (X, 398-405), Scott reviewed *A Sporting Tour through the Northern Parts of England, and Great Part of the Highlands of Scotland* by Colonel T. Thornton of Thornville-Royal in Yorkshire (London, 1804). The passage to which Hogg alludes is the first paragraph of the review. Scott goes on to warn Col. Thornton, 'a hunting, hawking English Squire', of the perils of 'poaching in the fields of literature'.

**25(c) "O that mine enemy had written a book!"** see Job 31. 35. Hogg uses this quotation as the text for his sermon on 'Reviewers' in his *Lay Sermons* (1834).

**26(a) his deputy clerk** Scott was appointed a Principal Clerk of Session in 1806. 'The Clerk's function was to control the various legal processes being heard each day by the Court, to frame and prepare the orders of the Court for signature by the Lord President, and generally to supervise the arrangement and calling of cases' (*Sir Walter Scott 1771-1971, A Bicentenary Exhibition*, organised by the Court of Session, the Faculty of Advocates and The National Library of Scotland (Edinburgh: HMSO, 1971), p. 35). Another duty of the office involved the authentication of registered deeds. It was in this aspect of the job that he employed the assistance of William Pringle, Writer (lawyer) in Edinburgh. Pringle served as Extractor in the Court of Session and was promoted to the position of Deputy Clerk, which he held from 11 November 1808 until 31 March 1832. Pringle's Clerk's Mark was 'F.S.P.'; his Unextracted Processes can be found in the Court of Session Minutes, Scottish Record Office CS 228.

**26(a) Terry** Daniel Terry (1780?–1829), an English actor and playwright, adapted many of the Waverley novels for the stage. He became Scott's close friend and frequent correspondent. Lockhart provides the following sketch of his character:

> He had the manners and feelings of a gentleman. Like John Kemble, he was deeply skilled in the old literature of the drama, and he rivalled Scott's own enthusiasm for the antiquities of *vertu*. Their epistolary correspondence in after days was frequent, and will supply me with many illustrations of Scott's minor tastes and habits. As their letters lie before me, they appear as if they had all been penned by the same hand. Terry's idolatry of his new friend induced him to imitate his writing so zealously, that Scott used to say, if he were called on to swear to any document, the utmost he could venture to attest would be, that it was either in his own hand or in Terry's. The actor, perhaps unconsciously, mimicked him in other matters with hardly inferior pertinacity. His small lively features had acquired, before I knew him, a truly ludicrous cast of Scott's graver expression; he had taught his tiny eyebrow the very trick of the poet's meditative frown; and to crown all, he so habitually affected his tone and accent that, though a native of Bath, a stranger could hardly have doubted he must be a Scotchman. (Lockhart, II, 274.)

**26(b) he never would have been involved as he was** Scott's secret financial entanglements with the Ballantynes led ultimately to his bankruptcy in 1826.

**26(c) Constable** Archibald Constable (1774–1827) published many of Scott's novels and poems.

**26(c) tyrravy** anger; rage.

**26(d) Mr A Campbell** Alexander Campbell (1764–1824), organist, music teacher, and miscellaneous writer, edited *Albyn's Anthology* (Edinburgh, 1816–18), a collection of Scottish melodies and 'vocal poetry' to which both Scott and Hogg contributed. Poverty-stricken in his later years, he worked for Scott transcribing manuscripts. Scott wrote his obituary for the *Edinburgh Weekly Journal.*

**26(d) the two Irvings** One is William Scott Irving; see note for 13(b). The other may be John Bell Irving of Whitehill, who wrote ballad imitations.

**27(a) he never lets his left hand know what his right hand is doing** echoes Matthew 6. 3. Douglas Mack observes that when Hogg expresses a deep sense of moral importance or approval, he often echoes the Sermon on the Mount.

**27(a) Matturin** Charles Robert Maturin (1782–1824), the Irish novelist, playwright, and clergyman. His novels include *The Fatal Revenge* (1807), favourably reviewed by Scott, *The Wild Irish Boy* (1808), *The Milesian Chief* (1812), *Women* (1818), *Melmoth the Wanderer* (1820), and *The Albigenses* (1824).

**27(b) Calton Hill** open ground near the eastern end of Princes Street in the centre of Edinburgh.

**27(c) Peter Robertson** Patrick Robertson (1794-1855); advocate and judge. Scott called him 'Peter o' the Paunch' and refers to him as 'that humourous tub of tripes' (Grierson, XI, 144) and 'the facetious Peter Robertson' (*Journal*, p. 202). He was known as a convivial wit and wrote several volumes of what the *DNB* describes as 'indifferent verse'.

**27(d) Mr. Martin** the *Edinburgh Directory* for 1797–98 lists a Peter Martin of Bristo

Street, proprietor of a 'cabinet wareroom' on Chapel Street. (See *OED* 'cabinet
(4)—a room devoted to the arrangement of works of art and objects of vertu; a
museum, picture-gallery, etc. Obs. or arch.') There is, however, no conclusive
evidence that this is the Mr Martin to whom Hogg alludes or, for that matter, that
the brawl ever actually took place. Scott moved to 10 South Castle Street in 1799
and then to 39 North Castle Street in 1801, so it is not possible to date the
incident.

28(a) **'I cannot tell how the truth may be / I say the tale as 'twas said to me'** *The Lay
of the Last Minstrel*, II, 22.

28(b)–(c) **The author the publisher and the printers** Archibald Constable died in
1827, John Ballantyne in 1821, and his brother James in 1833.

29(b) **the Earl of Mansfield** William Murray, 3rd Earl (1777–1840).

29(b) **Laidlaw should not be seperated from Abbotsford** after Scott died, William
Laidlaw became factor at Balnagowan, the estate of Sir Charles Lockhart Ross.
He then went to live with his brother James in Ross and died there in 1845.

29(c) **my own brother** Hogg's younger brother David. Mrs. Hughes describes him
as 'a sensible, steady, unimaginative person, rather ashamed of his brother's
poetical fame, which he fears may interfere with his agricultural pursuits' (Mrs
Hughes, p. 258).

30(b) **All turned to tales and novels** Hogg does not mention the importance of
Byron's wildly successful verse romances in persuading Scott to turn to prose
fiction. The enormous popularity of Byron's narrative poems eclipsed Scott's
own, and he turned to novels to recapture his readers. In 1821 in an unsent letter
to Countess Pürgstall ( Jane Anne Cranstoun) he reflected honestly on the
reasons for this change:

> In truth I have long given up poetry. I had my day with the public and being
> no great believer in poetical immortality I was very well pleased to rise a
> winner without continuing the game till I was beggard of any credit I had
> acquired with the public. Besides I felt the prudence of giving way before
> the more forcible and powerful genius of Byron. If I were either greedy or
> jealous of poetical fame and both are strangers to my nature I might com-
> fort myself with the thought that I would hesitate to strip myself to the
> contest so fearlessly as Byron does or to command the wonder and terror
> of the publick by exhibiting in my own person the sublime attitudes of the
> fighting or dying gladiator. But with the old frankness of twenty years
> since I will fairly own that this same delicacy of mine may arise more from
> conscious want of vigour and inferiority than from a delicate dislike to the
> nature of the conflict. (Grierson, VI, 506.)

30(c) **Joanna Baillie's** Joanna Baillie (1762-1851) was a Scottish playwright and poet
whose two volumes of *Plays on the Passions* (1798 and 1802) elicited both contro-
versy and praise. She and Scott first met in 1806, when Scott visited her at
Hampstead, and their friendship lasted until his death. He sponsored the production of her play *A Family Legend* in Edinburgh in 1810, and they corresponded
regularly. In an undated letter of 1814, Scott describes his plans for 'Joanna's
Bower':

> I intend in humble imitation of the Hermit Fincal in the tales of the Ginij to
> dedicate a seat to you in my bowers that are to be. I hope John Richardson
> gave a favourable account of them. I assure you though I cannot pretend to

walk under their shade (*sic*) of them yet I might find some which would shadow me were I to lie down neath them and you must be aware that this is the more classical and interesting posture of the two. In the meantime we look bare enough. But I will take care they shall make the most of their time and grow very fast if you will promise to come down with your sister and see them next season.   (Grierson, III, 536).

**30(d) Let Abbotsford therefore be secured to his lineal descendants** Hogg expresses similar sentiments about Abbotsford in a letter to William Jerdan of 27 December 1832:

> Alas what can I do in this wilderness towards the furthering the subscription to comemorate Sir Walter. They have made me a member of committees in London Glasgow and Edinr but I can do nothing. Only as I have written to them all I request and beseech that in the first place the estate house library and armoury of Abbotsford may be secured to him and his lineal heirs for ever for that is a great and splendid monument of his genius and research and the monument that will always be visited in after ages in preference to any other and people will be proud to possess a stem of the yew trees which he planted with his own hand. Indeed the idea of raising stone and lime monuments to Sir Walter appears to me quite ridiculous with the exception of something in Westminster Abbey and Abbotsford stick by that to him and his lineal heirs for ever. I am the more anxious about this as the next lineal heir to the present Sir Walter is likely to be Wat Scott Lockhart. All other monuments are vain. He has raised two monuments to himself in building and literature which are far beyond what any other architect can produce (NLS, MS 20437, fols 42–43.)

Abbotsford was made over to Scott's son Walter and his heirs male as part of Walter's marriage settlement. At Scott's death, he became second Baronet of Abbotsford, but both he and Charles died childless. Sophia's daughter Charlotte (1828–58) married James Robert Hope in 1847. They added Scott to their surname when she inherited Abbotsford from her brother in 1853.

### Familiar Anecdotes of Sir Walter Scott

**33(a) Lines to Sir Walter Scott, Bart.** Hogg's letter to Bloodgood of 22 June 1833 (see Note on the Genesis of the Texts, pp. xlviii–xlix) contains the following passage:

> There is likewise a poem of mine which I would have liked much to have added to this work. It was written about 1820 and addressed to Sir Walter on first hearing that he was made a baronet but I cannot lay my hands on it and where to direct you to find it I cannot tell. I know it was published at the time but whether in a Magazine or in the fourth vol of my Poetical works published by Constable I am quite uncertain

In the event Bloodgood did not include the poem in his edition of Hogg's *Familiar Anecdotes of Sir Walter Scott* (New York: Harper and Brothers, 1834); but, in the light of the above letter, it is reprinted here from *The Poetical Works of James Hogg*, 4 vols (Edinburgh: Constable, 1822), IV, 133–40.

**33(b) Albyn's son** Scotland's son: see note for 8(c).

**33(c) when first we met** another account of this first meeting appears in the opening pages of *Familiar Anecdotes*.

**37(a) That has been done by half-a-dozen already** many of these were published in periodicals. Hogg's letter to Lockhart of 20 March 1833 (NLS, MS 1554, fols 75–76) mentions two sketches of Scott's life: Allan Cunningham, 'Some Account of the Life and Works of Sir Walter Scott, Bart.' in *The Athenaeum*, 6 October 1832, pp. 641–53; and Robert Chambers, 'Life of Sir Walter Scott', *Chambers's Edinburgh Journal*, 1, supplement (6 October 1832). For an extensive list of contemporary memoirs and biographies of Scott, see James Clarkson Corson, *A Bibliography of Sir Walter Scott: A Classified and Annotated List of Books and Articles Relating to his Life and Works, 1797-1940* (Edinburgh: Oliver and Boyd, 1943; rpt. New York: Burt Franklin, 1968), pp. 25–43.

**37(a) his son in law** see note for 11(a).

**37(b) I shall in nothing extenuate or set down aught through partiality and as for malice that is out of the question** this echoes words spoken by Othello immediately before his death: 'Speak of me as I am. Nothing extenuate / Nor set down aught in malice' (*Othello* v. 2. 351).

**37(b) out of the question** at this point the manuscript reads: '(then copy the whole of the Reminiscences of him in The Altrive Tales)'. Bloodgood's edition of the *Familiar Anecdotes* (New York, 1834) responds by printing a somewhat altered text of the reminiscences of Scott that Hogg included in the version of *Memoir of the Author's Life* published in *Altrive Tales* (London: Cochrane, 1832), pp. cx–cxxi. Douglas Mack comments as follows on the alterations for the New York printing:

No doubt some of the changes can be attributed to Bloodgood, but many of them appear to be authorial. Possibly Hogg noted some revisions on a copy of *Altrive Tales*, and enclosed this copy when he sent his manuscript to Bloodgood. (Hogg, *Memoir of the Author's Life* and *Familiar Anecdotes of Sir Walter Scott*, ed. by Douglas S. Mack (Edinburgh: Scottish Academic Press, 1972), p. 136.)

In the present edition, these reminiscences of Scott are reprinted at this point from the altered version of the New York edition of 1834. The manuscript resumes on p. 43 of the present edition's text: see note for 43(b).

**37(b) the field at Ettrick-house** the meeting actually took place in 1802. At this time, Hogg leased the farm of Ettrickhouse, where he had spent his earliest years.

**37(b) the Ramsey-cleuch** Scott stayed at this farm, tenanted by Walter and George Bryden, on his expedition to Ettrick Forest in the summer of 1802. The famous conversation about the long and short sheep took place here: see pp. 38–39.

**37(c) the SHIRRA** see note for 10(b).

**37(c) "Minstrelsy of the Border"** the first two volumes of Scott's *Minstrelsy of the Scottish Border* were published in 1802 and received widespread praise. In collecting the ballads, Scott conflated variants, added emendations based solely on guesswork, and substituted his own revisions for the sake of poetic improvement. Hogg contributed considerable material published in volume III (1803) and in subsequent editions.

**37(d) William Laidlaw** see note for 14(b).

**37(d) our cottage** the residence at Ettrickhouse, where Hogg lived with his parents.

**37(d) the ballad of Old Maitlan'** *Minstrelsy* III (1803), 1–41. Hogg sent Scott a copy of the ballad through Laidlaw in spring 1802. Scott included an extract from Hogg's letter to him of 30 June 1802 in his introduction to the ballad in *Minstrelsy*, III, pp. 9–10. Some scholars have suspected Hogg of forging the ballad, but this argument has been discredited by Andrew Lang, *Sir Walter Scott and the Border Minstrelsy* (London: Longmans, 1910), which also provides a detailed account of its transmission. Hogg's poetic version of the visit to his mother and the excursion to Rankleburn is found in his 'Lines to Sir Walter Scott, Bart.', written on the occasion of Scott's knighthood, and reprinted in the present volume (pp. 33–36).

37(d) **Andrew Moor [...] Baby Mettlin [...] the first laird of Tushilaw** Andrew Muir was servant to the Rev. Thomas Boston, minister of Ettrick from 1707 to 1732. Hogg mentions him in *The Mountain Bard* as his source for 'Auld Maitland'. A Mr Anderson was first Laird of Tushielaw from 1688 to 1721 or 1724. Baby Maitland may have learned the ballad from a manuscript copy in the late seventeenth century.

38(a) **George Warton an' James Stewart** unidentified.

38(b) **a stanza from Wordsworth** Kenneth R. Johnston suggests that Scott may have quoted from 'The Danish Boy' (1800). The fourth stanza seems relevant:

> A harp is from his shoulder slung;
> Resting the harp upon his knee,
> To words of a forgotten tongue
> He suits his melody.

38(b) **the Messrs. Brydon** see note for 40(c), on Mr. Brydon of Crosslee.

38(c) **speir** (or speer); to ask or inquire.

38(d) **the *short sheep* [...] the *long sheep*** Scott used this conversation in the first chapter of *The Black Dwarf* (1816), thus confirming in Hogg's mind the identity of the Author of Waverley. In a note to that novel, Peter Garside observes that the 'short sheep' were of the blackface breed and the 'long sheep' were Cheviots, thus called because of particularly long bodies and tails. (*The Black Dwarf*, ed. by Peter Garside (Edinburgh: Edinburgh University Press, 1993), p. 209).

38(d) **a bard of Nature's own making** Hogg cultivated the image of natural genius. In *The Queen's Wake* (1813), the Bard of Ettrick, Hogg's own self-representation, uses as his motto 'Naturae donum', and Hogg's seal carried the same motto and a harp.

38(d) **Mr. Walter Brydon** see note for 40(c), on Mr. Brydon of Crosslee.

39(b) **Johnie Ballantyne** see note for 7(d).

39(b) **Rankleburn [...] the farms of Buccleuch and Mount Comyn** 'Buccleuch Church (Site). Only grass-grown wall-mounds now survive to mark the site of this church, which served the parish of Rankillburn until this was joined to the parish of Yarrow after the Reformation. The church was already ruinous by 1566'. 'Buccleuch Mill (Site). No structural remains survive'. (Royal Commission on the Ancient Monuments of Scotland, *Selkirkshire*, (Edinburgh: HMSO, 1957), pp. 35 and 76. The farm of Buccleuch is on the Rankle (or Rankil) Burn, a tributary of the Ettrick. The farmhouse is very near the Buck Cleuch, from which the Dukes of Buccleuch, chiefs of the clan Scott, derive their name. The story is told as follows in the guidebook *Bowhill, Selkirk, Scotland: Border Home of the Duke of Buccleuch and Queensberry, K. T.* ([Selkirk: Buccleuch Estate, c. 1990]), p. 2:

> Ancient Ettrick Forest [...] was a favourite hunting ground for the Kings of Scotland who used Newark Castle, two miles North of Bowhill, as a hunting box. Various Scotts had been active Rangers from the 12th century and, according to legend, it was in a deep 'Cleuch' or ravine in the Rankil

Burn, in the heart of the forest, that a certain young Scott seized a cornered
buck by the antlers, after it had turned on the king's hounds, and threw it
over his shoulder: hence the origin of the name Buccleuch (Buck-Cleuch).
An early Scott of Buccleuch is one of the main characters of Hogg's novel *The
Three Perils of Man* (1822). Originally, this character was called 'Sir Walter Scott of
Buccleuch'; but Sir Walter Scott of Abbotsford persuaded Hogg that this was
somewhat tactless, and the character's name duly became 'Sir Ringan Redhough
of Mount Comyn'. See pp. 9–10 for Hogg's account of this conversation.

**39(c) old Satchells** Walter Scott of Satchells (1614?–1694?) was the author of *A True
History of Several Honourable Families of the Right Honourable Name of Scot, in the Shires of
Roxburgh and Selkirk, and Others Adjacent: Gathered out of Ancient Chronicles, Histories, and
Traditions of our Fathers*, (1688; reprinted Edinburgh: Balfour and Smellie, 1776).
The rhymed text, written after a long career as a soldier, was dictated, either
because the author could not write or because he was blind. He describes himself
on the title-page as

> An old Souldier and no Scholler,
> And ane that can write noe,
> But just the letters of his Name.

The quotation cited by Hogg actually reads:

> If Heather-tops had been Meal of the best,
> Then Buckcleugh-mill had gotten a noble grist.   (p. 43.)

**39(c) the chief's black mails** *blak-maill* and *blak-meill* were used in Older Scots (from
1530) to signify 'a payment enacted or made in return for protection from spolia-
tion or injury; an illegal exaction'. *Meal* (meaning 'corn', 'grain') is pronounced in
Scots either 'mail' (mel) or 'meal' (mil) (*Scottish National Dictionary*).

**40(a) ancient consecrated helmet** perhaps an ironic reference to the enchanted helmet of Mambrino, *Don Quixote*, I, 21.

**40(c) the Pechs (*Picts*) [...] the latchets of our shoes** Douglas Mack observes that in
chapter 23 of *Rob Roy*, Scott describes his Highland hero in similar terms:

> Two points in his person interfered with the rules of symmetry—his shoul-
> ders were so broad in proportion to his height, as, notwithstanding the
> lean and lathy appearance of his frame, gave him something the air of being
> too square in respect to his stature; and his arms, though round, sinewy,
> and strong, were so very long as to be rather a deformity. I afterwards
> heard that this length of arm was a circumstance on which he prided
> himself; that when he wore his native Highland garb, he could tie the
> garters of his hose without stooping; and that it gave him great advantage
> in the use of the broadsword, at which he was very dexterous. But cer-
> tainly this want of symmetry destroyed the claim he might otherwise have
> set up, to be accounted a very handsome man; it gave something wild,
> irregular, and, as it were, unearthly, to his appearance, and reminded me
> involuntarily, of the tales which Mabel used to tell of the old Picts who
> ravaged Northumberland in ancient times, who, according to her tradi-
> tion, were a sort of half-goblin, half-human beings, distinguished, like this
> man, for courage, cunning, ferocity, the length of their arms, and the
> squareness of their shoulders.

Scott's comment may also allude to the depth of the Catrail or Picts' Work Ditch (or Dyke), which Scott mentions in chapter 8 of *The Black Dwarf*. It is an ancient earthwork supposed to have extended fifty miles across Roxburghshire and Selkirkshire from Gala Water to Peel Fell. In the early nineteenth century, it was thought to have demarked part of the Roman-Caledonian border (Royal Commission on the Ancient Monuments of Scotland, *Selkirkshire* (Edinburgh: HMSO, 1957), pp. 126–27).

> The work consists of a double mound with intervening trench [...] in its broader parts, taking from the centre of one rampart to the centre of the other, [it] measures from 23 feet 6 inches to 18 feet 6 inches, whilst the breadth of the ditch is 6 feet, and the slope from the centre of the rampart to the centre of the ditch-bottom 10 feet. (Sir George Douglas, *A History of the Border Counties* (Edinburgh: Blackwood, 1899), pp. 23–24.)

**40(c) the old castles of Tushilaw and Thirlstane** Tushielaw Tower is a dilapidated ruin of a manor house probably from the sixteenth century. Thirlestane Tower is a ruin of a later sixteenth-century castle located about a mile from the hamlet of Ettrick: Royal Commission on the Ancient Monuments of Scotland, *Selkirkshire*, (Edinburgh: HMSO, 1957), pp. 56–57.

**40(c) Mr. Brydon of Crosslee** Walter and George Bryden, cousins of William Laidlaw, occupied the farm of Ramsey-cleuch.

> Before the friends parted, Scott made a note of Hogg's address, and from that time never ceased to take a warm interest in his fortunes. He corresponded with him, and becoming curious to see the poetical Shepherd, made another visit to Blackhouse, for the purpose of getting Laidlaw along with him as guide to Ettrick. The visit was highly agreeable. The sheriff's *bonhomie* and lively conversation had deeply interested his companion, and he rode by his side in a sort of ecstasy as they journeyed again by St Mary's Loch and the green hills of Dryhope, which rise beyond the wide expanse of smooth water. It was a fine summer morning, and the impressions of the day and the scene have been recorded in imperishable verse [see note for 25(a)]. Dryhope Tower, so intimately associated with the memory of Mary Scott, the 'Flower of Yarrow,' made the travellers stop for a brief space; and *Dhu Linn* [...], with Chapelhope and other scenes and ruins famous in Border tradition, deeply interested Scott. [...] the horsemen crossed the ridge of hills that separates the Yarrow from her sister stream. These hills are high and green, but the more lofty parts of the ridge are soft and boggy, and they had often to pick their way, and proceed in single file. Then they followed a foot-track on the side of a long *cleugh* or *hope*, and at last descended toward the Ettrick, where they had in view the level green valley, walled in by high hills of dark green, with here and there gray crags, the church and the old *place* of Ettrick Hall in ruins, embosomed in trees. [...] The travellers went to dine at Ramsey-cleugh [...] and Laidlaw sent off [...] to Ettrick House for Hogg, that he might come and spend the evening with them. The Shepherd (who then retained all his original simplicity of character) came *to tea*, and he brought with him a bundle of manuscripts, of size enough at least to shew his industry—all of course ballads, and fragments of ballads. The penmanship was executed with more care than Hogg had ever bestowed on anything before. Scott was surprised and pleased with

Hogg's appearance, and with the hearty familiarity with which *Jamie*, as he was called, was received by Laidlaw and the Messrs Bryden of Ramsey-cleugh. Hogg was no less gratified. 'The sheriff of a county in those days,' said Laidlaw, 'was regarded by the class to whom Hogg belonged with much of the fear and respect that their *forbears* looked up to the ancient hereditary sheriffs, who had the power of pit and gallows in their hands; and here Jamie found himself all at once not only the chief object of the sheriff's notice and flattering attention, but actually seated at the same table with him.' Hogg's genius was sufficient passport to the best society. His appearance was also prepossessing. His clear ruddy cheek and spar-kling eye spoke of health and vivacity, and he was light and agile in his figure. When a youth, he had a remarkably fine head of long curling brown hair, which he wore coiled up under his bonnet; and on Sundays, when he entered the church and let down his locks, the *lasses* (on whom Jamie always turned an expressive *espiègle* glance) looked towards him with envy and admiration. [...]

Mr. Laidlaw thus speaks of the evening at Ramsey-cleugh: 'It required very little of that tact or address in social intercourse for which Mr Scott was afterwards so much distinguished, to put himself and those around him entirely at their ease. In truth, I never afterwards saw him at any time apparently enjoy company so much, or exert himself so greatly—or prob-ably there was no effort at all—in rendering himself actually fascinating; nor did I ever again spend such a night of merriment. The qualities of Hogg came out every instant, and his unaffected simplicity and fearless frankness both surprised and charmed the sheriff. They were both very good mimics and story-tellers born and bred; and when Scott took to employ his dramatic talent, he soon found he had us all in his power; [...] The best proof of Jamie's enjoyment was, that he never sung a song that blessed night, and it was between two and three o'clock before we parted.'

Next morning, Scott and Laidlaw went, according to promise, to visit Hogg in his low thatched cottage. [...] The Shepherd and his aged mother— 'Old Margaret Laidlaw,' for she generally went by her maiden name—gave the visitors a hearty welcome. [...]

From Hogg's cottage the party proceeded up Rankleburn to see Buccleuch, and inspect the old chapel and mill. They found nothing at the kirk of Buccleuch, and saw only the foundations of the chapel. [...] Hogg trotted up behind, marvelling at the versatile powers of the 'wonderful *shirra.*' They all dined together with a 'lady of the glen,' Mrs Bryden, Crosslee; and next morning Scott returned to Clovenford Inn, where he resided till he took a lease of the house of Ashestiel. (Carruthers, pp. 128–32.)

**40(d)  this retentiveness of memory** Carruthers writes:

Thomas Campbell used to relate, as an instance of Sir Walter's extraordi-nary memory, that he read to him his poem of *Locheil's Warning* before it was printed; after which his friend asked permission to read it himself. He then perused the manuscript slowly and distinctly, and on returning it to its author, said: 'Campbell, look after your copyright, for I have got your poem.' And he repeated, with very few mistakes, the whole sixty lines of which the poem (which was subsequently enlarged) then consisted. (Carruthers, p. 154.)

**41 (a) Skene of Rubislaw** James Skene of Rubislaw (1775–1864) was a legal friend of Scott's from his earliest days at the bar. They were both involved in organising the Edinburgh Light Dragoons, and Skene was a frequent visitor at Ashestiel and Abbotsford and, after Scott's bankruptcy in 1826, a source of considerable solace to him. Lockhart quotes Scott's *Journal* entry for 4 January 1826:

> Mr and Mrs Skene, my excellent friends, came to us from Edinburgh. Skene, distinguished for his attainments as a draughtsman and for his highly gentlemanlike feelings and character, is Laird of Rubislaw, near Aberdeen. Having had an elder brother, his education was somewhat neglected in early life, against which disadvantage he made a most gallant fight, exerting himself much to obtain those accomplishments which he has since possessed. Admirable in all exercises, there entered a good deal of the cavalier into his early character. Of late he has given himself much to the study of antiquities. His wife, a most excellent person, was tenderly fond of Sophia. They bring so much old-fashioned kindness and good-humour with them, besides the recollections of other times, that they must always be welcome guests. (Lockhart, VI, 184–85.)

**41 (a) leistering kippers in Tweed** various footnotes to Hogg's text were added in *The Domestic Manners and Private Life of Sir Walter Scott* (1834), the British pirated edition of *Familiar Anecdotes*. The following footnote is added here:

> Sir Walter alludes in the notes to his collected work by Cadell, to his "fire hunting" expeditions. Hogg enables us to fill up the outlines of one of them.

**41 (a) the Rough haugh of Elibank** Elibank was a ruined tower on the Tweed three miles from Scott's cottage at Ashestiel. A *haugh* is flat land beside a river.

**41 (b) Rob Fletcher** possibly James Fletcher, gamekeeper to the Duke of Buccleuch.

**41 (b) my ballad of "Gilman's-cleuch"** this poem was included in *The Mountain Bard* (1807) but probably written by 1803. It consists of seventy-four quatrains.

**41 (c) one of Southey's, (The Abbot of Aberbrothock)** the poem is entitled 'The Inchcape Rock' and was published in Southey's *Metrical Tales and Other Poems* in 1805. Scott and Southey visited each other that year.

**41 (c) old Mr. Laidlaw of the Peel** Robert Laidlaw held the tenancy of the Peel Farm adjacent to Ashestiel. 'Laird Nippy', as he was known, sublet the sheep farm portion of Ashestiel from Scott.

**41 (d) "turning up sides like swine"** *Domestic Manners* footnotes 'Guy Mannering'. In describing the night-time salmon fishing in chapter 26, Scott writes 'He turns up a side like a sow'. Both he and Hogg may be playing with a traditional proverb: 'Swine, women, and bees cannot be turned' (John Ray, *English Proverbs* (Cambridge: W. Norden, 1678), p. 212).

**42 (a) " 'An' gin the boat war bottomless, / An' seven miles to row' "** from 'The Weary Pund o' Tow', a song of mid-eighteenth century origin. The last stanza reads:

> But if your wife and my wife
> Were in a boat thegither,
> And yon other man's wife

Were in to steer the ruther;
And if the boat were bottomless,
And seven miles to row,
I think they'd ne'er come hame again,
To spin the pund o' tow.

(Robert Chambers, *The Songs of Scotland Prior to Burns* (Edinburgh: Chambers, 1862), pp. 203–05.)

**42(a) Ashiesteel** see note for 12(c).

**42(a) Sir Adam Ferguson** see note for 4(b).

**42(b) Loch-Skene and the Grey-mare's-tail** the trip took place in the summer of 1817. Loch Skene is in Dumfriesshire, and the Grey Mare's Tail is a nearby steep waterfall in Moffat Dale. Scott describes the scene in the Introduction to Canto Second of *Marmion*:

There eagles scream from isle to shore;
Down all the rocks the torrents roar;
O'er the black waves incessant driven,
Dark mists infect the summer heaven;
Through the rude barriers of the lake,
Away its hurrying waters break,
Faster and whiter dash and curl,
Till down yon dark abyss they hurl.
Rises the fog-smoke white as snow,
Thunders the viewless stream below,
Diving, as if condemned to lave
Some demon's subterranean cave,
Who, prisoned by enchanter's spell,
Shakes the dark rock with groan and yell.
And well that Palmer's form and mien
Had suited with the stormy scene,
Just on the edge, straining his ken
To view the bottom of the den,
Where, deep deep down, and far within,
Toils with the rocks the roaring linn;
Then, issuing forth one foamy wave,
And wheeling round the Giant's Grave,
White as the snowy charger's tail,
Drives down the pass of Moffatdale.

Scott also wrote of the trip in a letter to Mrs. Hughes of 9 or 10 October 1828:
I dined with the Ettrick Shepherd and an excellent rural feast we had he had not forgotten your kindness. On this occasion I visited my old acquaintance the Grey Mare's Tail in a tremendous storm of wind and rain— the path was a perilous one but the sight of the torrent tumbling from an immense height into a bottomless cauldron swelled by rain and contending in its fall with a tempest of wind was very grand indeed. The solid rock on which we stood rocked to the roar [of] wind and wave. I wished you to have seen it.   (Grierson, XI, 7.)

Carruthers quotes Laidlaw's description of the expedition:

'We proceeded with difficulty up the rocky chasm to reach the foot of the waterfall. The passage which the stream has worn by cutting the opposing rocks of greywacke, is rough and dangerous. My brother George and I, both in the prime of youth, and constantly in the habit of climbing, had difficulty in forcing our way, and we felt for Scott's lameness. This, however, was unnecessary. He said he could not perhaps climb so fast as we did, but he advised us to go on, and leave him. This we did, but halted on a projecting point before we descended to the foot of the fall, and looking back, were struck at seeing the motions of the sheriff's dog *Camp*. The dog was attending anxiously on his master; and when the latter came to a difficult part of the rock, *Camp* would jump down, look up to his master's face, then spring up, lick his master's hand and cheek, jump down again, and look upwards, as if to shew him the way, and encourage him. We were greatly interested with the scene. Mr Scott seemed to depend much on his hands and the great strength of his powerful arms; and he soon fought his way over all obstacles, and joined us at the foot of the Grey Mare's Tail, the name of the cataract.' (Carruthers, p. 135.)

Hogg uses this scene as the setting for his ballad 'The Grousome Caryl', published in *Blackwood's* in 1825 and later in *A Queer Book* (1832). After depositing the souls of the fiends in Galloway as 'the worste helle they knew', Hogg returns to the Grey Mare's Tail for the benediction of his last two stanzas:

> Maye the Lorde preserve bothe manne and beiste
> That treade this yirde belowe,
> And littil bairnis, and maydenis fayre,
> And graunt them graice to growe;

> And may never ane reude uncouthlye gueste
> Come their blessit bowris withynne;
> And neuer ane caryl be seine againe
> Lyke him of the Greye-Meris Linne.

(*A Queer Book*, ed. by Peter Garside (Edinburgh: Edinburgh University Press, 1995), p. 119.)

**42(b) if not rode by Clavers** John Graham of Claverhouse, 1st Viscount Dundee (1649?–1689), as commander of a troop of cavalry, was proud of his extraordinary feats of horsemanship in pursuit of Covenanters over bogs and up precipices in the south-west of Scotland in 1678 and following. In *The Brownie of Bodsbeck* (1818), Hogg includes an instance of Claverhouse's remarkable riding. His somewhat ignominious departure from Edinburgh, during which he rode halfway up the Castle Rock, is commemorated and inaccurately glorified by Scott in 'Bonnie Dundee'.

**42(b) Moffat** town in Dumfriesshire.

**43(a) "The Mountain Bard,"** see note for 8(d).

**43(a)–(b) Bless'd be his generous heart [...] my cradle sung** Hogg repeats this quotation from *The Queen's Wake* on pp. 59-60 (where he also quotes an additional 30 lines of the poem). For *The Queen's Wake*, see note for 8(c). The quoted passage comes from the 'Conclusion' to *The Queen's Wake*, in which Scott tunes the long-silent harp of the Bard of Ettrick and Yarrow, author of the traditional Border ballads, and thus revives 'the ancient magic melody' of the Scottish poetic tradition. If, as Douglas Mack speculates, 'Possibly Hogg noted some revisions on a copy of *Altrive Tales*, and enclosed this copy when he sent his manuscript to Bloodgood' (in New York) (*Memoir of the Author's Life* and *Familiar Anecdotes of Sir Walter Scott* (Edinburgh: Scottish Academic Press, 1972), p. 136), then the repetition of this passage from *The Queen's Wake* suggests that Hogg may not have reread very thoroughly. See also note for 37(b).

43(b) **The only foible I ever could discover** the manuscript continues here.

43(b) **Buccleuch [...] Harden** see note for 3(d).

43(c) **the chiefs of Haliburton and Rutherford** see note for 6(a).

43(d) **Bowhill [...] Duke Charles** see notes for 4(a) and 3(d).

44(b) **If ye reave the Hoggs o Fauldshope / Ye herry Harden's gear** see note for 4(c).

44(d) **refused to let a dish be set on our table** *Domestic Manners* adds the folowing footnote:

> Sir Walter, practical, and with a strong grasp of real life in his poetry, was always endeavouring to live in a world of fiction. His Abbotsford, the dinner here narrated, and the reception of the king at Edinburgh were continuous efforts to transplant himself into another age—not unlike children playing Crusaders, Reavers, Robinson Crusoes, &c.

45(a) **"Johnie Cope are ye wauking yet"** see note for 5(c).

45(a) **his weak foot** see note for 23(d).

45(a) **his straight forward bass voice** *Domestic Manners* adds the following footnote:
Which means, we suppose, a voice that never varied its notes; no—

winding bout<br>
Of linked sweetness long drawn out.

45(c) **the parliament house** the building dates from 1639. From the Restoration in 1660 until the Union with England in 1707, it housed the Scottish Parliament, Privy Council and Supreme Court (Court of Session). Scott was appointed a Principal Clerk of the Court of Session in 1806. A traditional Scottish proverb proclaims '"There's nae place like hame", quo' the deil, when he fand himsel i' the Court o' Session'.

45(c) **Castle Street** see notes for 6(b) and 27(d).

45(c) **Abbotsford** see note for 6(c).

45(d) **Yarrow** the valley of the Yarrow River; location of Bowhill.

45(d) **Melrose or Dryburgh** the ruin of Melrose Abbey is located in Roxburghshire, near Abbotsford. Scott incorporated stones from it in the construction of his house and celebrated its beauty in *The Lay of the Last Minstrel* (II, 1):

> If thou would'st view fair Melrose aright,
> Go visit it by the pale moon-light;
> For the gay beams of lightsome day
> Gild, but to flout, the ruins gray.
> When the broken arches are black in night,
> And each shafted oriel glimmers white;
> When the cold light's uncertain shower
> Streams on the ruined central tower;

> When buttress and buttress, alternately,
> Seem framed of ebon and ivory;
> When silver edges the imagery,
> And the scrolls that teach thee to live and die;
> When distant Tweed is heard to rave,
> And the owlet to hoot o'er the dead man's grave,
> Then go—but go alone the while—
> Then view St David's ruined pile;
> And, home returning, soothly swear,
> Was never scene so sad and fair!

The ruin of Dryburgh Abbey in Berwickshire houses Scott's tomb. James VI and I dissolved the abbey and transformed it into a temporal peerage under the title of Cardross for John, Earl of Mar. (Francis Grose, *The Antiquities of Scotland* (London: Hooper & Wigstead, 1797) I, 103–11).

**45(d)–46(a) billious complaint** beginning in 1816, Scott suffered periodically from severe abdominal cramps caused by gallstones.

**46(a) accompanied by pangs most excrutiating** *Domestic Manners* adds the following footnote:

> This fact—which we do not recollect to have seen noticed before, accounts for some inequalities of temper we have heard laid to Sir Walter's charge— his uncourteous treatment of Lord Holland, &c. Before blaming any one for such freaks, we ought always to inquire into the state of the stomach.

**46(b) Sir Alex^r Don** see note for 5(d).

**46(c) The Marquis of Queensberry** Charles Douglas, 5th Marquis of Queensberry (1777–1837), was married to a daughter of the 3rd Duke of Buccleuch. From 1810, the Dukes of Buccleuch were also Dukes of Queensberry.

**46(c) Croupier** one who sits as assistant chairman at the lower end of the table at a public dinner (*OED*).

**46(d) THE THREE PERILS OF MAN** see note for 9(b).

**48(d)–49(b) the article alluded to [...] the paper [...] a review of modern literature in the Edin^r Annual Register** see note for 20(c).

**49(a) Southey** see note for 20(b).

**49(b) THE SPY** see note for 20(c).

**49(b) Mr Shuffleton** see note for 20(d).

**50(b) John Ballantyne** see note for 7(d).

**50(b) James Ballantyne** see note for 21(d).

**50(c) determined to keep me down** *Domestic Manners* adds the footnote: 'What a horrible conspiracy!'.

**50(c) BROWNIE OF BODSBECK** see note for 21(d).

**51(a) your tale o' Auld Mortality** see note for 22(b).

**51(c) Mr Blackwood** see note for 22(c).

**51(d) a proverb about the Gordons** Douglas Mack notes David Buchan's suggestion that the proverb might have been 'Never misca' a Gordon in the raws o' Stra'bogie'. That is, do not criticise someone on his own turf. (Hogg, *Anecdotes of Sir W. Scott*, ed. by Douglas S. Mack (Edinburgh: Scottish Academic Press, 1983), note to p. 49.) In *Scots Proverbs and Rhymes*, Forbes MacGregor interprets it to mean 'Don't speak badly of a man among friends. The Gordons were the principal clansmen about Strathbogie, in north-west Aberdeenshire'. (Edinburgh: Gordon Wright, 1983), p. 41. Another possibility might be 'The Gordons hae the guiding o't', suggesting that Scott will acquiesce in order not to offend. Robert Chambers, *Popular Rhymes of Scotland* (London and Edinburgh: W. & R. Chambers, 1870), p. 130.

**52(a) Hunt of Eildon** see note for 23(a).

**52(c) he subsequently copied the whole of the main plot into his tale of Castle Dangerous** the two novels share similar plot elements: a prolonged siege of a Scottish castle, a woman offered as prize, a lady in disguise, and a happy ending. Scott cites as his own sources Barbour's *Bruce* and David Hume of Godscroft's *History of the Houses of Douglas and Angus.* Although Scott was writing under enormous pressure of debt and failing health in 1831 when he was working on *Castle Dangerous,* Hogg's charge of plagiarism cannot be substantiated.

**52(c) Joe Miller jokes** Hogg refers to *Joe Miller's Jests: or, the Wit's Vade-Mecum: being a collection of the most brilliant jests and most pleasant short stories in the English language: the greater part of which are taken from the mouth of that facetious gentleman whose name they bear,* compiled by John Mottley (London: T. Reed, 1739). The actual Joe Miller lived from 1684 to 1738.

**52(c) John Murray of Albemarl Street** see note for 24(b).

**53(a) his cottage on the banks of the North Esk above Lasswade** see note for 10(b).

**53(c) Jeffery** see note for 10(d).

**53(c) Brougham** Henry Brougham (1778–1868) was one of the founders of the *Edinburgh Review* in 1802, along with Francis Jeffrey and Sydney Smith. He later served as Queen Caroline's chief defence counsel and was appointed Lord Chancellor in 1830.

**53(d) this review of Marmion** Francis Jeffrey's largely disapproving review of Scott's *Marmion* appeared in the *Edinburgh Review,* 12 (April 1808), pp. 1–35. At this point *Domestic Manners* adds the following footnote:

> We have heard this story with a variation. Jeffrey, in his review of Marmion, while praising the author's talents highly, introduced some censure. Going to sup with Scott, he, in the honesty of his heart, took the proof-sheets of the review with him and read them aloud. Mr Jeffrey's manner is unfortunate, and he was considerably Scott's junior. Scott and all his friends (his wife in particular) took the matter in high dudgeon. The review was not modified.

**53(d) Curwin** probably Henry Curwen of Workington Hall, West Cumberland, and Belle Isle, Windermere. His daughter Isabella married Wordsworth's son John.

**54(b) Who was lady Scott originally?** see note for 11(d).

**54(c) a nobleman of very high rank** *Domestic Manners* adds the following footnote:
> This impression, strange to say, was encouraged by Sir Walter. Falconbridge was contented to be a king's bastard. The anxiety to be connected with nobility by a wife's illegitimacy, is a step beyond this, in aristocratical devotion.

**54(c) Glen-Finlas** see note for 24(c).

**54(c) William Erskine (lord Kineder)** see note for 24(c).

**54(d) a far better reader than he was sensible of** *Domestic Manners* adds the following footnote: 'Just'.

**54(d) The Marmion M.S.** the manuscript of *Marmion* (MS Adv. 19.1.16) is presently owned by the National Library of Scotland. For a detailed study of its composition and revision, see J. H. Alexander, *Marmion: Studies in Interpretation and Composition* (Salzburg: Univ. Salzburg, 1981).

**55(a) St. Mary's Lake** see note for 25(a).

**55(b) Grieve and Morison** John Grieve (1781–1836), hat manufacturer and minor poet, provided shelter and other assistance to Hogg during his first months of residence in Edinburgh in 1810. Hogg dedicated *Mador of the Moor* to him. For Morrison, see note for 24(d).

**55(c) Sir John Hope** if Hogg's chronology is correct, this is General John Hope (1765–1836); he was not knighted until 1821.

**55(d) "it's no little that gars auld Donald pegh"** in an early incident in 'The Renowned Adventures of Basil Lee' from *Winter Evening Tales* (2 vols, 1820), Hogg's title character, then a drunken grocer in Kelso, mistakenly sells a glass of vitriol rather than whisky to a Highland drover. He is startled when the High-lander, whom he feared had died of the dose, returns a month later asking, in these words, for more of the same. See *Winter Evening Tales*, I, 1–99 (p. 12).

**55(c) yon Lewis stories of your's** in another section of 'The Renowned Adventures of Basil Lee' the wandering hero, returning from America, leaves his ship and resides on the Isle of Lewis for a month. There he experiences a series of startling supernatural encounters apparently not unusual amongst the inhabitants of Lewis, who 'with the beings of another state of existence [...] have frequent intercourse': see *Winter Evening Tales*, I, 1–99 (p. 65).

**56(a) a humorous poem in M.S.** probably 'The Search After Happiness', written at the end of 1816 and first published by John Ballantyne in February 1817 as Number 5 of *The Sale Room*.

**56(a) a new holland shirt** *Domestic Manners* adds the following footnote:
> It appeared in the "Sale Room," a four-penny literary weekly, published by John Ballantyne. It is a circumstance not generally known, that a commu-nication to this publication signed Christopher Corduroy, was the first thing that attracted Scott's notice to Lockhart, of whom he previously knew nothing.

**56(d) Mrs Hogg** see note for 16(c).

**56(d) Mount-Benger** see note for 16(a).

**57(b) the Cooper of Fogo** see note for 16(a).

**57(c) his own house in Maitland-Street** see note for 16(d).

**57(d) Nought's to be won at woman's hand** from 'Tak Your Auld Cloak About Ye', a traditional song which Robert Chambers finds earliest in Ramsay's *Tea-table Miscellany* (1742) but suspects originated in the sixteenth century. Hogg quotes from the last stanza:

> Bell, my wife, she lo'es na strife,
>     But she would guide me, if she can;
> And, to maintain an easy life,
>     I aft maun yield, though I'm guidman:
> Nocht's to be gain'd at woman's hand,
>     Unless ye gie her a' the plea;
> Then I'll leave aff where I began,
>     And tak my auld cloak about me.

(Robert Chambers, *The Songs of Scotland Prior to Burns* (Edinburgh: Chambers, 1862), pp. 113–15.)

58(a) **Hugh John Lockhart** see note for 17(b).

58(b) **a braw gown!" [...] made for me in Paris** see note for 17(b).

58(d) **a fourpenny cut** in the terminology of printing, a 'cut' is an engraved plate, or the results of that plate; i.e. the printed page. *The Spy* did indeed sell for fourpence per issue. Scott (or Hogg) may also be invoking the eighteenth-century usage of cut as 'chance' or 'hazard'.

59(a) **two poems of Leyden's** see note for 19(d).

59(a) **when I was living in Nithsdale** see note for 8(b).

59(a) **Broadmeadows** see note for 8(b).

59(b) **engaged me to Lord Porchester** see note for 8(b).

59(b) **pendicle** a small piece of ground, a cottage, etc. forming a dependent part of an estate; in later use especially such a part separately sublet.

59(c) **the Queen's wake** see note for 8(c).

60(c) **Alan Cunningham** (1784–1842); Scottish poet, editor, biographer, and assistant to the sculptor Francis Chantrey. His *Remains of Nithsdale and Galloway Song* (1810), supposedly collected by R. H. Cromek but largely written by Cunningham, brought him to the attention of Scott and Hogg.

60(c) **Captain J. G. Burns** James Glencairn Burns (1794–1865), son of the poet, was an officer in the Indian service. He was one of the guests at Scott's farewell banquet at Abbotsford on 17 September 1831.

60(d) **he once promised to do it** in *Anecdotes of Sir W. Scott*, Hogg tentatively identifies this work as *Queen Hynde* (p. 8).

61(c) **composed a song for the corps** see note for 23(c), and the Appendix to the present edition (pp. 77–78).

61(c) **Donald M'Donald** see note for 23(d). In that version, Hogg claims that Scott discovered the authorship of the ballad from its publisher.

61(d) **Sir C. Sharpe** most likely Sir Cuthbert Sharp (1781–1849), En0glish antiquary and historian, knighted in 1816.

61(d) **Mr Gillies** Robert Pearse Gillies (1788–1858), Scottish advocate, poet, editor, and translator and a rather feckless friend of both Hogg and Scott, often in financial distress. He wrote about Scott in *Recollections of Sir Walter Scott, Bart.*, (London: Fraser, 1837) and in *Memoirs of a Literary Veteran*, 3 vols (London: Bentley, 1851). In the latter, he credits himself for introducing Hogg to Edinburgh society and credits Hogg, 'with the help of Glenlivat', for invigorating both that society and Scottish literature (II, 134). Gillies admired Hogg for his originality and 'genuine decision of character': 'yet after all these extraordinary performances, he remained in his demeanour, appearance, and manner of speech, *integer purus*, the same unalterable Ettrick Shepherd, who but a few years ago had driven his herd of "*nowte*" to All Hallow Fair, and borrowed scraps of paper in the shops to write his first pastorals for the printer' (II, 244).

62(b) **a blank verse poem [...] The latter half only was mine** in *Memoirs of a Literary Veteran* (III, 52) Gillies refers to Hogg as 'my good old collaborator the Ettrick Shepherd', but he does not provide any details of their collaboration.

62(c) **his deputy clerk** see note for 26(a).

62(c) **laughing and chatting with me all the while** *Domestic Manners* adds the following footnote:

We recommend this to the special notice of Mr Wallace of Kelly.

**62(d) Terry** see note for 26(a).

**63(a) the author of the celebrated novels** see note for 11(d).

**64(a) The publisher the author the two printers** see note for 28(c).

**64(a) the corrector of the press** Daniel M'Corkindale, foreman of the printing house of James Ballantyne and Company, died in 1833.

**64(b) Miss Ferrier's novels** Susan Edmonstone Ferrier (1782–1854), a Scottish novelist and friend of Scott from 1811, wrote *Marriage* (1818), *The Inheritance* (1824), and *Destiny* (1831). Her father, James, was a Principal Clerk of the Court of Session with Scott. William Blackwood sent Margaret Hogg a copy of *The Inheritance* when it was published, and Hogg responded enthusiastically: 'In short if the author of *Marriage* and *The Inheritance* be a woman I am in love with her' (letter to Blackwood of 28 June 1824, NLS, MS 4012, fol. 184).

**65(b) Matturin** see note for 27(a).

**65(c) our friend Kirkpatrick Sharpe** Charles Kirkpatrick Sharpe (1781–1851), Scottish artist, antiquary, and poet contributed to the *Minstrelsy of the Scottish Border* and edited James Kirkton's *Secret and True History of the Church of Scotland* (1817), ironically reviewed by Hogg in 'A Letter to Charles Kirkpatrick Sharpe, Esq. on His Original Mode of Editing Church History', *Blackwood's Edinburgh Magazine*, 2 (December 1817), 305–09. Hogg pretends to admire Sharpe's perverse cleverness in making the Covenenters seem so depraved that the reader inevitably adopts the contrary view.

> Charles Kirkpatrick Sharpe, with his antiquarian tastes, personal oddities, and aristocratic leanings, was a special favourite with Scott. He was a kind of Scotch Horace Walpole (so considered by his illustrious friend), but much feebler; perhaps stronger with the pencil, but infinitely weaker with the pen. (Carruthers, p. 148.)

**65(d) the present termination of the ballad** the original version of 'The Witch of Fife' (1813) ends at line 272, as the ill-fated husband renounces wine and women before he is burnt 'skin and bone' by the English at Carlisle. For the third edition (1814), Hogg added 52 lines in which 'the auld gudeman' is rescued by his wife, and the poet admonishes, 'And nevir curse his puir auld wife/ Rychte wicked altho scho be'.

**66(a) All turned to tales** see note for 30(b).

**67(a) the noblemen and gentlemen in London** Hogg visited London early in 1832 and was thoroughly lionised. Although in his letters home he repeatedly claimed to be desolate and lonely, he seems in actuality to have enjoyed a rousing good time. In a letter to his wife of 21 January 1832 he writes:

> I have no news save that I am very well. Indeed it is almost a miracle that I keep my health so well, considering the life that I lead, for I am out at parties every night until far in the morning... You will see that a great literary dinner is to be given me on Wednesday, my birth-day, for though the name of Burns is necessarily coupled with mine, the dinner has been set on foot solely to bring me forward and give me *eclat* in the eyes of the public, thereby to inspire an extensive sale of my forthcoming work. It was mooted by Lockhart, Murray, Jerdan and Galt, who have managed the whole business, and will be such a meeting as was never in London. ... But do not be afraid, for vain as I am, it will not turn my head; on the contrary, it has

rather made me melancholy, and I wish it were fairly over. Sir John Malcolm has been chosen to the first chair, and Lord Leveson Gower to the second, and among the stewards there are upwards of twenty noblemen and baronets. And all this to do honour to a poor old shepherd. (Quoted in Mary Gray Garden, *Memorials of James Hogg, the Ettrick Shepherd* (Paisley: A. Gardner, [1884]) pp. 251–52.)

**67(a) With regard to his family** see note for 11(a).

**67(d) I knew him a great deal better than Sir Walter did** see note for 12(b).

**68(c) Lord Mansfield** see note for 29(b).

**68(d) Laidlaw should not have been separated from Abbotsford** see note for 29(b).

**68(d) my own brother** see note for 29(c).

**69(b) our poor friend Irving** see note for 13(b).

**70(b) Morrit of Rokeby some of the Fergusons and I** see notes for 14(d) and 4(b). Sir Adam Ferguson had two brothers and three sisters.

**70(c) Mr Paterson** see note for 14(b).

**71(a) the Sutherland family** Elizabeth Sutherland married George Granville Leveson-Gower in 1785. He became Marquis of Stafford in 1803.

**71(a) the collossal statue of Wallace** see note for 15(b).

**71(b) every one do that which is right in his own eyes** see note for 15(b).

**71(b) Miss Porter's work The Scottish Chiefs** see note for 15(c).

**71(c) Lord Peter [...] King Henry's messenger to Piercy Hotspur** 'Lord Peter' may refer to Peter the Great of Russia who supposedly travelled in his dominions disguised as a commoner. Hogg alludes to this belief in *Confessions of a Justified Sinner.* In *1 Henry IV* (IV. 3) the King sends Sir Walter Blunt to Hotspur's camp to offer reconciliation and pardon. In the ensuing Battle of Shrewsbury, Douglas kills Blunt, 'Semblably furnished like the king himself' (V. 3. 21).

**71(c) Oman's Hotel** as Hogg does not specify a date, it is not possible to locate precisely which one of Charles Oman's establishments witnessed this event. From Marie W. Stuart, *Old Edinburgh Taverns* (London: Robert Hale, 1952), pp. 82–83:

> Charles Oman [...] took over Bayle's [in Shakespeare Square] in 1803. [...] Oman's move to the New Town was a lucky one and his progress toward becoming one of the city's leading and most enterprising hotel-keepers can be traced in old directories. In 1805 he removed again to West Register Street but took with him the memory of Bayle's old associations, calling his premises the 'New Club Tavern.' In addition to it he opened a hotel at 14 Princes Street in 1810, changing in 1815 to 22 St. Andrew Street. It was about this time that he was patronised by the Right and Wrong Club, 'perhaps the most ridiculous club ever founded in any city,' according to James Hogg, its leading light. [...] The demolition of Shakespeare Square and the opening up of the eastern end of Princes Street by the Regent Road and the Regent Bridge gave the city an important new thoroughfare, so in 1821 Oman went back to the neighbourhood once dignified by Bayle's and became proprietor of the Waterloo Hotel at a rental of £1,500. But four years later he turned ambitiously to the more exclusive West End, and three months before his death he opened yet another hotel at 4 and 6 Charlotte Square.

For more details on the Right and Wrong Club, see Hogg's *Memoir of the Author's*

*Life* and *Familiar Anecdotes of Sir Walter Scott*, ed. by Douglas S. Mack (Edinburgh: Scottish Academic Press, 1972), pp. 46–47.

**71(d) as a particular judge in these matters** in 1827 Hogg founded the St Ronan's Border Games, held annually at Innerleithen. Earlier, in 1815, he joined with Scott to organise a football match at Carterhaugh between players from Yarrow and Selkirk. See David Groves, *James Hogg and the St Ronan's Border Club* (Dollar: Mack, 1987).

**72(a) Mr Martin** see note for 27(d).

**72(c) Chauntry** see note for 13(a).

**72(d) "The Three Perils of women"** Hogg's novel was published in 1823 as *The Three Perils of Woman; or Love, Leasing, and Jealousy*. Hogg was indeed living at Mount Benger, but there is no evidence that Scott agreed to correct the proofs.

**73(a) unless it be for a few minutes amusement** *Domestic Manners* adds the following footnote: 'This must have been "leein' Johnie." '

**73(a) The Whig ascendancy in the British cabinet** see note for 18(d)–19(a).

**73(c) the little inn on my own farm** see note for 17(c).

**73(c) Altrive** see note for 17(c).

**73(c) His daughter was with him** see note for 17(c).

**73(d)–74(a) a certain gamekeeper** a letter from William Laidlaw to Scott of March 1820 may lend some credence to Hogg's story of the 'rascally gamekeeper', although there is a ten-year interval between Laidlaw's letter and Scott's caution to Hogg:

> I have no doubt that His Grace would bring our friend the Shepherd and his concerns before you, and I am anxious to know if it is the duke's intention to render him a little more comfortable at Altrive. You know that Hogg built the cottage there, at his own expense (with an allowance of wood, perhaps), and he likewise built a considerable addition to Mount Benger, and a barn—all which cost him a great sum of money, quite disproportionate to a holding of £7 a year, even at a nominal rent. The cottage was intended for a bachelor's abode, and is very inadequate to what is now required by the bard's family; and I see that if His Grace does not think of giving him some allowance as an addition, it will most likely banish him from the district with which his poetry and feeling are so closely associated. I mention all this because I have observed that there is a prejudice against him among the subagents since Christie left the service, or rather, since the late duke's death. One of them said to me, when I mentioned Hogg's genius and amiable character, *Cui bono?* I, too, say, *Cui bono?* What is the use of all his poetry, and the rest? Now, from R.'s usage of him, there is every reason to suspect that he is a *cui bono* man too, and Hogg stands a bad chance among them, and I believe the duke knows nothing about the truth of the matter. (Carruthers, p. 176–77.)

**74(a) Fielding's tale of Black George** see note for 18(a). *Domestic Manners* adds the following footnote:

> And yet Scott could bow down and worship this boy idiot—the plaything of a rascally game keeper—who valued a moorfowl more than a poet—because he was a Duke!

**74(d) the greatest man that ever that country contained** *Domestic Manners* adds the following footnote: 'Bravo Hogg.'

**75(a) his last ilness** see note for 19(a).
**75(c) epigraph** from Horace's 'To Delius' (*Odes* II. 3):

> All go one way: shak'd is the pot,
> And first or last comes forth thy lot,
>     The Pass by which thou'rt sent
>     T' Eternal banishment
>                         *Poems of Horace* (London: A. Brome, 1671.)

*Domestic Manners* adds the following footnote:

Saul among the prophets! Hogg quoting Latin!

# Index

Abbotsford: 6-7, 10, 14, 15, 16, 19, 28–29, 30, 45, 54, 56, 68, 70–71, 73, 75

Addison, Joseph: 19, 58

Altrive: 15, 17, 33, 73

Ashestiel: 12, 42, 54

Baillie, Joanna: 30

Ballantyne, James: 21, 23, 24, 26–27, 28, 50, 52, 54, 61–62, 63–64, 72–73

Ballantyne, John: 7–8, 20, 21, 26, 27, 39, 48, 50, 63

Blackwood, William: 51

Bowhill: 4, 43, 46

Boyd, Mr.: 8, 59

Broadmeadows: 8, 13, 59, 69

Brougham, Henry: 53

Brunton, Davie: 13–14, 69

Brydon, of Crosslee: 40

Brydon, George: 38

Brydon, Walter: 38-39

Buccleuch, 4th Duke of (Charles William Henry Scott): 4–5, 27, 43–46

Buccleuch, 5th Duke of (Walter Francis Montagu Douglas Scott): 17–18, 73–74

Buchan, 11th Earl of (David Stewart Erskine): 15, 71

Burns, James Glencairn: 60

Burns, Robert: 5

Byron, 6th Baron (George Gordon Noel Byron): 23

Campbell, Alexander: 26

Campbell, Thomas: 41
   *The Pleasures of Hope*: 41

Carpenter, John ( Jean Charpentier): 11

Castle Street (Scott's house at 39 North): 6, 45, 48, 72

Chantrey, Sir Francis: 13, 72

Clarty-Hole: 6–7, 30

Claverhouse ( John Graham, Viscount Dundee): 42

Constable, Archibald: 26, 28

Cunningham, Allan: 60

Curwen, Henry: 53

Don, Sir Alexander: 5, 46

Douglas, Robert (Minister of Galashiels): 6

Drumlanrig Castle: 73

Dryburgh Abbey: 45, 71

*Edinburgh Annual Register*: 20-21, 49–50

Eildon: 36

Elliott family: 5

Erskine, William (Lord Kinneder): 24, 54, 64

Ettrick Forest: 10, 33, 38

Ettrickhouse: 37

Ettrick Shepherd: 3, 31, 36

Fauldshope, Hoggs of: 4, 44

Ferguson family: 70

Ferguson, Sir Adam: 4, 11, 15, 42, 44

Ferguson, Col. James: 16, 57

Ferrier, Susan: 64

Fielding, Henry: 18, 74

Fletcher, Rob: 41

Galashiels: 14

George IV: 27

Gillespie, Thomas: 24

Gillies, Robert Pearse: 61–62

Gordon Arms: 17, 73

Grey Mare's Tail: 42

Grieve, John: 55

Haliburton, family of: 6, 43

Harden, family of Scotts of: 4–5, 43–44

Harden, 12th Laird of (Hugh Hepburne-Scott): 3, 4, 44

Hogg, David (brother of author): 29, 68

Hogg, James
   *The Brownie of Bodsbeck*: 22, 25, 50–51
   'Donald M'Donald': 23–24, 61, 79–81

## DATE DUE

| | | | |
|---|---|---|---|
| | | | |
| | | | |
| | | | |
| | | | |
| | | | |
| | | | |
| | | | |
| | | | |
| | | | |
| | | | |
| | | | |
| | | | |
| | | | |
| | | | |
| | | | |
| | | | |
| | | | |
| | | | |
| | | | |
| | | | Printed in USA |

HIGHSMITH #45230